DREAM KEEPER

Dark Dreamer

Book One

Amber R. Duell

For Ian

May the Sandman bring you good dreams every night!

The Sandman

The invisible dome that encased the Dream Realm burned blue beneath my gloved hand. My magic ached to be released from its rigid confinement to return to the spiritual place deep in my chest, where it could fuel dreams once again—but this barrier was the only thing standing between me and the Nightmare Realm. Or, more specifically, from the things lurking there. Grotesque or beautiful, animalistic or humanoid, it didn't matter. Each and every nightmare held their own special brand of terror waiting to ensnare an unsuspecting Dreamer.

From this close to the wall, I could easily see into the Weaver's realm. Rolling hills stretched into the distance, and a small stream snaked through the low plains, which were colored in muted greens and blues. The knee-high grass tinkled an eerie, hushed melody as the breeze rippled across it. Hooked barbs, hard as steel and sharp as razors, grew along each blade, invisible to the naked eye. Beyond the hills lay an endless array of landscapes with their own vicious traps.

None of the Weaver's creatures roamed among the swaying grass tonight—at least none I could see. Still, something felt different. A layer of anxiety prowling beneath the calm.

I ignored it the best I could and continued my nightly security inspection—if not to protect the Dream Keeper, then to protect *her* world. Although, if I were being honest with myself, it was no longer the Day World I was concerned with saving from legions of deadly nightmares.

It was the Dream Keeper herself—Nora.

Nora, who would be hunted for the dream I'd placed inside her five years ago—the exact contents unknown even to me. She held the end of an invisible leash keeping the nightmares in the Night World, and the Weaver wouldn't hesitate to regain control of it. Even if that meant helping the creatures slip their collars entirely.

I rolled my shoulders and turned my attention back to the barrier. The worry I carried was ridiculous, a waste of time better spent elsewhere. Nothing more than paranoia. The shields were secure, the Weaver still bound to his realm, and the key to unraveling it all was safely hidden in Nora's mind.

Even still, my magic knotted inside me. *Wrong, wrong, wrong,* it seemed to whisper, insistently. Tendrils of it slid down my arms, flowing from my fingertips. The glimmering beach vibrated beneath my feet, and thousands of pieces of sand floated into the air. Two feet. Three feet. Four. Until the air was filled with sparkling flecks. With a deep breath, I flung my arms out wide, fingers splayed to propel a fresh layer of my magic into the existing barrier. It shot outward, clinging to the dome, and strengthened it in a flash of blue.

With the beach undoubtedly safe for Nora, I looked inward. The cords connecting me to each Dreamer that knew the legend of the Sandman spanned out like a million silver harp strings. Some connections glowed bright, their owner already asleep. Others idled, dull and dreamless, while the person on the other end remained awake.

I knew exactly where to find the cord that led to Nora. Even if I hadn't found it every night since we met, the dream I gave her was made of my magic, and it begged to return home. I tugged off my gloves and reached out as if to touch her cord— as if it were a tangible thing, instead of something spiritual. The silver and navy flecks covering my pale hands shimmered brilliantly.

Unlike Nora's cord.

"What's taking you so long?" I whispered to myself. She was never awake this late. We met in the same place on the other side of the realm like clockwork.

Suddenly, a shadow raced toward me in a blur of black and yellow fur, and I froze. Baku was my only ally in the Night World, even if it was by default. "Enemy of my enemy" and what not. But he knew the rules. He wasn't supposed to be here when I was expecting Nora to arrive. If she ever discovered there were darker things outside of these walls, it would invite trouble.

The chimera dug his tiger paws into the sand, skidding to a halt before me. Baku snorted through the elephant trunk situated between his ivory tusks. Large ears flapped twice on either side of his brindle face, and his cow-like tail snapped back and forth behind him.

I stopped breathing the moment I met the worried gleam in his eyes.

"Something's going on in the Nightmare Realm."

It wasn't a question. Baku spent most of his time on the other side of the barrier which meant he had a front row seat to whatever had happened and there was no reason to challenge his judgment. "Wh—"

The Weaver's maniacal joy shot through me, snaking around my fear, strangling it, and I staggered back a step. I hadn't been able to feel the Weaver since the binding. His magic was always traceable, but *never* his emotions. Dread pooled in my gut. I tried to shove the other sensation out, to pull instead on his location, but his magic registered in every direction. It was like trying to pinpoint the dream cord of an insomniac.

A streak of gold shot across the sky. It splintered its way through the stars, spreading, thinning, and fading. Magic thrummed through my veins, frantic to escape. To rise and protect. To defend. Baku pranced nervously at my side.

"Sandman." A gentle voice traveled down the cord. "Help me sleep."

"Nora." Her name fell from my lips as a single, strangled breath. I clenched the leather gloves in my hands. She hadn't asked for my help in years. *Years.* I gaped at the barrier in awe, utterly perplexed. Checking on the Weaver was important, but so was aiding Nora. If one was safe, they both were. I swallowed hard and drew a leather pouch from my belt loop.

"Find the Weaver," I told Baku. I tugged my gloves on again and snapped the hood of my tunic up over my brown curls. "I'll be right behind you."

Baku gave a curt nod and rushed back through the barrier without pause. Even if he had his hands—rather, paws—full, trying to devour a thousand nightmares tonight, Baku would help me find answers.

The cord between Nora and I grew taut as I careened along it to her bedside. Despite my best efforts not to, my breath still hitched when I caught sight of her platinum hair against the dark sheets. I reached a gloved hand out to brush a few strands from her temple but curled my fingers at the last moment. *You shouldn't*, I admonished myself. *This is off limits.*

I didn't creep around in bedrooms, and I certainly didn't touch anyone without their knowledge. Not even Nora. *Especially* not Nora—even if my chest did ache for the smallest hint of physical contact. It was my own fault we never touched, never high-fived or hugged or held hands. It was one of my rules, my lies, to keep distance between us. A lot of good they did. My body still jolted every night at the first glimpse of her and the adrenaline coursed through me long after she woke every morning. I'd spent an eternity watching people dream of love, but I never understood the appeal until Nora. None had come before her and I knew with absolute certainty that none would come after.

"I don't know why you needed to call me tonight," I said, keeping my voice low. Though she could neither hear nor see me, I fumbled for the edge of my hood, retreating into its shadow.

"But, my magic will take you to the beach. You'll be safe there." Please *be safe there*. "I'm sorry, Nora. But I'll see you soon." Reaching into the ever-present pouch, I pinched a bit of sand between my fingers. "Remember to keep a true heart and a true mind, and that the power of the dream is yours."

Then, I promptly sprinkled the glimmering flecks over her eyes and whispered, "Sleep."

My throat seized, and I choked back the awful truth of what she was, of what I made her, and what consequences we might be facing for it now. After escorting Nora's consciousness to the beach, and once I'd ensured that she was safely inside the barrier, I slipped through the surrounding shield into the perilous terrain of the Nightmare Realm. I flew through the tall grass toward the center of the Nightmare World amid a chorus of harsh metal clinks. The tiny barbs stabbed through my pant legs and pricked against my leather boots. Each cut into my skin was like a slap with a hot poker, but it was a small price to pay for a chance at reaching the Weaver's Keep in time to stop whatever was happening. The scent of burning wool ravaged my senses. *His* magic. Strong and undeniable. A sure sign that his binding must have worn thin—*too* thin, given how little time had passed.

The Day World was still warded against the Weaver's power and would remain so. That is, as long as he didn't find Nora. However, just because he couldn't open the doors without prying the information from the Dream Keeper's mind, that didn't mean he couldn't knock.

Chapter Two

Nora

Shadows danced in the soft warmth of the white mini-lights strung around my bedroom. I hopped around my bed, fumbling with the buckle on my sandals, and tossed my purse in the corner. Something hard—probably my phone—thwacked against the light blue wall.

"Whoops," I muttered, then growled at the metal hook locking my footwear in place. There were places to go, people to see. Or, rather, *one* person, and it was already hours past our usual meeting time. I jerked at the stiff strap. "Get off."

Finally, it popped, and I kicked it triumphantly into the corner with my bag. The other came off without any trouble, and my stomach fluttered in anticipation. I tugged off my jean shorts and stepped into a pair of plaid pajama bottoms, leaving on the ribbed tank top I wore out tonight. Who cared that a glob of nacho cheese stained the front? The Sandman certainly wouldn't.

Climbing beneath the cool sheets, I dragged in a long breath and released it slowly. A small grin played on my lips as I stared at the lights hanging overhead. Then I shut my eyes and waited. Waited for sleep to claim me. To deliver me. But my body was too tense, and my mind still flipped through the day's events—as ridiculously boring as they were. When the highlight of your day was painting your nails a new color, what was there to mull over?

After a handful of long minutes, I opened my eyes again and bit my lip. I could ask. It had been… Actually, I couldn't remember the last time I asked him for anything. Even this. But I had to be up early for work tomorrow and we'd already missed out on hours together. A grin crept across my face.

"Sandman," I whispered, and closed my eyes again in preparation. "Help me sleep."

It came swiftly then, sweeping me gently from my world to another as easily as the breeze carries a feather. I curled my toes, feeling the powder-like sand of the Sandman's beach beneath my bare feet, and opened my eyes. The endless blanket of bright stars, the luminescent waves, the Sandman… This place, this dream, was like coming home.

"Sorry I'm late," I called with a smile in my voice. The light aroma of lilacs filled my lungs and I sighed, content. "Natalie and Emery dragged me to a party to celebrate our final first day of summer vacation." By this time next year, we would all be high school graduates and legal adults—neither of which I was ready to think about. I stretched my arms over my head and fought a yawn. "Sandman?" There was no reply. I dropped my arms and spun, searching for a glimpse of the familiar black-clad figure. This was our spot—the place directly below the brightest star.

My brows lowered in confusion. So why wasn't he here? He was *always* here. "Where are you?"

The only sound was the soft hush of waves lapping the shore. I turned again, squinting down the beach, but there was no hooded figure in sight. My heart skipped a beat. The dream seemed to yawn open, the emptiness pressing in on me from all sides. He had to be here somewhere. A pit formed in my stomach, and I staggered back, unsteady. *He had to.*

The beach was an addiction I didn't know how to cure myself of—didn't *want* to cure myself of. For every time I had to pretend this place didn't exist, the Sandman was there to absolve me of the lies. There to make me feel like I was good and sane and normal. It didn't matter that he was *also* the reason I didn't feel any of those things were true when I was awake. The Sandman was my anchor, holding me firm when life tried to wash me out to sea. Without him… I swallowed hard. Without him, I would be a ship without sails.

"Sandman!" I jogged down the water's edge, my pulse drumming in my ears. "I'm here."

But he wasn't.

***

Three thirty-two.

The clock on my nightstand glowed green, the colon blinking in a slow, torturous rhythm. I tapped my fingers on my stomach. The Sandman had never been a no-show before. And if he wasn't there, maybe that meant *they* were right, and he wasn't real.

No.

I refused to believe that. My mother meant well, but I couldn't face a lifetime of pill-pushing psychiatrists. One white-haired doctor tossing around words like *personality disorder* and *delusional* was enough. By the time the final doctor deemed the Sandman a simple outlet for me to process my parents' divorce, the damage was done.

Don't worry about it, he said. *It will pass*, he said.

That was five years ago.

The divorce was a distant memory. My father moved across the country and my mother remarried, but the Sandman became a permanent fixture. One I'd learned to never, ever talk about.

What's going on? I pushed the thought toward the Sandman even though I knew he couldn't hear me. There was only one call that reached from this side of the Dream World to his, only one cry capable of bringing him here, but it never stopped me from trying.

I flung the sheets back with a huff and grabbed an oversized Lund Valley Community College sweater from the end of my bed. Natalie hoped we would go there together next year but… I wrinkled my nose and glanced at the dresser drawer where my sketchbook was carefully tucked between scarves. If I went to college at all, it would be for art, but that was a big *if*. No one in my family knew I drew, and if my mother was going to let me major in something "impractical," she would want to at least see my work. Unfortunately, each page featured a majestic beach and a man hidden beneath a hood. Both things I was supposed to have forgotten long ago.

Tugging the sweater over my head, I made my way through the dark hallway toward the stairs. My mother and step-father were both working the night shift at the hospital and my sister could sleep through anything, yet I found myself tip-toeing down the hall.

I paused outside Katie's door and listened to the steady, heavy breathing on the other side. Part of me wanted to wake my sister up to talk about what happened, but the other part of me—the part that remembered the piercing fluorescent lights of a therapist's office—knew better. Katie had teased me about the Sandman when we were younger, but she never treated me differently. However, now we were older. Barging into her room to complain that my *imaginary friend* hadn't shown up that night might alienate the last blood relative I could rely on.

Although Katie annoyed me like no one else, I loved her more than I was irritated with her. I needed my big sister on my side—even if it meant hiding a huge part of my life. So, I stepped away from her door and crept silently downstairs to the kitchen.

Maybe because I was about to steal someone's box of frozen Thin Mints.

Sorry, not sorry.

Mist curled out of the open freezer, and I reached behind the chicken before a shrill, heart-wrenching scream tore through the house, squeezing the air from my lungs. It was made of nails and teeth and death. Of danger and fear. My eardrums rattled. Each nerve stood at attention, electricity buzzing over my body.

"Katie?" I yelled, frantically abandoning my pursuit of the cookies.

Confusion laced the edges of my shaky voice, but I was already racing across the kitchen. Instinct twisted my gut, telling me to turn and run, to save myself, but I couldn't. Not if my sister was in trouble. Not if someone had broken in when no one was home to help. Not if Katie was hurt and scared. I propelled myself up the stairs to the second floor, my skin itching me to go faster, faster, faster. Katie's door was still shut at the front of the hallway. My breath shuddered, and I reached for the handle, pausing with apprehension. The metal was cold in my palm.

"Katie?" Her name came out as a crackling whisper and I forced myself to inhale. Then exhale. Inhale again. My hand shook as I twisted the knob.

I eased the door inward. Without a barrier between us, the sound cut through me like a knife. I slapped a palm against the wall, hitting the light switch, and flinched at the sudden brightness. At what it might reveal.

Katie lay flat on her back, her eyes shut tight, with the sheets snarled in a ball at the end of the bed. Sweat poured down her face, plastering her pink hair to her skin. The wild scream continued, unrelenting, her jaw stretched wide, her neck muscles protruding. But everything else was in its rightful place. Nothing was broken. The lock on the window hugged its latch.

I stepped into the room and spun, bumping into the dresser. My pulse thrashed; it mimicked Katie's scream in pendulum beats. Loud then muffled then loud again. "Katie?" My voice felt tight. I knelt on the mattress and shook my sister's broad shoulders. "Wake up."

The scream cracked. Katie sucked in air as if she were drowning and began again, just as terrified. I used the back of my wrist to wipe the moisture from my forehead. My nails dug into her shoulders, and I shook her rigid body with every ounce of strength I had. The more I yelled her name, the more desperate, more savage, my voice became. Black spots danced in my vision. Nightmares were one thing, but this was something else. Something beyond that. I shook the dizzying fear away and darted into the bathroom across the hall.

I returned with a Dixie cup of cold water and leapt onto the bed. The water hit Katie's face with a splash. "Come *on*," I shouted to no avail.

I fumbled for Katie's cell phone on the nightstand. If our mother didn't know what to do, she could send someone who did. My thumb hovered over the direct number to my mother's unit when a quick, metallic burst of air whooshed in from the hallway. A shiver ravaged my spine, and Katie's pitch reached new heights. I slipped from the bed, my hip smashing into the floor. The phone fell from my hand, seemingly in slow motion. I lunged for the door, and slammed it shut, leaning my back against the wood.

I couldn't think.

Couldn't... I couldn't...

The walls seemed to shrink, boxing me in. Trapping me.

Above the screech, a deep chuckle rumbled in the hall. My heart rose to my throat, and I dove for the phone where it had landed on the rug. I managed to dial *nine* before Katie's scream cut off. Palpable silence penetrated the room. My rapid breathing mixed with my sister's, and I edged up onto shaking knees. Katie rolled onto her side with a twitch.

"Katie?" My voice came out as a squeak.

She snuggled into the pillow, and her breathing returned to normal. *Okay.* She was okay. I turned my attention to the space at the bottom of the door. There was probably no one out there anyway. My sister's screams threw me off after a confusing night, that's all. I was merely tired and scared and was likely imagining the whole thing.

But before I called anyone, I *had* to be sure.

With the phone clutched in my hand, I crawled across the room to where the bright yellow handle of Katie's tennis racket leaned against the wall. I gripped the hard foam and held it to my shoulder. I didn't want to leave Katie alone but what choice did I have? I couldn't call for help if no one was out there. My mother would have a field day.

Clenching my jaw shut to keep my teeth from chattering, I dialed two *one*'s before opening the door. If anyone was on the other side, it would only take a single touch to call for help.

I eased out, holding the racket in front of me, and flicked on the hallway light. The stillness slammed into me like a brick wall. "Okay, okay, okay," I chanted under my breath. This was stupid. And yet… at five-foot-three and a hundred and ten pounds, an intruder wouldn't necessarily need to be armed to overpower me.

My nerves exploded with a burst of adrenaline, and I leapt from room to room until each light bulb on the second floor glowed. I checked every closet, under every bed. The racket shook in my hand. There was nothing. No one. An irrational spike of anger zipped through me at the possibility of my brain's betrayal.

My body moved on its own accord, taking me downstairs one tentative step at a time. One million potential fates I might encounter, if there was someone lying in wait, coursed through my thoughts. The joints in my fingers locked around the phone with my thumb still over the green call button. My tongue was sandpaper against the roof of my mouth, and I crept through the living room.

The freezer was still open, rattling in an attempt to keep the internal temperature down. I chomped down on my lip and inched my way forward to shut it. The rarely-used alarm system beside the back door taunted me—if only I remembered the code.

It seemed like it took ages to finish searching the house. I looked everywhere from the coat closet to beneath the bathroom sink, but it had only been eleven minutes since I had woken up. No time at all, really. I gripped the back of a dining room chair to stay on my feet.

There was no intruder. Katie had a nightmare, and my mind deceived me.

Again.

Always.

Only this time, it wasn't part of my subconscious. I wasn't asleep. Katie had screamed. There was a blast of air. Someone had laughed.

I swallowed the fear rising in my chest.

No one *believed* they were crazy. I wasn't sure what it meant if I thought I was unhinged but constantly persuaded myself to believe I wasn't. Was I? Wasn't I? Not even the doctors could agree on an answer. My sanity was a double-edged sword, and I was fighting to maintain balance on the tip.

I dashed back to Katie and climbed in bed beside her, nestling close. I tucked the wrinkled sheet around us both and tried to ignore the nausea curdling in my stomach. Katie was older than me, bolder and more confident, but in that moment, she felt as fragile as blown glass. I wrapped an arm around her waist and squeezed my eyes shut. My ears strained to hear the slightest sound that could signal danger, but no one else was in the house.

No one had laughed.

The Sandman wasn't real.

I balled the back of Katie's T-shirt in my fist. He was real enough to me, and I needed him. *Please, Sandman,* I called in a silent plea for the second time tonight—the one only he could hear. *Help me sleep.*

Chapter Three

Nora

"Crap," I grumbled, rummaging through the papers littering my desk. "Crap, crap, crap."

If I hadn't hit snooze so many times, waiting for the Sandman to come to the beach, I wouldn't have been running so late.

"The power is mine." Ha!

Over the years, I repeated his mantra a million times. The words became such a part of me that I forgot the knowledge existed; they were as natural to me as breathing. The power of the beach was his, I knew, but my dreams—the dreams he claimed I would have if he weren't there—that was mine. But if it were true that I could control things when the Sandman wasn't there, he would have appeared. I clenched my jaw, shaking out a book. My name tag had to be here somewhere. I slammed the hardcover down and gripped my rolling stomach.

Idiot.

Heat tingled my cheeks. Relying on him, missing him, needing him... It was ridiculous. He was part of me, and anything that he could give me, I could give myself. My lungs burned, reminding me to inhale, and I sucked in a dry breath. I needed to get my act together, to get to work, and to stop being my own worst enemy.

My name tag fell from between two notebooks and clicked against the desk. I scooped it up, pinned it on my white dress shirt, and tucked the hem into my khakis. I was *so* late. I flew out of my bedroom, and straight into Paul.

My step-father still wore baby blue scrubs that smelled of rubbing alcohol and latex, his dark hair sticking up at odd angles. "Hey kiddo, what's the rush?"

"I'm running late for work." I forced a smile—something I would have to do all day if I didn't want endless reminders from my boss that a good attitude was 'an essential part of good customer service.' Besides, my step-father was a good guy. Better than my biological father, actually. Nice. Involved. *There.*

Paul made a low "hmm" in the back of his throat. "You didn't drink and drive last night, did you?"

I threw him a scowl. The fact that my mother practically shoved me out the door to go to the party should've been a good indicator. "Natalie drove, and she drank soda all night."

"Had to ask," he grumbled. "Fatherly duty and what not."

I rolled my eyes, but a genuine smirk quirked my lips. "Yeah, yeah. Mom asleep? Tell her I'll do the garbage when I get home."

"I'll take it out." Paul yawned and stepped around me into the bathroom. "Have a good day."

The bathroom door clicked shut behind him, and I glanced toward Katie's room. There were only ten minutes left before my shift started, but the screams still echoed in my ears. A raw, frightening thing. I bit my lip and inched forward to peek inside. The hinges creaked a baleful tune as I nudged the door open enough to slip inside, making the hair on my arms rise in anticipation.

The sheets were pulled up to her shoulders, her mass of bubble gum hair spread across the pillow, exactly how she was when I left sometime near dawn—after jolting awake for a third time.

"You up?" I whispered, creeping toward the bed. Katie's chest moved up and down in a steady rhythm, but she had to be more than breathing. She needed to be *okay*. I poked her shoulder. "Hey."

She growled without opening her eyes, "The house better be on fire."

"I wanted to check on you before I left."

Katie rolled over to face the wall. "Shoo."

I stuck my tongue out at her. Katie was okay, even if her voice sounded a bit hoarse. She was fine, but I wasn't. Not really. My head felt hollow without the Sandman's support, my body heavy. "I'm going, I'm go—"

On the maroon pillowcase, completely invisible without the line of sun coming through the window, were flecks of glittering sand. My knees wobbled. I leaned closer and ran a finger through it. The dust was soft, almost a powder, and shone as brightly as a diamond. I stared, unblinking, at the tiny sparkles stuck in the grooves of my fingertip.

These particles… They played such a big role in my life the last few years. Every night I walked on it. Sat on it. Drew in it. At thirteen, I spent six hours trying to make sand castles from the loose particles, but they refused to stick to one another. At fifteen, I made dozens of snow angels across its surface and, with a flick of a certain someone's wrist, it morphed into actual snow. Heck, last week, I used it to play a game of tic-tac-toe. I would know it anywhere. This was *his* sand.

What was it doing on Katie's pillow? The Sandman had ignored my call while I lay awake for hours waiting for sleep to take me. Unless he *had* come… But then why wasn't he at the beach?

"*Nora.*" Katie flung the sheet over her head. The movement kicked the remaining granules into the air. "Go. Away."

I clutched my hand to my chest and sprinted to the car.

***

My fingers still trembled as I parked behind Howell's Furniture and Decor. Twenty-four hours ago, I had everything under control. Dreaming about the Sandman was one thing, but disembodied laughter, sand on Katie's pillow… I drew a deep breath and blew it out slowly through puckered lips.

What looked like sand could have been Katie's makeup. She liked glitz and glam. That was it. Eye shadow. I shoved the car keys into my purse and nodded to myself in the rearview mirror.

Since I was seven minutes late, I didn't need to draw more attention to myself and decided to jog around to the main doors, instead of knocking on the back. I saw my boss through the glass and cringed. She was usually doing paperwork in the office this early.

"Hey, Lisa," I called over the cowbell clanging against the door. "Sorry I'm late. It won't happen again."

"I hadn't realized." Lisa, a tall woman with wisps of grey in her hair, glanced up from where she leaned over the desk. She held the phone up to one ear, covering the bottom half as she spoke. "You look... chipper."

I stifled a groan. If by chipper, she meant like a member of the walking dead, then yes. "Long night." *Strange night. Strange morning.*

"Come meet your new coworker." She sidestepped the desk to reveal a boy no older than myself in a swivel chair. "This is Ben. He'll be working the sales floor with you this summer."

Ben glanced up from the paperwork and smiled so warmly it locked me in place. It was a smile of hopes and dreams. Promises. His violet eyes gleamed with a thousand flecks of starlight, and the fluorescent lights that reflected in his pupils stretched into seemingly endless mirrors. A mop of thick, curly ash-brown hair framed high cheekbones, and a narrow nose stopped above the softest looking lips.

I swore his breath caught at the same moment mine did. Looking at him, I felt like I was missing a place I had never been. The way he watched me sent lava racing through my veins. I knew him. *Somehow,* I knew him. The longing for something I didn't understand quickly bubbled into panic, and one foot slid back toward the doors.

"Hello," he said with the sweetest of smiles.

One word, two syllables, and the air evaporated from my lungs. His voice tugged at a vital memory. I nearly stumbled backward into a coffee table but caught myself on a column. I couldn't place the voice exactly. It wasn't anyone I knew, but the sound ached deep in my marrow. I wrung my purse straps, the stiff leather digging into my palm, and forced myself to walk toward the desk.

"Randy," Lisa snapped into the phone. "This isn't funny. Where are you? Call me back." She slammed the receiver down.

I shifted between my feet. "Everything okay?"

"Randy ran the deposit to the bank over an hour ago. I swear, if he went back home to sleep..." Lisa picked the phone up again and dialed. "I'll watch the floor while you give Ben a tour."

"Tour?" I swallowed hard. Howell's wasn't hiring. Someone called at least once a week to ask, and the answer was always no. Maybe if someone was lucky, they needed help with deliveries, but never the sales floor. The walls around my composed facade trembled, threatening my sanity. "What happened to Josh?" I asked.

"He's moving to afternoons." She rounded the desk and held the phone out in front of her to speak directly into the receiver. "Randy, if I have to leave one more voicemail, I swear to God..." She slammed the phone down again.

Ben slid his stack of papers across the desk. "I'm done filling these out."

"Great. Thanks," Lisa said. She motioned him out of her chair and plopped down in his place. "If you have any questions, Nora can fill you in."

I glanced sideways, my eyes level with Ben's shoulders. A spike of nerves shot down the back of my neck, trailing all the way down my spine, and I arched my back against the tingling discomfort. Hints of toned muscle flexed beneath the rolled sleeves of his dress shirt when he reached out to shake my hand. Tattooed specks of navy blue and silver covered his hands, the granules thinning out as they spread up his forearm and disappeared beneath the fabric. It was hard to believe Lisa hired him looking like he did. Crazy contact lenses *and* tattoos? I wasn't even allowed to put unnatural color in my hair. I scowled at the mix of emotions warring inside my head—intrigue, comfort, fear. He looked down at me, oozing charm and mystery and everything that would've drawn my friends closer. I stepped away.

The familiar sensation prickled again, begging me to move toward him, and I stopped myself mid-wince. Five years spent teaching myself to run as a default setting, to block out the fantasies, and yet ignoring his hand was one of the hardest things I'd done in a long time. I took a deep breath, letting it out through the corner of my mouth while pressing a hand against my diaphragm—a technique one of the doctors said might help if I felt stressed. My mother insisted I try, and usually they were right. Today, however, it did nothing.

"After you," he said and tucked his arms behind his back.

I fought against a barrage of crazy ideas—ideas crazier than the one I had when I saw the sand on Katie's pillow. Were my dreams leaking into reality? *No.* The Sandman wasn't real in this world. He wasn't. The stress was simply getting to me.

Ben smiled again, a shy grin, and my defenses cracked.

Lisa waved a frantic hand toward us while holding the receiver to her ear. I sighed and turned my back on them both. *Deep breaths.* Deep breaths and a shred of sanity would get me through the day, then tonight I could ask the Sandman directly if there was more to what I was seeing.

Of course, that was assuming he showed up.

Squaring my shoulders, I led Ben through a collection of couches and chairs. "This is where the living room sets are. The customers can order anything they see here. Lamps, rugs, tables." I flicked a ring of fabric samples tied to the arm of a recliner. "Color swatches and prices are attached to everything, so you don't need to memorize them."

"Got it."

He was close. Too close. His energy curled toward me, and I sidestepped an end table to put space between us. "The dining room sets are in there." I pointed through a wide doorway to the left. "Most tables come with four chairs unless the ticket says otherwise, but they can order more."

"All right."

I picked up the pace, motioning to another room at the back. "Desks, bookcases, cabinets, entertainment centers. Basically, office furniture and miscellaneous things that don't fit out here."

"Should I be writing this down?" A hint of a smile laced his voice.

"Maybe," I snapped, then cringed. He was probably trying to diffuse the tension sparking between us. One of us had to— my shift didn't end for another eight hours. I stopped at the end of the aisle. "That way," I murmured, jerking my elbow at the staircase.

He started toward the narrow, sloping steps, his tattooed hand gliding over the rail. Unspoken words pressed against me. I frowned and watched him climb higher alone. Something about the way he moved left me immobile. For a split second, I saw a man in loose cotton pants and a hooded tunic. The image was gone faster than it came, but the damage was done. I couldn't un-see it.

When the curly haired boy stopped halfway up, I jumped. My teeth clacked against each other in an attempt not to say anything. Ben wasn't the Sandman. Because the Sandman *did not exist*.

"Is something wrong?" he asked innocently.

I lifted my chin, cleared my throat, and sprinted up the first few steps. *Not crazy, not crazy, not crazy.* "Where are you from, Ben?"

He resumed his ascent. "All over, really."

A small, cynical noise escaped my throat before I could stop it. He hadn't done anything wrong. This was my problem, my instability, not his. I couldn't take it out on him because he happened to remind me of someone else. Maybe his family moved around a lot. Maybe he really was from all over. My fingers tingled at the memory of the sand on Katie's pillowcase, and I crossed my arms, pressing them into my sides.

"Dreamer, Dreamer," whispered a low, rasping voice behind me. I spun around, gripping the railing, but no one was there. A metallic taste coated my tongue. "Not a screamer," said the voice, this time right in my ear. Cold dread oozed down my spine. "Snapped his neck and—"

"These stairs," Ben said too loudly, chasing away the whispers. "Bit of a hazard."

I blinked the shock away. "Yeah, they're not the best." I dragged in a breath and shot the rest of the way to the second floor with terror rippling across my back. "Bedroom sets." I forced lightness into the words, but it rang false, even to me. Ben shifted closer. He smelled of lilacs and crisp morning air. I shut my eyes and held my breath against the memories it stirred, but the aroma lent me a moment of clarity, of comfort, offering stability to my voice. "It saves the customer more if they buy the whole thing, but they can buy individual pieces if they want. There's a chart on the back of the tag for pricing." The scent grew overwhelming, tightening my stomach with something other than fear. My gaze fell on him. He ducked his head and reached up to pinch the air beside his temple in a familiar gesture. For a moment, I imagined him tugging at a hood. "You..." I paused. He what? *Ugh.* I needed to take a mental health day.

"Nora," Lisa shouted.

"Up here," I called back, thankful for the interruption.

She popped up in the archway below. "I'm going to run home and see if Randy is there. Can you watch things for me while I'm gone?"

"I..." *Don't leave me alone with him.* "Okay. No problem."

"I'll be back soon," she said, already disappearing.

Ben stepped up beside me. "She's..."

"Yeah," I agreed. There wasn't really a word to describe Lisa, but she was a good boss when she wasn't trying to micromanage everything. Or everyone. "Anyway." I shrugged, diffusing some of the tension between my shoulders. "That's it for the sales floor. I'll show you the stock room after Lisa comes back so we can watch for customers."

His arm brushed against mine, and I nearly jumped out of my skin. "What do we do now?" he asked.

"We wait." I started back down the stairs, my eyes darting from one side of the stairwell to the other. My ears prickled but the voice was gone, if it had ever been there to begin with. I let out a slow breath. "Come on. I'll show you how to check the system to see if something is in stock."

Ben's eyes burned into my back, and he followed me silently to Lisa's desk. Not in a way that bothered me, but in a way that should have. I rolled my shoulders. I didn't know Ben. There wasn't a voice in the stairwell. Katie had a nightmare. No one laughed.

Didn't, didn't, didn't.

I threw myself into the rolling chair, still warm from when Lisa sat in it and clicked the power button on the computer. "It takes a minute for this to get going."

"Okay." He grabbed a chair from the other side of the table used for customers and swung it around to sit beside me.

My finger rapped on the mouse. Twenty minutes down. Seven hours and forty minutes to go. My stomach grumbled, and I brushed my long bangs down to hide the side of my face.

"Hungry?"

"Not at all," I lied. Even if he did notice the rumbling, he didn't have to comment.

He laughed. "Liar. When did you eat last?"

The screen popped up with a system update. I flung myself back in the chair. *Of course.* "This is going to take all day," I said, ignoring his question. The last thing I ate was a grilled cheese sandwich yesterday afternoon and a handful of chips at the party. If Natalie and Emery hadn't guilt-tripped me into going out, I would've chowed down on leftover beef stew before bed. Then my cookie heist was interrupted, but it was none of his business. "While we wait, I can show you—"

"The vending machines?" His eyes glimmered, and my face warmed. "Excellent idea. I already know where they are."

"That's not—"

But he was already out of his seat, striding toward the break room in the back. I leaned my head against the headrest. It wouldn't hurt to eat, but my appetite had vanished along with my sanity. My mother couldn't find out. For two months before the first psychiatric visit, I rarely ate, only wanting to get back to the Sandman. Now, if I so much as left a few bites on my plate, she hovered near my door at night to make sure I wasn't in bed too early. Falling asleep before nine on one of those nights almost guaranteed her looking up the phone number of a doctor again. I dragged my hands down my face. Three years without mentioning the Sandman, and she still refused to let it go.

"Pick your poison." Ben dumped an armful of snacks on the desk. "Each one equally delicious and peanut free."

My eyes narrowed. "Are you allergic to peanuts?"

"No." He lifted a hand to his temple again, tugging at air, and plunked down beside me. He focused on the bags as he arranged all of them to face up. "Pretzels? They had loops and sticks."

I snagged the closest bag—the sticks—and pried it open without looking away from him. There was no way he could have known I was allergic to peanuts. None. Just like there was no way he was a fictional person that lived in my head. Peanuts are a common allergy; maybe he was used to looking out for someone in his family.

"So how did you talk Lisa into hiring you when there were no openings?" I asked.

He held his hands up to his chin. "My charisma?"

"Ha. Ha." My lips curled against my will.

"What? You don't think I'm fascinating? Perhaps I should try harder." He batted his long eyelashes. "How about now?"

I slapped a hand over my mouth before I could laugh a mouthful of pretzel into his face. "I think you should save it for the customers."

A siren wailed in the distance. Whatever spell he cast, broke. The smile fell from my face, and I surged up from the desk. I needed to put some space between us. It was too easy with him, like I wasn't pretending. No good could come of that; my secrets were too important to risk.

I opened one of the doors, wedging a piece of wood beneath it to let in some fresh air, and the siren grew louder, followed by another. "I wonder what's going on," I said more to myself than anything.

Ben was at my side then, his expression tight. A rock settled in my gut. I didn't know him well enough to know where his thoughts were but seeing him like this unsettled me.

"Let me guess. You have a warrant out for your arrest," I joked.

His smile was taut, his eyes following the flashing lights when they turned the corner and whizzed by the store. "Why? Are you into bad boys?"

I snorted. "In your dreams."

His eyes flashed, the tiniest of true smiles breaking through. "Maybe in yours."

My heart squeezed. I opened my mouth to speak but the blast of sirens stole my ability to think. To breathe. I tore my eyes away from his, from the secrets written there—and they *were* there, ringing through every bone in my body.

A black Toyota flew into Howell's gravel parking lot in a cloud of dust. The driver slammed the vehicle into park before it came to a full stop, jerking the car to a halt. Lisa's father climbed out, his face beet red.

"We're closing up," he said in his usual raspy tone. "Go on home. We'll call you when we're ready to reopen."

"What happened?" I asked, craning my neck to follow the police. Ben stood as still as a statue beside me.

Lisa's father brushed by us without another word and flipped the row of light switches. A large ring of keys swung on his belt with a bright orange tassel. *Lisa's keys.*

"Grab your things," he barked.

Katie's screams rose up in the back of my mind again, a faint, distant ringing, mingled with a deep chuckle. I shook my head. It was fine. Everything was fine.

"Are you okay?" Ben asked.

"Yep." I bolted toward the desk where I set my purse.

If Lisa's father wanted us to leave, that was fine by me. Between Ben and the creepy, nonexistent voice playing mind-games with me, I was more than ready to go home.

Where Katie had screamed. And another nonexistent voice chuckled.

I swallowed my secrets, shoved down my doubts.

Fine.

I'm absolutely fine.

***

When I swept through the front door, my mother poked her head over the kitchen counter, her brunette ponytail limp. "What are you doing home?"

I shrugged and kicked the door shut with my heel. "I thought you were in bed."

"I forgot to put dinner in the crockpot." She glanced at the television. *Breaking News* scrolled across the bottom of the WNOX 11 station. "Shouldn't you be at work?"

"There was..." I started. The reporter stood outside a small ranch house that was surrounded by yellow tape. Countless police lights flashed in the background and an ambulance was backed into the driveway. Officers lingered near the door, speaking with two men in suits. "Turn it up."

My mother set the cutting board down. "Did something happen at the store?" she asked, ignoring the scene on TV.

The reporter motioned an older woman forward. I strained to hear what he said, focusing on his lips, but only caught a *thank you.* I darted around the recliner and knelt in front of the entertainment center, tapping the volume button. "And you were the one who discovered the body?"

"Yes," the woman answered in a shaking voice. "Some of their mail was delivered to my house. I have a key, so I went in to set it on their table, and he was on the couch." She placed her hands on her chest. "His neck was snapped at the most hor—"

One of the people in suits—a bald man with dark skin and silver glasses—touched her shoulder. "That's enough." The reporter opened his mouth to object, but the detective pointed a finger at him. "This is an open murder investigation. You know better."

Open murder investigation. My heart dropped, and I gripped the edge of the television stand. The detective ushered the woman away. The reporter turned back to the camera, his face grim. He lifted a finger to his ear and nodded.

Behind him, the EMT's wheeled out a stretcher. The camera zoomed in to reveal a woman with an oxygen mask on. I gasped, slamming a hand over my mouth. It couldn't be...

"Is that Lisa?" My mother's voice rose to a near screech.

I nodded, my body numb. She was fine when she left the store. Did she walk in on the murderer? But the other woman found the body, and she appeared fine. So, what happened? The blood drained from my head, and I shuffled back to plop on the couch before I fainted.

His, the woman had said. Randy. Randy was dead. Murdered. His neck... *His neck.* The voice from the store echoed in my ears. *Dreamer, Dreamer, not a screamer. Snapped his neck and—*

It knew. The voice knew.

My mother jammed the power button, but I could still see the image of Lisa on the stretcher. My hands shook. If by some miracle I wasn't losing it, I had somehow gained psychic abilities overnight.

Insane, insane, insane.

"Nora? Are you okay?"

Tiny wrinkles formed at the edges of my mother's eyes, and she chewed on the inside of her cheek. I knew that look. It was the I'm-worried-you're-about-to-snap look. The one she got right before she started suggesting I be reevaluated.

"Howell's is closed until further notice," I said in a flat voice and cleared the lump from my throat. *Act normal.* It didn't matter my boss was just killed or my other boss was on the way to the hospital. Any sign of weakness, of an oncoming emotional break, in front of my mother, spelled disaster. I stood and rubbed at my eyes. "We were out late last night, and I had to wake up early, so I think I'll go back to bed for a little while."

"Oh? Are you sure you don't want to stay up? You can help me chop the carrots." She hovered at my shoulder, and I shook my head. "How was the party anyway? Did you have fun?"

I hid my wince behind a yawn. She didn't need help with the carrots, and she certainly didn't care about the party. She only wanted to make sure the horrible news didn't send me swan-diving off the deep end. More than anything, she feared the resurgence of the Sandman, which, in turn, meant she lived in terror of major change. After all, he was born from the stress of her divorce so, why wouldn't her remarriage, Katie moving away for college in the fall, or my final year before graduation bring him back? *Because he never left.* Her list of possible triggers hadn't included people-I-knew-being-murdered before, but I was willing to bet it now held the number one spot.

I forced a smile, skirting around her. "It was lots of fun, Mom."

"Good, good," she said, relieved. But her eyes followed me all the way up the stairs.

Once inside the safety of my room, I dug my sketchbook from its hiding place and threw myself into the desk chair. My hands shook as I flipped through pages full of blues and purples and silvers. Past dozens of sketches of the Sandman—that brought an image of Ben to the front of my mind. Those vivid violet eyes belonged among the other images. I could already feel my hand gliding over the sheet of paper, making the perfect sweep of his eyelashes. Could visualize the thrill that would spark through me, shading those impossible irises until they reflected the same mysterious glint as the real things.

But, instead, I slid the black pencil from the box. The tip scratched against the page with a sharp rush. My hand moved feverishly, leaving harsh, angry lines in its wake. When I was finished, the colored pencil slipped from my grip and rolled off the edge of the desk, clattering to the floor.

The words *Dreamer, Dreamer* swallowed the page. They stared up at me. Mocked me. I slammed the notebook shut and clasped my hands over my ears as if it would stop the voice from coming back.

Chapter
Four

Nora

The television blurred as I clicked through the channels. Every time I tried to sleep, Katie's scream haunted me. I refused to ask for the Sandman's help again, though. After two full nights without him, I couldn't stomach it if he ignored my call. False hope only led to disappointment; I wasn't going to risk confirming he had vanished completely.

But my body languished with news I couldn't share with anyone but him. The Sandman didn't yet know that I had watched police cars race past Howell's on their way to a murder scene. Didn't know it was Lisa's house where Randy was found murdered. His neck snapped. Just like the voice whispered in the stairwell. Impossibly. Unbelievably. *Why would I hear that? Of all things, why that?*

I hauled the blanket off the back of the couch and wrapped it around myself. *This was so not healthy.* Anything was better than sitting in my living room, feeling sorry for myself, but I couldn't find the energy to move.

The cushions shifted near my feet. "Hey," Katie said around a spoonful of cereal. "What are you watching?"

"Nothing yet. Here." I tossed my sister the remote.

We hadn't spoken about the other night. I wasn't sure Katie remembered having a nightmare, or if she blamed her hoarse voice the next morning on too much singing in the shower. Really, it could have been either, but it was hard to imagine that she could forget a nightmare that vivid.

"I'm surprised you're up," I glared at her puffy eyes, willing her to give me the smallest opening to ask. "It's before noon."

"Well, someone likes to blast the television at the crack of dawn," she said.

The surround sound wasn't *that* loud. "It's not the crack of dawn; it's almost eleven."

"Precisely." Katie slurped another spoonful of breakfast, and I cringed. "I could've slept until two, and still made my date with Jen by four."

I glared at her. "Don't you want to enjoy summer vacation? You're only here for a couple more months."

"I *am* enjoying it." Katie leaned into the cushions and flipped the channel, "Nothing exciting happens before lunch."

"Whatever."

"Howell's is still closed, right?" Katie asked.

"Yep." My stomach churned at the thought of going back there. Paul found out from a coworker that Lisa was fine—the sight of Randy's body triggered a severe asthma attack—but I imagined it would be a long time before she reopened. It would be impossible to walk past the office without remembering all the mornings I found Randy taking a nap inside. Impossible not to wonder how different things could've been if he came back to the store to sleep instead of going home.

"That's so bizarre. I mean, why would someone kill your boss? I heard nothing was missing from the house, and there were no signs of forced entry. That's super fishy. My money is on the wife. She had the opportunity, and I'm sure they'll dig up a motive."

I bolted up and snatched the remote from Katie's hand. "Her name is Lisa," I snarled, pointing the remote in her face, fighting off a flash of heat. "And she didn't kill anybody."

"Alright, alright." She held her hands up in surrender while balancing her bowl on her lap. "Sorry, it's just the biggest thing to happen in Cedarbrook in a long time. I didn't mean anything by it."

"Yeah?" I snapped and threw myself back into the cushions. "Well, maybe you should think before you open your mouth. What if whoever killed him followed him from the store? He was taking the deposit to the bank before. If I wasn't late, maybe I would've seen something."

"Or been killed too," she said.

"Katie!"

She rolled her eyes. "Sorry. You're right. Shutting up now. How's mom taking it?"

"Like mom," I grumbled. *Staring holes into me.*

Silence stretched between us. Katie always knew exactly which of my buttons to push, and exactly when to back away. Only this was a *big* button; my boss' murder wasn't a joke, and I wasn't ready to talk about it. But I could only turn my phone off for so long before Emery showed up at the house. And Natalie, if I didn't reply to her texts before she got back from her family trip to California. I swallowed a groan.

"Sooo, what are you doing today?" Katie finally asked.

I tucked the blanket under my armpits. "This."

"Oh no. You're not going to sit around the house moping again. Weren't you just lecturing me about enjoying vacation?" She hopped up and tapped my knee. "Get dressed."

I wasn't moping. I was processing. And avoiding. My friends weren't the only reason I turned off my phone. Multiple news outlets called to get inside information on Randy like I would know anything about his personal life, and a Detective Bell wanted to ask me a few questions. My parents took his calls.

"Where are we going?" I asked.

"Shopping," Katie sang to the ceiling.

"For what?"

"I'll have a dorm room to decorate soon. Maybe I'll get some new clothes, too," Katie called over her shoulder on the way to the staircase. "Who cares? Mom told me she left some money in the jar. We'll hang out at the mall, grab some lunch, and then you can drop me off at the theater to meet Jen."

I narrowed my eyes. "What you're really saying is that you want me to chauffeur you around all day."

"Maybe." She winked at me over the railing. "But I've been having these creepy dreams, so I need to get the hell out of this house."

I felt the blood drain from my face. *Dreams?* Plural? And *creepy?* Creepy was the furnace kicking on when you were alone in the cellar. It was a portrait with eyes that followed you around the room. It absolutely was not something that made a person scream, like Katie had screamed. I swung my legs off the edge of the couch and untangled myself from the blanket. My head swam, thoughts clouding. "Wh… What do you mean? Creepy dreams?"

"I call dibs on the shower," she yelled in a high sing-song voice.

The Sandman was gone, Katie was having bad dreams, and that voice in the stairwell… *Dreamer, Dreamer.* I rubbed my forehead against the distant echo of it. All of that couldn't be a coincidence, could it? When I shivered, it had nothing to do with the air conditioning.

***

The sweet aroma of sesame chicken mixed with burnt cheese from the pizzeria behind us. Half of the people jammed into the food court were our age, but I only recognized a handful of them. A handful too many, that is. I prodded my fries around my tray, dunking the occasional one in catsup before eating it. Three boys from my school, juniors, stared in our direction. I tried to ignore their loud whispers, catching only bits and pieces.

Body.

Murder.

It was no secret I worked at Howell's but there was no reason I should know anything. Except the voice knew. *Didn't exist. Didn't happen.* My foot bounced under the table.

"Where to first?" Katie scooped fallen guacamole off a plastic wrapper and shoved it back into her taco.

"This was your idea." And a horrible one at that.

"Ask her," one of the boys said a bit louder.

"No way. You do it."

Katie slammed her palms down on the table and twisted toward them. "Take one step toward this table and you'll be the ones on the news tonight."

A fry flew to the back of my throat, sending me into a coughing fit. The guys bolted, disappearing into the center of the mall, before I regained my composure. "I can't believe you just did that," I wheezed.

"Why? They deserved it," Katie said around another bite of taco. "Anyway, like I was saying. Should we start on the top floor and work our way down?"

"Let's go see what new—" The words stuck in my throat as I spotted Ben walking straight toward our table, a white bag hanging off his wrist. His curls bobbed around his forehead as he focused on the phone in his hand. "Crap."

"New crap? That's vague," Katie said with a snort.

I slid lower, the wire seat grating against my spine. I bowed my head to hide behind my hair. With hundreds of people in the mall, why did he have to be the one in my current vicinity? The last thing I wanted was to be reminded of Howell's or the Sandman. This trip was supposed to get my mind off those things.

"Who are you hiding from?"

Crap. Crap. Crap. "Ben."

"Ben?" Katie shouted and sat up straighter to scan the crowd over my head.

"Shut up."

Quickly, I glanced in Ben's direction, with the feeble hope he was too engrossed in his phone to notice, but it was too late. His head snapped up and our eyes met. Ben's perfect lips parted in surprise and his hand rose to his temple, grabbing at air again. Recognition rippled from my head to my toes but I willed the sensation away. Why did he have to be so impossibly attractive? Even with the weird contacts and tattoos that made no sense, I couldn't help but be drawn to him. Maybe he merely reminded me of the Sandman because I needed to see him so badly. It certainly wasn't because they looked alike; I had never seen an inch of the Sandman that wasn't hidden beneath black cloth.

"Ben, from work?" Kate asked, practically bouncing in her seat.

I gave a small nod. He was two feet from our table now; I had to say something. Perhaps, that we were just leaving or that I had to pee. Any excuse to avoid a conversation.

"Hey," he said brightly.

I slid up in the chair. "Hi."

"How are you?" His eyes never left mine while he waited for an answer.

"Um," I stammered. "I'm... okay. Good. You?"

The corners of his lips curled sympathetically. "Same."

I dropped my gaze to the tattoos on his hands and arms. Looking closely, his fingertips were solid navy blue. It wasn't until after the first knuckle that any hint of silver played along his skin. The specks were more condensed there, spreading out and swirling together the higher up they climbed on his arm, until the cuff of his T-shirt got in the way.

"New phone?" I blurted, hoping for his quick answer and even swifter exit.

He shrugged and dropped the phone into the bag. "I figured it was time to join the twenty-first century."

"You didn't have a phone before today?" Katie asked, her brows raised. I kicked her under the table. "Ouch. What?"

Ben kept watching me, waiting. For what, I wasn't sure, but it felt like more than a few words of casual conversation. "I should have checked in with you sooner. Lisa mentioned you've worked with them for almost a year, so I figure this must be hard."

"Well, you're here now, right?" Katie asked, offering a wide smile. "We're done eating, and I was just about to drag Nora to the jewelry store. Want to come along?"

I shot daggers at Katie from across the table. *I'm going to throttle you*, I promised with a steady gaze. My pursed lips vowed it would be a long, long process. Either she thought I had a secret crush on Ben, or she was developing one herself—not that I could blame her. No part of me wanted to spend the afternoon with him trailing us from shop to shop, though. The corner of my eye twitched. Well, *almost* no part of me.

Regardless, I was definitely not done eating.

"I'm sure he has better things to do than follow us around the mall," I said with a stiff smile.

"I don't!" Ben cut in fast, his voice overlapping the end of my sentence. A rogue blush colored his cheeks. "I mean, if you don't mind me tagging along."

Katie nudged me with her toe and scowled, "Yeah, it's totally fine with her."

Ben beamed, "Here, let me."

He scooped up our trays and headed toward the garbage cans. I eyed the half-eaten food before whipping around to my sister. "What are you doing?" I whispered through my teeth.

Katie shrugged. "He's hot."

"Hot? Since when do you like guys with tattoos?"

"First of all, I meant for you. When it comes to guys, he's not my type, but a girl *can* appreciate beauty when she sees it." Katie squinted at Ben from across the food court. "Secondly, what tattoos? How much have you seen of him exactly?"

"Katie," I snapped. I was in no mood for her games. Not about this. "Seriously? Are you blind? He's covered in them."

"Is he?" She wagged her eyebrows.

"And who wears colored contacts like that?" I added, my voice struggling to stay level.

"Been staring into his eyes, have you?"

I drew in a breath and clenched my hands under the table. If we weren't in public, there was every possibility that I *would* strangle her. Wasn't there some sort of sister code about this stuff? Her baby pictures were *so* coming out the next time Jen came over for dinner, especially the one where she decided to go streaking down our street when she was two. It was currently stuffed in the back of the hutch where my dearest sister assumed no one would find it. I cocked one eyebrow, a dare for her to try anything else.

"All right, all right. You're going to have to tell me all about the tattoos later, but his eyes are brown. If he's going to go through all the trouble of colored contacts, he could've picked something fun. Like red. Oh, or cat eyes. That would be cool."

"You're not funny."

Ben approached the table again with his hands in his pockets—his eyes unmistakably violet. "Ready?" he asked.

***

Cards full of cheap earrings and necklaces lined the walls of the jewelry shop. Mirrors hung every few feet, interspersed by spinning racks. I broke away from Katie and slowly scanned all the jewelry that I would never wear. Ben kept a respectable distance between us, but it wasn't enough to keep me from fidgeting. Something inside me rustled, a living thing writhing beneath my skin, determined to undermine my decision to stay away from him. However, practice made perfect, and I had years of experience, pretending to appear calm and collected.

I glanced at the cashier—a brunette in a floral shirt—and stepped up to a clearance rack at the end of the counter. A magazine was open on the glass case. The girl's eyes drifted closed, her chin slipping off her palm, before she caught herself from face-planting on a perfume ad. I knew exactly how she felt. She raised a hand in a small, embarrassed wave. Ben, of course, gave her one back.

My eyes grazed over beaded necklaces without really seeing them, latching on a zebra print sleep mask with *Sweet Dreams* embroidered in purple. Katie asked something on the other side of a podium, but her words were far away, drowned out by the memory of her scream echoing in the recesses of my mind. It grew louder and louder. I couldn't decipher Ben's answer to her over the upbeat music coming from the ceiling speaker. My pulse raced, a loud *whomp, whomp, whomp* against my eardrums, seemingly in time with the bass.

"Nora?" Ben touched my wrist with gentle, warm fingers. The sensation tore through me, pushing at the macabre chorus until it was nothing more than a faint ringing in my ears. "Are you okay?"

"Yeah." I turned back to the rack, unable to stand the weight of his stare. It felt as if his gaze burrowed into me and latched onto something hidden. Secret. An enemy invasion and yet, for some reason, a welcomed homecoming. "Yeah, I'm fine."

"You look tired."

I shrugged.

"Are you worried about what happened with Randy?" he asked in a quiet voice. "Or is something else bothering you?"

"Nora." Katie scooted between us with a wide blue headband. "Does this clash with my hair?"

"It's perfect," I told her, and Katie bounced away. "If you want to look like cotton candy," I added under my breath.

Ben chuckled. The sound snapped me awake, warming me to him just a little.

"Don't you want anything?" he asked, glancing around at the myriad of ornamentation.

"No. I try to go through life unnoticed… and everything in here draws attention." I bit my tongue. Did I really say that out loud? Next thing I knew, I would be telling him my whole life story. *Ugh.*

"I noticed you," he said quietly, tugging on one of his curls.

Heat flooded my cheeks. What was I supposed to say to that? Thank you, but don't? Because I was ten pounds of crazy in a five-pound basket. This was the worst time imaginable for someone to take an interest in me, and an even worse time for me to *maybe* be interested back. He was nice. And hot. But I had to figure myself out first. Once I stopped seeing Ben as the Sandman, there might be a chance. Until then, I couldn't afford more confusion.

"Hello?" Katie asked the cashier. "Hey."

"I was thinking—" Ben froze, his eyes wide. I followed his gaze to where my sister reached over to shake the brunette's arm.

The girl leapt from her stool and stumbled back. "Get them off." Her voice cracked. "Get them off. Get them off!"

I stepped forward cautiously, my hands raised. "Get what off?"

"Get *them* off!" She repeated it a dozen times, her voice rising with each scream. Carefully manicured nails dug into her tanned forearms, the white tips disappearing. She dragged her hand back with a horrendous *rip*. Layers of skin disappeared. Bright red blood streamed toward her elbow, dripping on the tile floor.

My feet were cemented to the ground. Suddenly, Ben leapt over the counter, shaking the cashier's shoulders, and pried her fingers away. "Wake up." It was a command, calm and careful. But her eyes were wide open, fixed on the gashes on her arm. "Come on. Wake up," he urged.

"*Off.*" The cashier shoved Ben away with more strength than a girl her size should possess and snatched a glitter pen from the counter. "*Off, off, off.*"

Ben tripped on the fallen stool, knocking them both into the corner. "There's nothing there," he said through his teeth. "Wake up."

"*Get them off!*" She pierced her left hand with the pen. Blood oozed around the tip.

Katie screamed. The old shriek rose up in my mind to join it until I could hear nothing else. My body shook, and I stretched across the counter to grab the girl's good hand. To stop her. To give Ben an extra second to restrain her. But before I could reach her, the girl yanked the pen out. In one swift movement, she shouldered Ben through the counter's gate and into my side. We knocked over a podium as we fell, landing in a tangled heap.

The cashier stabbed again. And again. And again. One blossoming bead of blood after another, moving up, up, up her arm. "*Off! Get them off!*"

"Stop!" I shoved the fallen podium off my foot, but it used time I didn't have. I saw what was coming. I saw it, and there was nothing I could do. Time slowed. The scream in my head rose up, muffling my shouts. "Katie, stop her. Stop her!"

But my sister was frozen in slack-jawed horror, as the girl plunged the pen into her throat.

The world stopped in a spray of crimson.

Katie bolted from the store into a gathering crowd. Ben wrapped strong arms around my waist and dragged me away. It all happened so fast, so immediately, that we reached the doors before the body toppled with a sickening thud. It was only after Ben took my face in his hands and held my gaze that I realized the scream was no longer an echo. It wasn't Katie's. It was mine—torn from some place deep inside. The crowd surged around us, rushing this way and that, calling for help. It snuffed the air from my lungs, and I swallowed against a raw throat.

"It's okay. You're okay," Ben said. I moved back a fraction of an inch, but he held fast. "Keep looking at me, Nora. Don't look in there. Look at me. You're okay. I'm here."

I was too shocked, too utterly depleted, to do anything but lean on the bit of strength he offered. Something shimmered behind his starlit eyes, an undercurrent of blue. The hint of an inner glow peeked out, before fading into the depths.

"Nothing is okay," I breathed, unsteady.

Nausea took hold, and I broke away, running to the nearest garbage can. I dry heaved over the pile of rotting food. The stench wafting up from inside did nothing to help. Saliva filled my mouth, and I let it drool from my bottom lip.

"Dreamer, Dreamer, couldn't free her." It was the same velvety voice from Howell's. A voice like distant rolls of thunder, warning of an oncoming storm. "Saw a beetle who tried to eat her."

I heaved again. This time it wasn't in vain.

Chapter Five

The Sandman

A rendering of worlds.

A distortion of nature.

A binding of power.

The Weaver and I had lived through it all together, until the day I trapped him in his realm, snipping the last strand of friendship. I sat on the beach, head in my hands, immersed in the actions of the sand-made figures in front of me. It was as if they were part of a play—these replicas of the Weaver and me. For hours, I watched as we created our realms, clear in purpose, content with our differences. I was the light, he, the dark. The balance was satisfied, and our world was better for it.

But we weren't the only beings that had to live in it. I forced the sand to skip over the parts featuring creatures more ancient than us, molded from anger and violence. They were dormant now, irrelevant. But they weren't completely unrelated either. One in particular was the catalyst that changed everything.

I waved a hand at the scene of us reaching for a blade in unison, and it scattered. A lump formed in my throat. Binding the Weaver gave me no pleasure when once, a millennium ago, we were friends. I raked my hands down my face as longing spread through me. It had been a mistake to watch the past—to allow myself to remember with this much clarity. No matter how guilty I felt now, it was the right thing to do. The *only* thing to do. Locking the Weaver in the Nightmare Realm saved millions of lives.

And yet...

I pressed my fingers against my eyelids.

And yet...

A sound like nails on a chalkboard wrenched me from my turmoil. Razor sharp talons clawed at the fabric of the barrier before me. The magic glowed blue beneath each tapered point as it held the line, buffering each blow. I kept my eyes on the reptilian nightmare and scooped up handfuls of sand. It fell in showers from between my bare fingers, swirling and twisting into kunai throwing knives. They hovered in the air around me, dozens of gleaming, pointed tips aimed at the beast.

"Come on," I whispered the challenge as I stood.

My muscles twitched, my nerves tingling. Nora could never see this. I felt her on the other side of the beach at the same moment the barrier strained, and this needed to be over before she came looking for me. I spent countless hours reinforcing the protections between the Dream and Nightmare Realms after what happened at the mall. Although they were stronger now, they were not completely unbreachable. No magic was.

The Weaver knew exactly what he was doing. While Katie's nightmare and Randy's death came as a surprise to Nora, she wasn't quite as emotionally vulnerable as he would've liked. The

Weaver needed the shock of today, the blood and the carnage. The things that called to nightmares like hopes called to dreams. He was turning Nora into a flame in the middle of the dankest dungeon.

I supposed I should be glad it attracted a mindless nightmare instead of a more sophisticated creation, but I couldn't find it in me to be grateful. Intelligent or not, the scaled creature was perfectly capable of ripping a hole in my barrier. The magic around the Dream Realm was as secure as I could make it, but even the strongest metal bent with enough exposure to heat.

A high-pitched shriek rippled across the starry sky. If I didn't act soon, the commotion would attract others. I filled my lungs and blew a handful of sand at the wall. It opened for me, a mere pinhole in the scheme of things, and a forked tongue slipped through followed by the tip of a green scaled nose. The barrier fogged with the creature's hot breath. A single clawed toe slipped inside, and the barrier creaked under the pressure.

I sent the first wave of knives soaring forward. They whizzed through the air, hitting their mark one after another. The giant lizard reared back, exposing a yellow underbelly. The next set of knives rustled my clothes as they flew past me. They hadn't yet hit when padded steps thundered across the invisible domed ceiling.

Black and yellow fur streaked across the sky, and the lizard squealed the most human of sounds. A breath fell from my mouth. *Thanks, Baku.* I lifted another handful of sand and blew it at the breach. The space glowed with blue light, and I turned before it faded to match the rest of the wall, tugging my hood up. There was little worse than watching Baku devour his meals.

The sound, maybe.

Definitely, the sound.

Besides, I had a promise to make good on. I told Nora I would see her soon, though she never heard me say it, but we hadn't met in days. Day Walking didn't count. Even with Nora's ability to see the marks on my arms, she didn't know me in the Day World. How could she? She had never seen me in the Night World. I needed to be more careful with what I let slip around her. There were things I shouldn't know as Ben but taking form in her world—being near her in a way I never could before—it was too easy to forget. The extreme amount of energy it took to be there didn't help my focus either.

With a sigh, I ripped the gloves from inside my tunic and strode across the beach, leaving the gnashing teeth and tearing flesh behind.

***

Nora's pink sweatpants stood out against the silver sand, where she sat at the edge of the beach. The thin white fabric of her T-shirt allowed the lines of a black bra to show through, and I forced myself not to look. Her wet hair was twisted into a high bun, beads of water still clinging to the messy ends. A line creased the space between her brows.

I hated that line and the fact that I was partially to blame for it. I hated that I hated it.

Nora was the Dream Keeper. That's all she was ever supposed to be. I didn't dare give voice to anything more because it was undoubtedly impossible. I loved her enough to recognize I couldn't give her more than a few stolen hours every night, and she couldn't give me more than a handful of decades before she passed away. It wasn't fair to either of us, but the heart never cared about *fair.*

It was enough that I was her refuge. That I was the one she turned to every night since that first call, five years ago. It *had* to be enough. But it wasn't…not really. I didn't want to be her dirty little secret. To be the thing she had to keep hidden from everyone she loved because the truth would mean more doctors.

My chest ached. That's what I had to be for her—hidden. I took a silent, deep breath, and approached. "Hello, Nora."

Her voice was distant, cool, when she replied, "Hello."

"I'm sorry I'm late." I swallowed hard and knelt in front of her. My hands balled into fists on my thighs—as much from nerves as they did to make sure I followed the rules. The feel of her skin beneath my hands was ingrained in me now. A taste of a drug I would always crave. "I came as soon as I could."

She said nothing for so long, my pulse echoed in my ears. The barriers had thinned more than I expected, and with the Weaver playing hide-and-seek... Hurting Nora was the last thing I ever wanted to do but losing her trust could be deadly. We were bound together, a team, whether she knew it or not—what one of us did affected the other.

It was quickly becoming obvious my time of sheltering her from the truth was ending, though. How much damage would the Weaver inflict before she remembered our first meeting? It was easy to let her forget that night. Anyone could've called out to me at that moment and become the Dream Keeper. If I hadn't been so desperate, I would never have chosen someone so young, so vulnerable, for the task. But fate intervened.

I had explained things the best I could at the time, saying that a bad man was trying to hurt her world, and I needed a safe place to hide the key to his cell. Nora had glared into the shadows of my hood with wide, curious eyes, and granted me permission when I asked for it. But it was a game to her. An adventure in the storybooks. A *dream*. She didn't know the gravitas of the danger.

She couldn't have because as soon as I removed the information from my mind and placed it into hers, I collapsed—broken in every way from the battle with the Weaver.

The balance was upended when I turned his own magic against him, binding him to the Nightmare Realm. Although our circumstances were vastly different, the results were the same: two weakened sides of the same coin. A fact I was both grateful for and loathed. I betrayed the Weaver the night we met to discuss things, but his excuses for invading the Day World were never going to make a difference. I don't remember how I did it—Nora carried that knowledge now—so the Weaver couldn't use the same methods against me. And, though binding him was a necessary evil, it is only right that I suffer for betraying someone I once called a friend.

"Where were you?" Nora asked in a voice so lifeless I hardly recognized it.

"I..." *Not yet.* I couldn't tell her yet. There was still time for me to fix things first. "You were about to have a nightmare," I said softly. It didn't answer her question, but it wasn't a complete lie, either.

"A nightmare." She was quiet for a heartbeat, her eyes narrowing. "I can't remember the last time I had a bad dream."

"I've always kept them away." Something I would not be able to do much longer. Worse yet, the Weaver knew it. Yesterday. Tonight. Tomorrow. On and on, the attacks would continue until he either got what he wanted, or I found a way to rebind him. This was just the beginning of the nightmare. The prelude. My gloves strained against their stitching. This was a battle I wasn't prepared to fight a second time.

"My boss was murdered. Someone snapped his neck. You'd know that if you were here, of course." Nora's green eyes swept over me, dull and distant. "Then today I watched a girl at the mall stab herself to death with a pen."

There was nothing I could say, nothing I could do, to make her forget what happened. I knew because I saw it too. The Weaver's wicked joy slammed into me both times, but never soon enough for me to pinpoint his target. All I could do was make sure I was nearby in case he sent a sleepwalker after Nora. Not to kill her, of course—if she died, the dream died with her—but to persuade her in the only way the Weaver knew how: torture.

"I'm sorry," I said again, letting my sincerity coat each word.

"You don't happen to know anything about it, do you?"

I stared out from beneath my hood, my heart racing. "Why do you ask?"

She turned her head away from me. "No reason."

With a clenched jaw, I shoved the image of the cashier from my mind and grabbed a handful of sand. Nora needed to talk about what happened but doing it here would only draw more attention to herself. Besides, Baku was ravenous, but he could only eat so many nightmares in a single night.

The sand shifted and swirled as it took shape. First a pair of sneakers, followed by legs, a torso, arms. I stared at my own face, and the sand lifted my image's lips into a smile. My stomach dipped. It was stupid to be jealous of myself, but a seed of discomfort planted itself anyway. Ben could be there for her in a way I couldn't. The fact that she would never know that particular truth... was sand in my wounds.

At that thought, I cleared my throat. Now was the wrong time to go looking for hope. Walking in her world may have taken more out of me than I could afford, but not going left her vulnerable. I had to concentrate on protecting her from the Weaver. Nothing else.

"That's Ben," Nora said in a flat, distinctly unhappy voice. "Katie and I ran into him today at the mall."

That wasn't intentional—the being spotted part, anyway. I meant to watch from afar in case the Weaver tried anything. Not that it mattered in the end. I drew a deep breath and pushed aside the growing guilt. "And?"

Nora shrugged one shoulder. "And nothing. He works at Howell's."

"*Nothing* doesn't show up in your dreams." Especially not the first one the sand finds. Those are the most important ones— the ones that give Dreamers the peace they need to truly rest.

She flicked a hand at Ben's abdomen, and the image scattered. "It's not a big deal."

"You must like him." I bit my tongue. Hadn't I just decided not to go seeking hope?

"Are you *jealous?*" She smirked, but it fell as fast as it came.

Of course, not—I'm much cuter, I almost joked, but I didn't want her to ask me to prove it. It was hard enough to resist showing myself. I wasn't sure why I bothered to hide anymore; it was meant as another way to keep a wall between us, but that wall had crumbled to dust. There was nothing *other* about my face besides my eyes. Nothing to scare her.

However, she now knew me as Ben. Would she feel lied to? Betrayed?

"Don't worry," Nora said with a sigh. Her nose wrinkled in the way that never failed to fill me with adoration, and she pinched her own cheeks, trying not to smile. "You're still my favorite, and I'm sure you're just as cute. If I ever saw you, I would probably dream about you too."

She thought I was cute? My hand twitched with the impulse to reveal myself, but before I could move, a familiar throb pulsated through my marrow. The Weaver was close. If Nora didn't stop dwelling on what happened, she would light his path right to our doorstep. I grabbed a second handful of sand and willed it into my own creation. A butterfly glided through the air to land on her knee.

"I truly am sorry, Nora," I said in a strained voice. "There were some things I needed to take care of. I didn't mean to stay away."

She nodded and turned her attention to the fluttering wings. "It's okay. Maybe not the *best* time for you to go M.I.A." Her nose wrinkled again, but this time her eyes lacked the playful glint that always accompanied it. "But you're back. That's what matters."

Nora hadn't looked this lost or confused since before we agreed she should lie to her mother about my existence. I felt just as horrible about it then as I do now, but I saw what those doctors were doing to her. The bright-eyed, care-free girl I knew faded slowly. She withdrew from all but two of her friends, tossed her astrology books in the dumpster behind the school, and quit the swim team in her freshman year. Though Nora still sketched, there was always a tightness around her eyes on the rare occasions she talked about it. Everything that might relate to me or this place put her under a microscope, so she replaced the slide that *was* her life with one that could withstand the scrutiny. But her manufactured existence lacked the fiery spark of her soul.

I released another handful of sand and a dozen smaller butterflies took shape. They landed in her hair, fluttering around her with graceful ease.

She reached out a hand to let one rest in her palm. "Can I ask you something?"

"Of course."

"Do you think you'll—" She squinted around me. "What's that?"

The sea shrunk away from the beach, and a tendril of black fog inched across the receding water. "Wake up." The words flew from my throat in a stunned breath. "Nora, wake up."

The fog snapped forward, crushing the butterflies mid-flight. Nora gasped, and I lurched to my feet. Sand rose with me, snapping together to form a long blade in my hand. The curved metal gleamed in the moonlight.

"Wake up," I shouted.

"What?"

"Wake. Up." A whistle sounded above us, and the retreating water rose into a tidal wave. It rushed toward the shore, eclipsing the sky. "Nora!" I screamed in a rush of terror.

She vanished, and I flung an empty hand at the wave. A break wall shot from the shore and caught the impact before collapsing. The mist writhed against the beach, scraping against the sand trying to find purchase. With Nora gone, taking her piece of my power out of play, the Dream Realm was entirely dependent on me, and I held no fear of the Weaver—only of what would happen if he escaped. Without fear, he had nothing to hold over me. Fear was his power, his strength, his everything.

"Weaver," I called. Binding aside, he was forbidden from this place. There were no living things for him to kill here, but his presence was a poison, infecting the beach, tainting the dreams.

He had an entire world to govern—generals and soldiers, enemies and allies. There was no reason he should need mine or Nora's. "Show yourself."

The mist paused, and the Weaver's deep voice drifted from its center. "I'd love to, old friend, but it's a tight squeeze. Open a door so we can face each other."

"I will be dead before you step foot in here," I snarled.

A soft chuckle danced across the beach before the mist retreated beneath the water. I watched the last wisps vanish and exhaled. The sword disintegrated from tip to hilt. The barrier wasn't deep enough to keep him out—nothing I did was enough. It was a miracle I managed to bind the Weaver at all. My shoulders sagged. There was no guarantee I could do it again with the barriers and a Dream Keeper siphoning my power. Not when I had to resort to Day Walking to protect Nora.

The Weaver was still weak but keeping him that way meant weakening myself. It didn't matter who was right or wrong. It didn't matter that the Weaver had tried to unleash his beasts on the Day World. The universe always kept the balance.

For every light there was a shadow, for every dream, a nightmare.

Chapter Six

Nora

I swept through Howell's, systematically adjusting chairs around tables and fidgeting with the decorative centerpieces. The police left the entire store a mess. I rolled my eyes. As if they would find something hidden beneath a vase... But I was thankful for the busy work. It kept me away from the office and Lisa's elderly father, who hadn't moved from the desk all morning. The music from his portable radio drifted through the store and, try as I might, I wasn't able to block out the cheerful rhythm. It fed my anxiety, making me jerk and jump without reason. They may have had to reopen the store to survive, but I didn't need to come back. I shouldn't have. But then again, sitting home wasn't much better.

I paused near the back room where Ben was busy talking to a young couple about office chairs. He smiled and laughed and joked with them. All things I would probably never do again after what happened at the mall. Detective Bell interviewed Katie and me last night. He was the same dark-skinned man that interrupted the woman's TV interview about Randy. He was nice enough, promising we weren't suspects, ensuring it was important to speak with eyewitnesses, but that didn't stop him from giving me a distinct once over. With two strange deaths in the same short span of time and my connection to both, there had to be suspicions.

"Hey, you," Ben said, bobbing his head slightly.

I jumped, nearly dropping a set of fifty-dollar bookends. A breath shuttered out of me as I hugged them to my chest. Break these and it was goodbye fancy new colored pencil set.

"You break it, you buy it," he said with a grin.

I laughed dryly and set the ceramic pieces down on top of a TV stand. "I break it, *you* buy it for scaring me." I rubbed my hands together to hide my shaking fingers.

His grin widened. "If I wanted to scare you, I would have done something a little more fun than saying *hey you*."

My cheeks warmed. "Did you need something?"

"The computer says a rolling chair is in stock, but I'm not sure where to look."

We still hadn't finished the tour, and it was impossible to explain all the places in the back where the chair could be squirreled away. I chewed on the inside of my cheek. "I'll show you."

I led the way through the swinging doors to the back room with Ben following closely. The dry air tickled my nose, and I held my breath against the scent of wood and cardboard. We passed the motion sensor and fluorescent lights flickered to life overhead. The ones in the very back remained off. Randy was supposed to order more bulbs at the end of the month—I jerked again at the thought, quickly hiding it by pretending to trip over my own feet.

"Careful," Ben said, laced with concern.

I took a deep breath and slipped between two rows of large boxes. "Which model number do they want?"

He hesitated. "It's the brown leather one with an adjustable headrest. I can go get the number."

"No," I said, and he stuffed his hands into his pocket. "It's fine. I know which one you're talking about."

I steadied myself between the rows, gripping the rough, dusty boxes. Industrial staples poked precariously out of a few, and I squinted at the descriptions written on white stickers over the barcode. Last time I checked, there was one stuffed behind some mattresses, but if I could avoid climbing back there, I would. Besides, the longer I took in the back, the less time I had to spend out *there* talking to people. I was convinced half of the customers today were only here to be nosy.

A hard corner scraped my ankle through my khakis. I kicked at the offending cardboard until the overhang sat neatly on the shelf.

"I can get it," Ben offered.

I glanced up to where he stood at the end of the tight aisle, beneath the flickering bulb. It almost seemed like his tattoos glowed a bit in the split seconds between the light, which, of course, made no sense. It had to be a trick of the mind—or a special ink. Something. "Don't worry. I've done this a million times," I said. The hardest part was wedging a box out from between others, but once it hit the concrete floor, it slid down the row without much effort.

"But—"

"Please." I sighed and went back to reading labels. "It's been a rough couple of days, and I'm not in the mood to fight with you about which one of us should handle the manual labor."

He was quiet for a heartbeat. "I'm not trying to fight."

"I know," I admitted. He was trying to be nice, but with my mother's obnoxious, worried glances over dinner last night, that almost made it worse. I was flesh and bone just like he was, with good days and bad days, but on every single one of them, I was capable of carrying a stupid chair. A square box caught my attention at the end of the row, and I shimmied my way further down.

"If..." He paused. "If you ever need someone to talk to, you know, about what happened..."

The Sandman had annoyed me by not showing up and then asking me to leave, and the last few days *had* certainly left me with a lot to say, but I wasn't going to lean on Ben simply because he was available. The way he reminded me of the Sandman was too unnerving to allow anything more than necessary interactions between us. The mall was a mistake. I needed my sanity now more than ever and each time I looked at his handsome face, I wanted to picture it with a hood. "I already have people to talk to, but thanks."

"Your sister?" he asked.

"No. Katie will never talk about what happened again." Not that I blamed her in this case, but she had a way of pretending problems didn't exist. A family trait, I supposed. I couldn't help but wonder if she saw that spray of blood every time she shut her eyes too. If she heard the thump of the body hitting the floor whenever it was just a little too quiet. I leaned over a box and one corner caught me in the ribs. *Keep it together*, I begged myself.

Don't lose it in here. I backed up and bounced on the balls of my feet.

"I do have friends, you know," I said, forcing myself back to the present.

"I know."

The way he said it made me believe he did know, and not in the everyone-has-friends way. "I found the chair, so if you want to go cash the customer out, I'll bring it up."

He stood there another moment before stepping back. His footsteps echoed off the high ceiling, and I blew out a breath. The last thing I needed was for someone to make me feel so transparent. I had too many deep, dark secrets for that. I shuffled the box back and forth, waiting to hear the swinging doors open, when warm fingers grazed the back of my neck. I clasped a hand over the touch and spun. Boxes were stacked one on top of the other, leaving no room for someone to reach between.

"Ben?" I whispered, the hair on my arm standing on end.

A low, rumbling chuckle brushed my ear. I flattened myself against the boxes and closed my eyes. *It wasn't real.* This was what suppressing my feelings got me—another person in my head, tormenting me. Maybe my brain was simply wired differently. Maybe... maybe... I had no idea. Stress affected people differently, I was told. Hallucinations must have been my go-to coping mechanism.

Lucky me.

A warm brush of air sent goosebumps rippling over my skin.

"Get away from her," a voice hissed. I gripped the edge of the steel shelf. *Sandman?*

"Did you think you could hide her forever?" asked a rich voice with an undercurrent of fury.

I crept down the aisle, my heart jack-hammering in my chest. My knees shook, and I peeked between boxes. Ben's white shirt stood out in the unlit corner. His tattooed hands were balled in fists while he spoke. "Not forever. That's why I took precautions."

The chuckle rose again. "You're already failing."

"Am I?" Ben whispered with enough venom to make a viper jealous.

I snuck into an empty space between two cellophane-wrapped desks. Who was he talking to? I leaned on one desk for support and squinted. The corner was empty. I froze. Maybe the killer was Ben after all—maybe he followed Randy home before coming in and the girl... I didn't know about the girl. The cashier did it to herself, but if I was crazy for talking to someone in my dreams, then Ben was crazy for talking to shadows. Shadows that I heard as clearly as he seemed to. One thing was certain—he had no idea how far voices carried back here.

"You think you're safe from me because you don't hold it yourself." Something moved in the corner, a flash of gold slicing through the black. I slapped a hand over my mouth to keep from screaming. "You've convinced yourself that you have nothing to be afraid of, but I smell it on you, old friend. You reek of fear. My freedom isn't the only weapon I have against you anymore. It hasn't been for a while now."

Then the corner brightened a fraction, and Ben flexed his fingers. I sprinted down the aisle to the chair and gripped the edges of the box. I couldn't listen to another word. To another delusion. With a jolt, I yanked the box forward. It crashed down on my big toe, and I yelped.

"Are you okay?" Ben darted down the narrow aisle and bent to free my foot.

"Yes." I rubbed a dust-covered wrist over my forehead. He couldn't know I overheard anything—either he was crazier than I was, or I was officially ready for an institute. Choice A might put me in danger. Choice B meant outing myself. Neither option was all that appealing. I needed to get away from him, from everyone, and think before I opened my mouth.

"I need to go home early today," I said in a hushed voice as a frenzy of emotions withered in my gut.

Ben walked backward, guiding the chair from my path. "Okay."

"You've got that?" I said, motioning to the chair. "It's the right one?"

His eyes searched my face. Seeing. Too seeing. "Yes."

I bolted from the back, leaving Ben alone with his invisible foe. Only, he wasn't quite invisible—because I saw him. Sort of. Flashes of black and gold. A silhouette.

No. I saw nothing. *Nothing, nothing, nothing.*

"Nora!" someone called.

A moment later, I was tackled from behind. Black spots danced in my vision before I recognized the voice as Natalie's. My friend squeezed my waist, mumbling something about missing me into my shoulder.

"What are you doing here?" I asked, patting the arms that held me in place. Part of me wanted to let her hold me so I didn't fall over with relief, but touchy-feely wasn't really my thing. "I thought you weren't coming back from vacation until Friday."

"It *is* Friday." Natalie released me from the embrace and spun me around. "Why aren't you taking our calls? We've been trying to get a hold of you for days. Emery went to your house yesterday, but Katie said you weren't feeling well."

"I wasn't." I faked a cough, knowing full well she would see the lie. "See?"

"Oh no, don't you play those games with me, missy." She grabbed my hand and dragged me through the store. "You're avoiding us, so you don't have to talk about what happened."

That was exactly what I was doing. After the mall, the press intensified their efforts to get in touch with me and an unmarked police car sat at each end of the block now. Turning off my ringer, ignoring calls and texts, was the best way to prevent reliving the real-life nightmares. The Sandman had the beach on some sort of lockdown—he wouldn't say more than that. I only knew that much because he slipped up during one of the few brief moments we saw each other, mumbling something about barriers.

"We're not going to ask about anything," Natalie continued, "and I've secured you an early release." Lisa's father smiled and waved to us on our way toward the exit.

My stomach churned. "Where are we going?"

"Wait," Ben called, and I tensed. "You forgot your purse."

I turned slowly enough to register the look of shock and awe plastered over Natalie's face. A bolt of unexplained jealousy pierced my chest. I had no claim on Ben and I didn't want one. Did I? He was just talking to shadows, so, if for no other reason, I shouldn't let myself be interested. I couldn't risk *his* crazy feeding mine.

Besides, Natalie already had a boyfriend. Who I hadn't seen in ages because he graduated last year. And I was busy studying. Or working. Or, really, just having an overall aversion to the whole large-social-gathering thing. *Did* she still have a boyfriend? Surely, she would've told me if they broke up...

"Thanks." I plucked the straps from his hand. "See you later."

Natalie clutched my arm. "Who's this?"

"Natalie, Ben," I said with reluctance. "Ben, Natalie."

She held out her hand, and they shook. "We're heading to the carnival tonight at six," she told him.

"We're what?" I asked. There would be way too many people there—most with prying eyes and curious minds. I clutched my purse to my chest. If I thought the attention from Randy was bad, how much worse would it be now?

"Want to meet us there?" she said, ignoring me.

Ben quirked a mischievous smile. "You'll be there?" he asked me.

"I don't—"

"She'll be there." Natalie tugged me toward the doors again. "See you later."

We were outside then, peeling toward Natalie's rusted heap of a car. I threw myself inside, still hugging my purse, and slammed the door. "I can't believe you did that."

"Listen." She turned the key once, twice, and the engine turned over. "I've waited our whole lives to double date."

Date. With Ben? "No."

"Fine." She scrunched her curls. "Don't date him, but, just know, he's clearly interested. And besides, I can't uninvite him now."

I glared across the seat at her. First Katie, now Natalie. I almost didn't want to date Ben, based solely on principle. "I hate you."

"You love me." She moved to pinch the apple of my cheek, and I leaned out of reach. "Anyway, you'll never guess what my aunt did this year. Go on, guess."

Curses. Natalie always had the best stories after her family reunions. "Did she spike the punch bowl again?"

"That too." Natalie laughed, spitting out the latest story between gasps for air, until we turned into my driveway. Emery's van was parked on the street while she sat on my lawn, plucking blades of grass. I twisted my purse straps. They were my friends, and Natalie promised they wouldn't ask questions. Maybe Katie was right when she said I needed to stop hiding in my room. My bad luck had to be used up for the next few years…going anywhere should be safe.

As safe as the back room at Howell's.

I forced a wide smile and slid from the passenger seat.

"The lost has been found," Emery called. Her red hair was twisted back into a regal bun, making the worry etched on her face stand out.

"Hello to you too," I answered with as much cheer as I could muster.

"Come on," Natalie prodded. "There are movies, pizza, and a present from California waiting inside."

***

The present turned out to be a small amethyst charm on a thin chain bracelet. I fiddled with my birthstone through the chick-flicks they rented, forcing my attention to remain solely on the movie. They talked around me—summer jobs, family, gossip—and I tried to listen to that too. I tried to engage. It was harder than usual, though. The echoes of the voice in the shadows overrode them, chafing against my skull, until we finally left for the carnival.

Stalls peppered the park. The sugary smell of cotton candy and caramel corn filled the air, and huge lights buzzed with electricity. A rainbow of colored bulbs flashed on the Ferris wheel. Somewhere, someone squealed with joy, and I dug my nails into my palms.

"Hey there, pretty lady," called a man on a microphone. He stood beneath a striped booth with wooden rings in his hand. "Care to give it a try?"

Emery shrugged and stepped up to the counter. Her little brother loved it when she brought him home something. I leaned against Natalie to watch Emery toss the rings at the pins. "Are you having fun?" I asked.

"Yeah," Natalie said, giving me a playful shove. "Are you?"

"Yes." I ground out the word as a spinning ride started a few feet away and another shout rang through the crowd.

"I forgot to tell you earlier, but my grandma is visiting next month."

"Grandma B?" I brightened at the thought. Her grandmother was like the one I never had, and she knew how to spoil a girl. Nothing beat her chili, either. Or her pie. And that pasta chicken thing she made. I was going to need bigger pants. "How long is she staying?"

"Two weeks, and she wants to take us to Miami again." She wagged her eyebrows. "You know what that means?"

"Road trip," we sang at the same time and laughed.

A soft tap touched my arm and I whirled around, all humor instantly gone. "Hi," Ben said, rubbing the back of his neck.

My heart sputtered. He came. He *actually* came. And he looked down at me as if I had painted the moon in the sky. My cheeks burned at the wonderment written all over his face, and it struck me. Maybe Natalie was right. Maybe… Maybe he was interested. "You're here."

"Did you doubt me?" He nudged me with his elbow and gave me his starlit smile. The fire in my face spread down to the pit of my stomach.

Emery cheered for herself, and the man with the microphone handed over a neon green stuffed frog. Natalie backed away from Ben and me, smiling. "Ferris wheel?" she suggested to Emery.

I felt the weight of Emery's eyes on me, curious and wondering. Unless Natalie filled her in on one of my bathroom breaks, she had no idea who Ben was or what he was doing here. But she nodded. Later on, there would be questions. So many questions.

"Do you want to go on it too?" Ben asked, eyeing the ride with a hopeful expression.

Natalie winked at me, and they moved toward the surprisingly short line. Now that Ben was here, my desire to leave peaked. This place, with the crowds and loud music, was suffocating. As always. More than always. I didn't have the energy to pretend things were okay, but I didn't have the energy to fight against my friends' efforts either. "We don't have to," I said.

He shrugged one shoulder and looked up at the hanging seats. "I don't mind."

I did. We would be stuck in close quarters for several long minutes, and I wasn't sure how I felt about that. Or, at least, I wasn't sure how I was supposed to feel. "I'm sort of afraid of heights so…"

He smirked. "No, you're not." He motioned me forward, and I glared at him, too shocked by his surety to insist we stay on the ground. "I promise, I don't bite." He winked and added, "Hard."

I folded my arms across my chest and crinkled my nose. "Sorry, I've seen too many movies to want to hang out with a vampire."

"Fine, fine. No biting," he said with false disappointment. He took my hand and tugged me gently after my friends.

My feet dragged down the line. It felt as if my sandals were made of iron as I stepped into the swaying bucket. Ben slid in beside me, and the attendant slammed a bar across our laps with a deafening *clack*. We jolted backward and stopped to let people into the seat in front of us.

"Sorry if it's weird Natalie asked you to come today," I blurted. It wasn't safe for any words to leave my mouth with so many feelings happening at once.

His hands hung loosely over the metal bar. "Why would it be weird?"

"Because we barely know each other." Although it felt like we did. Maybe it was only weird for me. "And you just met her today."

The ride moved again, this time keeping a steady pace the entire way around. Natalie and Emery twisted in their bucket to look down at us. "You two behave," Emery shouted.

I blushed. What had Natalie told her in the last two minutes? Gross exaggerations, obviously. Ones she would pay for with copious amounts of cheesecake. "Ignore them."

Ben paused, then winked playfully and looked up at my friends. His arm slipped around my shoulders, warm and solid, and Natalie whooped before turning around. When they weren't looking, his arm slid away slowly. I fought the urge to draw it back. The image of him talking to the voice floated through my mind, and I gripped the bar instead. It wasn't the first strange thing he'd done. There was the knowing look on his face when the police flew past Howell's and his odd reaction to the girl with the pen.

"I've been wondering." I pressed my lips together. It wasn't something I could just say. "When we were shopping and… things happened, why did you tell that girl to wake up?"

The muscles in his jaw flexed. "She was nodding off before that, so I guess I just assumed."

"But to do what she did, she would need to be in REM sleep, and that doesn't happen until you've been asleep about ninety minutes." The cashier nodded off but was awake minutes before. That fact bothered me since. I refused to let the thought form before now because if I thought about it, I would be forced to think that something else was going on. Something strange and unexplainable. But that's exactly what was happening.

He nodded. "I see you're a sleep expert."

"I've done a little research," I said flatly.

He shrugged, sobering. "I don't know why I said that to her."

What about the back room was on the tip of my tongue, but I wasn't brave enough to hear him deny the truth outright. First, I had some questions for the Sandman. Mainly, if there was any validity to my thoughts. Then, *then*, I would corner Ben and ask him what he knew.

"How was the rest of work?" I asked to change the subject.

"Did you know there are twenty-seven shades of blue you can order furniture in?"

I cocked an eyebrow. "That boring, huh?"

"Of course. You weren't there," he bantered, but his expression shuttered. He stared out across the brightly lit area, his gaze hyper-focused as he scanned our surroundings. "How was not working?"

"Oh, you know." My hair floated around my face, pieces drifting into Ben's personal space. I gathered it into one hand and held it to the side, away from him. "Apparently we're having a sleepover at Emery's tonight, so the fun never ends."

He looked at me then. A look that knew everything I didn't say out loud. A look that said it was okay that I didn't mean it when I said it would be fun. One that said it was okay if I needed to break a little bit. And maybe I did, or maybe I had to do the impossible and swallow my pride. If I asked my mother to take me back to a doctor, she would. But for that brief second beside him, it didn't feel like I was cracking around the edges.

It drew me closer, the space between us shrinking. I needed that feeling. I needed it like I needed air in my lungs. The outsides of our thighs pressed together. Ben inhaled through parted lips, his eyes glowing as they watched my lips. Before I could think about what I was doing, I stretched up to kiss him. The world exploded in a shower of stars, the Ferris wheel no longer the only thing making me soar. It was everything. Every promise, every hope, every dream.

Ben's body stiffened, and I froze. What was I doing? It was my first kiss, and it was with someone I barely knew. It didn't matter that he felt familiar. He was little more than a stranger. I eased back, but his fingers grazed my jaw. He leaned into me, caressing my lips with his own. A small, almost pained, groan escaped him, and he broke away.

I gasped at the sudden loss of contact. Something tugged deep in my chest, tightening. My mind scrambled to make sense of what just happened. I kissed him. He kissed me back. It was right and wrong and everything between.

"Sorry," I breathed. "I'm an idiot."

Ben ran his middle finger over his bottom lip. "Don't be sorry," he said, his voice slightly husky.

I rubbed my face and groaned. There couldn't be a worse place than a carnival ride for me to make the first move. How much longer would I be trapped?

"Hey." He reached out and flicked my side-swept bangs back in place. "I mean it."

I scooted as far away from him as the bench allowed. "Sure."

We stayed that way—me squished in the corner and Ben staring down at nothing in particular—until the worker unlocked the bar imprisoning us. I bolted off the platform. My friends gaped, and I shoved my way out the exit. "I'm going to find the bathroom," I shouted, and didn't stop running until they were out of sight.

"Nora," Ben called after me. "Nora, wait! Please."

I ducked behind the game tents and gulped the sweet-scented air. "Stupid, stupid, stupid." I groaned. In all my life, of all the idiotic things I'd done, this was the worst. And Ben... He had no idea what he was getting into with someone like me. Unless he knew *exactly* what he was getting because he saw the same things I did. The Sandman hadn't known him but there was no denying what happened earlier today.

The Sandman. How was I going to tell him about what happened? I couldn't hide anything from him when he read my dreams. A kiss—my first kiss—would *definitely* show up. Especially when it was with someone I was maybe into, and when that someone was as hot as Ben was. The Sandman shouldn't care though. Even if he did, it shouldn't matter, but guilt nibbled at my insides anyway.

"Hello, Dream Keeper."

The voice froze me in place. It was louder than before, more direct and less frenzied. "You're not real," I whispered, swallowing.

"Of course, I am." The shadows shifted. A flash of black. A speck of gold. The same thing I saw in the back room. "Don't play hard to get, my little Sun-Kissed one. Give me what I seek."

"You're. Not. Real," I insisted. *Except Ben heard you too.* My eye twitched.

"There are two people who would beg to differ. Alas, you cannot ask them now, can you?"

I turned my back to the shadow and stepped toward the crowd. I wasn't going to stand there and let a bodiless voice twist the knife in my stomach. The deaths weren't jokes. *Those* were real, tangible things. It wasn't a hazy truth like the Sandman. Everyone acknowledged them, their loved ones living with the fresh scars of loss. I blinked against an imagined splatter of red.

"Your Sandman knows," the voice continued as if reading my mind. "He knows many things, Dream Keeper. Many things you do not. Dangerous things. Dark things. Things that will make you regret and things that will make you hate. Things you don't want to know but things you should. Things, things. Many things. Things that tie us together, little Keeper."

My head tilted back to watch the shadow from the corner of my eye. My heart threatened to explode from my chest. What did he know? What *didn't* I know? And why was he calling me a Dream Keeper?

"Let's make a deal, shall we?" The shadow pressed forward into the hazy outline of a man. "If you give me the dream, now, tonight, then I promise not to torment anyone else you're fond of."

I didn't know who—what—he was, if he was anything, but the offer made my entire body itch. *Torment.* I cringed. That was exactly what happened in the mall. The terror on the cashier's face was more real than anything. My stomach bottomed out. The shadowy-figure wasn't simply recapping the deaths. He was the reason for them. I shook my head to clear away the ridiculous, impossible thoughts, but they refused to go. My pulse throbbed through my body, and I dove back into the masses to find my friends.

Chapter Seven

The Sandman

The pewter-grey sky of the Nightmare Realm cast everything in long, twisting shadows. I tried to ignore the ones that moved and focused instead on the miles of blackness that stretched out before me on the other side of the barrier. The wall gave beneath my hand, wobbling across the entrance to the Day World. A thousand flecks of sand sputtered along the glimmering wall before going dull. Thousands more had already lost their magic while others struggled to hold the line. Only a few patches remained solid and titanium strong, mainly where it clung to the fabric of the Nightmare Realm. I would have thought the edges would fail first—especially since I just fixed this portion two nights ago.

I drew in a deep breath and squinted at the barrier. If it was fading this quickly, the Weaver was regaining his strength faster than I realized. I would need to double the thickness. Triple it.

And I still had to find him. In all the years I'd known him, the Weaver was never this hard to locate.

Baku paced behind me, his claws clicking on the stony ground. "You know," I said over my shoulder. "If there *are* any nightmares lurking nearby, they're not going to come out if they see you."

Baku twisted his head to stare at me and turned for another trek across the wasteland.

I smirked. "You would probably get a quicker meal if you hid until someone got it in their mind to attack me."

Baku brushed against the back of my legs, knocking me forward a step.

"Fine, fine." I laughed. "It was just a suggestion."

I reached into the leather satchel hanging at my hip and scooped up two handfuls of sand. I blew it out in front of me, and the grains froze in a sheet. Setting my fingertips against it, I pressed it into the existing barrier and smoothed it down with my palms. The magic absorbed it, drinking it in, until the area glowed blue, then faded to nothing but a mere shimmer.

Inch by inch the barrier shone with new power. I worked my way down, silently grateful Nora was sleeping at her friend's house tonight. She would be later than usual, if she came at all. It was already past three in the morning so when she finally closed her eyes, she might be too tired to dream.

Still, my gut twisted at the possibility of not seeing her. She never shut me out on purpose, but what if tonight was different? What if our kiss was too much and she couldn't stand the thought of seeing me? She ran off so fast I wasn't sure what to think.

I paused to rub the back of my hand over my tingling lips. When she kissed me, the cord between us had thrashed greedily.

It was impossible she hadn't felt it too. My only hope was that she hadn't understood, or had written it off as nerves. A lump formed in my throat.

Besides, it wasn't *our* kiss.

It was her kiss with Ben. Even if she did sense similarities between Ben and me, she would never believe it. Just like she would never have kissed me as my true self—it was probably my fault. I set up the rules. I lied. I omitted and pretended.

It was *definitely* my fault.

But my world had unfurled on the Ferris wheel. The kiss was everything I never knew I was missing and more. It would be wrong to coax her into talking about it tonight when she thought I was a neutral third party, but *damn it*, I needed to know where her thoughts were.

I would have to tell her the truth soon anyway, especially if I planned to continue Day Walking. Truthfully, the best thing to do was to stop going; I wasn't able to stop the Weaver from killing Randy or the girl in the shop, anyway. He had occupied the shadows at the edge of the carnival, lingering outside the lights too. I wasn't doing anything but complicating my friendship with the girl that held the key to my enemy's cage. That's all she could ever be to me. All that was fair. But it was a crushing reality. A pebble here, a boulder there, building up over the last year, but now it felt like a rock slide, on the brink of an avalanche.

I sighed and scanned my work again. The barrier was as clear as it was around the beach now and just as sturdy. Nothing was slipping out.

"That should hold until I recharge," I said to Baku.

"Should it?" the Weaver drawled.

My heart leapt into my throat, and I spun around. Baku was nowhere to be seen but my counterpart stood before me, larger than I remembered. His black hair was smoothed into a tight bun. A long, refined nose ran between his wide brows and below them, his eyes glowed molten gold. The perfect nightmare. Alluring enough to draw someone in, terrifying enough to turn them inside out. And it all but gutted me.

"You've made improvements since I was here last," he said. "But if you need to recharge after such a menial task…"

I bared my teeth.

"Tsk. So hostile." He scanned the wall behind me. The gold embroidery on his sleeveless black vest shifted on its own. Threads of gold and black ran off his left shoulder, hugging his muscular bicep before snaking down to his wrist, looping into a band. The loose ends strummed above his pulse point as if they shared his heartbeat. "Give me what I want, and I'll never bother you again."

"That's all you *would* do, Weaver," I said, my voice even more weary than I was.

Every time I turned around, he was testing me. Coming to the beach for no purpose other than to taint my sand, experimenting with his nightmares to find one to inhabit my slumber. Letting nightmares into the Day World was the last straw, but his antics stretched back to the very beginning. If only the playful intent behind it all had stayed the same, maybe then we could've avoided this mess.

I reached into my satchel for more sand and called power from my reserves. It would take more than I had to re-bind him, not to mention that I had none of his threads to use against him. The playing field was even. I could hurt him as easily as he could hurt me, and which one of us left in better condition came down to one thing: determination. Unfortunately, the Weaver loved power as much as I loved Nora.

"I have thousands of creatures that do my bidding. I have an *army*. What do you have?" His voice was low, bordering angry, but his muscles were loose, relaxed. "Don't you miss it?"

"Miss what?" I snapped.

The hard edges of him softened. "The way things used to be."

My eyes narrowed to slits. "Whose fault is it that they're different?"

"Ours," he said with a defeated sighed. Then his face hardened. "You alone won't be enough to keep me out after tonight."

After tonight. My lungs constricted. "What did you do?"

He grinned, running his thumb over his nails.

"Tell me," I demanded.

"The Dream Keeper is a pretty little thing," he said carefully. "I'd hate for anything to happen to her because you refused to cooperate."

Liar. I tossed the sand into the air but before it could take shape, he disappeared. I turned my focus inside, reaching for the cord that connected me to Nora. She was fine—alive and already asleep. How had I missed it? My magic was trained to catch her subconscious if I had enough power to spare, but I still *felt* it. Unless I was so drained tonight, I hadn't noticed.

The important thing was that she was safe.

I loosened a breath and fled the Nightmare Realm before the Weaver had a chance to change his mind about fighting. He was right—he had an army. Hundreds of years' worth of power prowled his lands and what did I have? A beach full of sand I was too tapped to properly wield? If I was going to beat him a second time, I had to reclaim my strength.

***

Nora strolled down the edge of the water. Her arms wrapped around her abdomen, and her lip trembled. She couldn't see me yet—not behind the secondary barrier I placed to divide my realm in two. One side was mine, the other hers. Separation. Distance. Neutrality. Yet another wasted effort.

I slid the strap of my satchel over my head and dropped it to the ground. Nora let her head fall back. Her shoulders rose and fell with a deep breath. I tugged on my gloves, flipped my hood low over my face and stepped forward.

She didn't see me coming until I was nearly beside her. When she did, she froze and looked at me like I was a stranger. Like the last five years never happened.

"I'm sorry," I blurted, my heart seizing. "I didn't think you would come tonight."

"I'm sleeping at Emery's," she said, hollow.

"Are..." I swallowed. "Are you okay?"

She shook her head. "I need to get some help."

"Help with what?" I asked, cautiously.

"I can't function like this. Hearing things, seeing you... I can't focus. It's like I'm floating out to sea without a paddle and no one cares because I've been adrift for years anyway."

My breath stuck in my throat. This was worse than the kiss. She meant help with me—to get rid of me. There was nothing the doctors could do to erase my presence, but it hurt all the same. I clenched my jaw until my teeth ached.

"Of course, people care," I said. "I care."

81

She choked on a sob. "But you aren't *real*, Sandman."

"I've always been real," I whispered.

But she either ignored the comment or didn't hear it. I was here—*really* here. No matter how hard she tried to block me out, I was as fixed as the sun. But, maybe that would be best. I could still protect her dreams from the other side of the beach, the side she never saw, and there would be no distractions.

"Are there other things like you?" she blurted, running her fingers down her arms.

My back straightened, my hands sweating. "I'm the only Sandman."

"That's not what I meant." She advanced two steps. "Is there anything else out there? Something that hurts people?"

"I'm not sure where this is com—"

"Where this is coming from?" she finished for me, her eyes flashing incredulously. "How about the fog last night for starters? You know more than you're telling me."

I swallowed hard. There were so many things I had to tell her that I didn't know where to start. If now was even the right time for it. "I..."

"What's a Dream Keeper?" she snapped.

My blood ran cold. "Where did you hear that?"

"A little birdie told me," she said carefully from between her teeth.

"The Weaver?" I asked before I could stop myself. Rage splashed against my insides. I knew he was up to something but talking directly to Nora? I expected him to be subtler than that. The stairwell and back room at Howell's... Did she hear him then? I thought he was trying to get to me, not her. Maybe if I hadn't been so busy, if I had taken a few minutes to listen to her that first night the Weaver pushed at the barrier between our worlds, I would have known. "Don't listen to him, Nora. He's dangerous."

Her eyes widened, her mouth dropping, then her face pinched. Suspicion lined her features. A flush of anger and fear colored her cheeks. I'd never seen that shade on her before. "What is a Dream Keeper?" she asked again in a low voice, enunciating each word with a stone-cold edge.

I couldn't lie. Not when she asked so directly. Not when she deserved the truth a long time ago. If she was going to learn it now, it was better that it came from me.

"You are," I whispered, my throat tight, and braced myself for her reaction.

She jerked back, eying me like I had just given her a death sentence. I prayed I hadn't.

"Nora—"

"No." She shook her head violently, her fingers digging into the hair around her ears. "Dream Keeper? As in keeping a dream? But he said if I didn't give it to him... And I... Then that means..." Her face fell, draining of color.

Then she vanished.

I stared at the indents her feet left in the sand and willed my lungs to inhale again. That could have gone better. Tomorrow felt like a lifetime to wait for a chance to explain.

Everything.

Before I lost her forever. I tugged on the cord that connected me to Nora, asking her to come back. Begging. But there was no reply.

Chapter Eight

Nora

Darkness enveloped the living room when I woke, leaving my friends as nothing but hazy outlines in the room. I sat up and took deep, shaky breaths. *Dream Keeper.* The title echoed through me over and over, alternating voices between the Weaver and the Sandman, until I slammed my hands over my ears. How could things have gotten so bad so quickly? Imagining the Sandman was manageable, but now I was twisting real life events to fit with my warped fantasy dream-life. *Sick.* I had to be.

But I could never actually ask my mother for help. No matter how much I needed to.

I climbed quietly to my feet so as not to wake anyone, and crept over throw pillows, then Emery. My foot knocked a plastic cup. "Crap," I muttered. Hopefully that was water—her mom was rather proud of the new beige carpet. My foot squished into the liquid, and I cringed as it oozed between my toes.

A night light glowed at the end of the hall. Emery's little brother had a hard time finding the bathroom without it, and I silently thanked him for that as I tip-toed across the tile. A quick stop at the store in the morning to get my own wasn't the worst idea. Maybe more than one. I should count the number of outlets in my room first. All I needed was to wake up to a stand of burnt out mini-lights. I wrinkled my nose. Or maybe I should just start sleeping with the light on and consider it problem solved.

With a quick flick of the bathroom light switch, I shut myself inside. My fingers curled around the edge of the sink, and I leaned forward to place my forehead on the cool mirror. *I've always been real*, the Sandman had said. *You are*, he had answered when I asked about a Dream Keeper.

The words overlapped, bumping and scraping against each other in a bid to be heard. Keeping a true heart and a true mind in my dreams should've meant the beach was safe. *Should have.* If I had remembered to keep both things, that is. I said I trusted the Sandman, but there was someone more important that I had to have faith in: myself. Self-trust was something I hadn't known in years, if ever, and it was becoming increasingly impossible to uphold.

But if I believed in myself, then I would have to believe what the Weaver said at the carnival—that he would hurt someone. He wanted me to give him a dream, but what did that mean? How would I give something like that away? It isn't a material thing I could hand over. More importantly, *why* did he want it? Maybe he wanted access to the Sandman, so he could hurt him. My heart sunk. How was I supposed to justify choosing someone that lived in my head over real people? *But* if one of them was real, so was the other.

Stop it. I couldn't let my delusions run wild. *None of this is real.* None *of it.*

I stood straight and splashed water on my face. "Okay," I said to my reflection. The soft lighting made me appear haggard; the dark circles beneath my eyes looked black, my cheeks, sunken. I was paler than usual, which until that moment, I hadn't thought was possible.

I couldn't stay at Emery's tonight. I wanted—*needed*—the comfort of my own bed. Using the hand-towel, I dried my face and reached for the light again when a shadow flicked near the toilet. My stomach lurched. I swung the door open and leapt into the hall. The shadow followed. My joints locked and I stood, watching little yellow fish float inside the sea-themed night light, willing the impossible away. The house was quiet. Quiet and still. I held my breath and listened. Silence.

Calm down. I sighed and dropped my head. *Everything is fine.*

At my feet, dark toe-prints lined the hallway floor, rows of dark circles staining the grey slate. Somehow, deep down, I knew. I knew it wasn't juice I stepped in. A collection of snapshots flashed before me. The police cars rushing by Howell's. Lisa on the news. The cashier with the pen in her hand. The spray of crimson as her body fell to the floor.

Blood.

It was blood. I could never mistake the sight of it. My stomach dropped.

"Natalie?" I called, my voice tight. "Emery?"

Let them be annoyed that I woke up them up. *Let them.* I took two halting steps back toward the living room. *Let's make a deal,* the Weaver had said earlier. My breath stuck in my throat. That wasn't real. It couldn't have been. But maybe. I swallowed hard.

"You awake?" I shouted down the hall.

Oh please, oh please, oh please.

The hallway tilted, and I lost my balance. My shoulder collided with the wall. I slid my way back to the living room and fumbled with the knob on the tall floor lamp.

I couldn't look.

I had to look.

"Guys?" I pleaded, tears welling in my eyes. "Someone say something."

The ice machine in the refrigerator grumbled, sending me straight into the air. The back of my hand knocked the lampshade. I steadied the rocking light with my other hand, and found the knob, twisting until the bulb clicked on. Light flooded the room, but my gaze stayed on the pleated white fabric of the shade. I waited. Held my breath. Prayed someone would grumble for me to turn it off. But no one did. Not after five seconds. Not after ten.

"Anyone?" I whispered desperately. The silence pressed against me. Pressed and pressed and pressed until, finally, I lifted my eyes.

My soul left my body.

Everywhere. The blood was everywhere—coating the walls, painting the furniture red, turning the floor into a swamp.

Emery's body was sprawled out in the same place as when I stepped over her. Her dull eyes stared up at the ceiling. Long, jagged cuts carved both forearms deep enough to see muscle and bone.

Natalie faced the hall from the recliner, two empty sockets staring across the room. Gleaming red streams coated her cheeks. Clutched in her hands were both eyes.

The room pulsated with light and dark. I fought against the lightheadedness. This wasn't real. Not real. Not...

Across the room, scrawled in blood on the bay window, was *DREAMER, DREAMER* beside a smiley face. Something clicked, every ounce of denial shattering. The surreal feeling fell away, replaced by a rage so blistering the scars would never fade. The scream that tore from my throat engulfed me, tore me down, down, down until I folded in on myself.

***

I rubbed my puffy eyes against the memory of red and blue lights flickering through the window. Highlighting the words written there. Reflecting off the pools of blood, too much for the carpet to absorb. Against flashes of ivory bone poking through skin and dull, lifeless eyes. *Eyes.* I choked back the swell of acid that ignited the back of my throat.

This was my fault. The Weaver wanted to make a deal, but I didn't listen. I tried so hard to convince myself that he wasn't real when I knew he was. If I had given him the dream, whatever it was, my friends would still be alive. Who else would he hurt to get to me? Who was next on his list? Knowing what I know now, would I say no if he asked again?

"Miss Gallagher, I need you to focus," Detective Bell said. I pressed my back against the steel chair and brought my feet up to the seat, burying my face in my knees. "If you want us to catch who did this to your friends, we need you to tell us what you know."

"Where's my mom?" I croaked, my throat still raw from screaming. "I want my mother."

"She's... filling out the paperwork. You're a witness, not a suspect so we can go ahead without her." He clicked his pen a few times, looking purposely down at his notebook. "You said you didn't hear anything."

"No." I lifted my head weakly. The past few hours cooled my fury to a simmer, waiting. Waiting for the second my head hit the pillow. For the Sandman to show his face. I wasn't sure what my answer would be if the Weaver asked again, but I had to end this before he got the chance. For that, I needed the Sandman's help. This wasn't about me anymore. It hadn't been since Randy was murdered, but now it was personal. Now I didn't simply want the Weaver to go away. I wanted him to pay. In flesh. In blood. In pain and death. And I wanted to be the one to do it.

I could only hope I had the willpower to not give in first.

I drew in a shallow breath. "No," I said again, louder. "I wasn't feeling well when I woke up, so I went to the bathroom. When I came back, I turned on the light..."

Detective Bell scooted his chair closer to the table. "Emery Williams' arms were sliced to ribbons, and Natalie Flores, the girl you've been friends with since preschool, clawed out her own eyes. They're dead. Gone. Horrifically murdered. They'll never get to see their families again. They won't graduate next year. They won't go to college, get married, have families. They won't grow old. Their lives are over, Nora. So, I say to you again, people aren't killed like they were without there being some noise. Likely *a lot* of it, based on the crimes committed. These were not pain-free deaths. If someone threatened to hurt you, if you give names, we can keep you safe."

I wanted to fall from the chair and melt into the linoleum. There was no noise during the murders. No struggle. No intruder. Emery's father double-checked all the doors and windows before we settled in to watch a movie. They were still secured when the police arrived. The *thing* behind their deaths cared nothing about locks. The note on the window left no room for doubt—not that I harbored any. I hadn't imagined the voice or invented fantastical theories. Everyone else saw the message.

It was real.

All of it was real.

"You must be a sound sleeper," Detective Bell said when I was silent.

"Apparently Emery's entire family is," I countered. How could I explain it was the Weaver without landing myself in a padded cell? Besides, I wasn't sure exactly how he killed them yet. Just that he did.

His scowl deepened. "A lot of people are dying under strange circumstances. Your boss." He ticked off a finger. "The cashier. Now your closest friends while you slept right beside them."

I swallowed against the rawness of my throat. "I haven't done anything wrong."

Detective Bell removed his glasses and pinched the bridge of his nose. "This doesn't look good. You understand that, don't you?"

"No. I don't. If I did anything to my friends, why wasn't I covered in blood? And, like you pointed out, how could I have pulled that off without waking someone up? In case it's missing from your file, Natalie was a super athlete. If I tried to gouge her eyes out, don't you think she would have knocked me into next week?" I took a ragged breath. I didn't know how the Weaver managed to do it so quietly, but I certainly couldn't have. It was impossible.

"Besides, you have the girl at the mall on surveillance. How can you possibly think I had anything to do with that?"

The detective cleared his throat. "Just because you didn't commit the murders tonight, doesn't mean you don't know who did. You could have let someone into Emery's tonight and locked the door behind them on their way out."

"I didn't," I said as hard and sharp as an axe.

He settled his glasses back over his nose. "Do you have a problem with anyone? Is there anyone that would want to hurt you by hurting people around you? An ex-boyfriend, maybe?"

As it turned out, I did have someone out to get me, but I answered, "I don't have any ex-boyfriends."

The door creaked open and a young officer looked in. "Detective?"

"What is it?"

"Her mother is demanding to be let in."

Detective Bell tossed his pen to the table. "We're done here. She'll be out in a second."

The officer nodded and disappeared.

"I really don't know anything," I insisted more gently.

He glowered. "I don't have time for lies when someone is out there terrorizing the town."

"Neither do I." I put my palms on the table to slide the chair away. "If I knew anything, I would tell you."

"There's one more thing before you go," he said, his tone softening.

I froze. What else could there possibly be?

"I apologize for withholding this from you, but it's important we find the person responsible for the murders. I didn't want to sidetrack you." He cleared his throat again and stared at his notepad. "Your sister is missing."

The words hit me like a brick. "What do you mean, *missing?*"

"Katie was in bed around one this morning, according to your mother. When we called to tell her about what happened, she looked in her room again, and your sister was gone. Her phone and purse were still in her room, and the back door was left ajar."

"Katie isn't missing," I half asked, half stated.

"I'm sorry." Detective Bell eased out of his chair, his lips pursed. "We're going to need you to take a drug test on the way out."

I blinked rapidly until I was able to focus on Detective Bell standing across the table. My sister was missing, and he was talking about peeing in a cup. "Are you sure she's missing?" I demanded. "Because Katie likes to sneak out for parties sometimes. Maybe she—"

"We've considered all the evidence," he hedged.

"But..." But *how?* "What evidence?"

"Excuse me." Detective Bell adjusted his tie and walked to the door. "Your mother is waiting, and I have a killer to find."

I splayed my fingers on the cool metal table. "It's probably the same person," I blurted. "Right? It has to be."

"We'll be in touch. Don't leave town," he said calmly, though the vein protruding from his forehead told another story.

Then he was gone, leaving me alone to remember how my legs worked. How anything worked. I couldn't breathe. Couldn't speak. The fire inside me roared again, and I knew. Whatever it cost me, whatever price I had to pay, I was going to kill the Weaver.

***

"Sandman," I screamed the moment my feet hit the beach.

He climbed from the glowing sea, water dripping freely from his hood. His clothes clung to him, accenting muscles I would never have guessed lay beneath all that fabric. "I'm here," he said, breathing hard and fast.

I paused, glancing behind him at the quiet waves. "What are you doing?"

"Fixing something." He shook out his gloved hands. "What happened?"

"They're—" *Tell him. Say the word out loud: Dead.* But I didn't want to say it. Didn't want to admit it and have it become real. I clutched my stomach. "Oh, God. I'm going to be sick."

The sky darkened, a hundred different shapes rushing in from nowhere, jostling together to blot out the blues and purples. Shadows fell over the Sandman's form. Slices of starlight cut through the dark masses.

My mouth hung open. "What the..."

"Whatever happened, don't think about it now or he'll come," the Sandman said, and dipped his hand into the sand.

I gripped his wrist before he could form a dream. "Don't think about it?" I hissed. "My friends were brutally murdered while I slept right next to them. My sister is *missing,* and I shouldn't *think* about it? I should pretend it's all okay? You think you can show me a pretty picture, and it will all go away? I promise you, Sandman, nothing will erase what I saw tonight. Ever."

"Nora," he croaked. The sand fell, lifeless, from his hand. "I... I'm sorry."

Pieces of individual shapes dipped lower in the sky—a hoof, a wing, a human-like arm—and I squared my shoulders. The Sandman's tendons flexed beneath my hand, and I jerked away.

I touched him, and he didn't disappear.

I glared at the place my hand had just been, unable to find the right question. Even if I could, I wouldn't have been able to process his answer with my mind torn in a million different directions. Did he lie? Was I missing something? What the hell was going on?

"I don't have the ability to protect you if those nightmares break through the barrier tonight." His voice was strained.

Nightmares. I lifted my head and shuddered. "Is that him? The Weaver?"

The sopping wet hood shook around his head. "No, but they belong to him."

"That bastard is going to pay for what he did." I bolted across the beach, charging toward the sea. "Right after he gives Katie back."

The Sandman stumbled after me and yanked me back with an arm around my middle. The touch sent electricity through my chest, shocking my heart. It was warm and relaxing yet somehow exhilarating—everything I ever imagined. But it wasn't the right time to feel calm. I needed to be angry. To cling to the hate.

"It's not him, Nora. They don't have your sister."

"But they're the Weaver's so they'll take me to him, won't they?" I growled. He wanted something from me badly enough to go through all this trouble—it seemed safe to assume he needed me alive. If not, I would've been victim number one. "I'm going to kill him with my bare hands."

"The Weaver can't be killed without disrupting the balance." He held me flush against his chest, and I felt each hammer of his pulse. It spurred my own, lighting a new kind of fire. He lowered his face to my neck and breathed in. "Please," he begged. "Don't antagonize them. We'll get Katie back."

"I don't understand." I stopped fighting against him, instead standing still as stone. "How did he get her?"

"If he has her, she's only here as much as you are. Her body is still in your world while her mind is trapped. If someone is prone to sleepwalking, the Weaver can turn them into a puppet; she could be anywhere."

"You're saying she kidnapped herself?" Katie hadn't sleep-walked in years. Not since the night she roamed the house with a flashlight and tried to suck up the *snake* with the hose of the vacuum. The dog had a bald spot on his tail for months. My body sagged against the Sandman. "I have to find her."

"We will." He backed away from me and reached into his tunic. His hand trembled around the ties of a black leather bag. "Take this."

I reached out slowly. "What is it?"

"Sand." He took my hand and set it in my palm. "Use it on your mother and step-father at night. It will keep them safe from the nightmares."

"But—"

"They only want the dream in your head. If you leave right now, I promise to tell you everything tomorrow." I had never heard his voice so low. "I need to do something to make this place safer for you, and I need to do it now."

"What dream hidden in my head?" My voice rose, wavering.

When he didn't reply, I opened my mouth to demand answers when a crack—half breaking glass, half thunder— rocked the beach. A small white line skated across a clear dome I never knew existed. Thick slime oozed beneath a giant worm slithering overhead. It reared back and slammed a sucker-like mouth against the barrier. Blue light flashed against the impact.

Dozens of rows of teeth clacked against the hard surface and a forked tongue lapped in search of a tangible flaw.

"Go," he urged.

I swallowed hard. "I want answers first."

"I'm sorry," he whispered. "There isn't time."

I shook my head, my stomach dipping. "I can't leave without my sister."

He gently clasped my face and turned me to him. Water dripped from his hood, pattering gently on his arms. Arms that looked strangely familiar beneath the clingy fabric. I squinted at the outlines of his muscles, took in his height. A name began to surface, a line connecting two dots, but the Sandman's thumbs grazed my cheekbones.

"Never doubt that I'll do whatever is necessary to make this right. Anything you ask, anything you don't, it's yours. All of me is yours," he promised.

I blinked slowly, a blush heating my cheeks, and eyed the worm again. "Will any of them get in?"

"They're only here for the dream."

I gripped his wrists, my gaze drifting upward. "Will you be here the next time I fall asleep?"

"I'll be here," he swore. "And I'll tell you the rest."

"You'll *show* me the rest," I corrected, grabbing the edge of his hood.

His hand flew up to grip my wrist, making sure I didn't try to remove the fabric. "I'll show you."

"Okay." The worm slammed its head down again, and I flinched. "Tomorrow," I agreed and woke up.

The lights above my bed blurred as I blinked the lingering sleep from my eyes. A quiet clicking filled the room. It took a good thirty seconds to realize it was my teeth. Longer to realize my entire body was shaking. Longer still to remember I needed to breathe. I dragged in a breath, the air burning my dry throat.

What was that thing?

Everything felt like a lie. My whole life. The Sandman was supposed to be my constant, but now…

Tomorrow. Tomorrow I would have answers.

My limbs were heavy and sluggish, but I forced myself to move. To climb out of bed and put one foot in front of the other on the cold floor. The dresser drawer seemed to weigh a thousand pounds. I sifted through my scarves until I found my notebook and clutched it to my chest.

As I reached for the colored pencils, the memory of the nightmarish worm trickled to the front of my mind. I gripped the edge of the drawer to steady myself. *No.* That thing would not grace a single sheet of paper. Instead, I would draw Natalie's mischievous grin and Emery's bright eyes. Katie's liveliness. The people in my life that I took for granted. The ones who saw beyond what my own mother saw and accepted me.

I leapt back onto my bed and flipped to the last page—the one that said *Dreamer, Dreamer*—and wrenched it out. This notebook was my lighthouse and would be filled only with happy things to chase away the dark.

The pencils clacked against each other as I dumped the box out onto the bedspread, the red landing on top. I flinched. *Pencil... Pen.* Bloody *pen.* I snatched it up and hurled it into the small waste basket beside my desk. My heart thumped wildly at the reminder, and I focused on the blank paper. *Good things.* I could do that. With a shaky hand, I lifted the pink pencil and began with Katie's hair.

That night, I sketched until my hand cramped. Until the first glimpse of sunlight broke through the window. Until each new drawing was speckled with fallen tears.

Chapter Nine

The Sandman

Flashes of orange lightning highlighted each curve of the clouds and rumbles of thunder followed closely on its heels. Despite there being no rain, the ground in this part of the Nightmare Realm was thick with mud. It sucked at my boots, squelching with each step through the empty field. Traces of the Weaver's presence lingered, his magic prickling against mine, and the strong metallic scent of it mixed with the lighter scent of burning wool. A new nightmare was born here recently. It was too bad Baku was nowhere to be found—he loved the new ones best.

I rubbed at the soft spot in front of my ears. The low, droning moan of the Blood Army followed me around geysers of boiling water, through a darkness alive with glowing eyes, and past a table set for an elaborate dinner party. Landscape after landscape, it lingered.

Luckily, there was no hint of the red mist that followed the army, nor any sign of their leaders. Rowan and Kail weren't mindless beasts like the ones the Weaver used as cannon fodder. They were carefully crafted with minds of their own—elite nightmares, nearly as terrifying as the Weaver himself.

With their mournful song echoing through my head, I followed the Weaver's trail of magic deeper into the storm. He could sense me as easily as I could sense him, and he was a step ahead. This being his home turf, it made sense, but bouncing around his realm was growing old—fast. If he considered my emotions rather than my mere presence, he might be convinced to stop.

I hoped—against every instinct I had, I hoped—that I could talk some sense into the Weaver. That we could come to terms. *Peacefully*. His word was his bond by choice, and it hadn't faltered once over the millennia. Mine, however, was another story. I had lied to him countless times about things I could no longer remember.

It was true I cut the last ties of friendship to him the night of the binding, but maybe he would believe me tonight. I had something worth bargaining for this time: Nora's safety in exchange for lengthening his leash.

A rustling drew my attention to the right. Another flash of lightning revealed thin strings reaching down from the clouds. I squinted and brushed my hood back. The strings shifted. Another rustle came from behind, and I turned just in time to avoid an oval hand aimed at my head. Raw wood carved into simple shapes formed a life-size marionette. It stumbled forward in a series of jerky movements controlled by seven white cords. A hint of sulfur clung to its body, identifying it as the Weaver's latest creation.

It rushed me, strings swaying, head down, arms pumping. I tossed a handful of sand out between us, and it swirled into a tall horizontal bar. The puppet's strings snagged on the steel, jerking its body backward where it clattered to the ground. The metal disintegrated into a pile of lifeless sand. Cords wrapped around the marionette's limbs, looping through its joints. I rubbed the space between my brows. *New and stupid.* I didn't have time for this.

"I rather liked that one," the Weaver said, on the other side of his nightmare. My muscles tensed, my eyes flying to the black and gold threads running from his vest sleeve to his wrist. "I see he needs improving though. I'll have to study him and make adjustments."

"You killed Nora's friends and took her sister." The words were out before I could swallow them. It wasn't the best start to a negotiation.

The Weaver rolled his eyes and approached his nightmare. He ran long fingers over a string, following it up toward the clouds. "I did."

"Weaver—"

"*Sandman.*" He glared at me, his gold eyes fierce. "You never could take a hint."

My lips parted. "What?"

"This." He motioned between us. "If I wanted to talk to you, I would've stayed home. Surprisingly, I don't feel like listening to your empty threats. Let me guess, you were going to start with *stop or feel my wrath.*"

"I wasn't—"

"I'm a busy man so let me make this easy for you." He leaned in and examined a knot around the marionette's elbow joint.

"Fetch the dream, and I won't have to bother the Dream Keeper again."

He might not bother her, but she would never be safe with his creatures running around the Day World. No one would be. "You know I can't do that."

"You mean you won't," he said and tugged a string free from where it caught on the puppet's chin.

I circled him, and the marionette strained to reach me. The Weaver slapped its forearm, stilling the nightmare. "You have an entire world at your fingertips," I started.

"Which is more than you have with miles of empty beach. I know, I know. You're like a dog with a bone, aren't you?" The Weaver plucked another string free from the puppet, and it climbed to one foot, the other still caught at the ankle. "Don't pretend you don't want more than this life. I feel your emotions the same as you feel mine. I know what it is you desire."

My lungs deflated, and my abdomen ached the same as if he sucker-punched me. In a way, he did. But our wishes weren't the same. He wanted to invade and destroy. I only wanted Nora.

"The impossible," I whispered. He had spent his entire existence striving for things outside our limits—pushing boundaries, working himself to the bone for *more, more, more*. More power. More territory. But this was the first time I wanted something I couldn't quite reach, and it shook me to my core. "We want the impossible."

"No!" The Weaver leapt around the limping nightmare, his hands in fists near his chest, imploring me to understand. "It isn't impossible, don't you see? You think only inside your little sandbox… If you released me and my nightmares, you would have the strength to stay with the girl in the Day World until you grew bored of it."

I winced against the earnestness in his voice. It was true, but that didn't make it right. Night beings ruled the realms through dreams and nightmares, influencing the Day World in our own way. We weren't meant to force ourselves on the mortals' conscious, but taboo or not, I would continue Day Walking until this mess was cleaned up.

"Or is that the problem? You're worried about tiring of the girl?" The sharp edge of his gaze softened. "You don't have to be. When you come back, you and I can work together again. It would be like old times."

Old times. A volley of memories pierced my mind like arrows, stretching back long before the Night World was cleaved in two. Before boundaries and bargains came between us. When we were both new to this existence—him, born in the Day World's shadow, the embodiment of mortal fears. And I, the manifestation of their optimism, their wishes and goodness. Different yet unified, we had laughed together, grown together, and combined our power for the common good more than once.

But the day we erected the wall between the Day and Night Worlds, something pivotal shifted between us. We drew a line in permanent ink and there was no washing the stain from our fingers. No matter how much either of us might wish to.

"We have to maintain the balance, and part of that is staying where we belong," I said, my voice hoarse.

He groaned and spun on his heels, working the last snarl in his puppet's string. "The balance always rights itself, Sandman. You should know that better than anyone. Just look at yourself—keeping me prisoner has turned you into one as well."

I pressed my lips into a straight line. He wasn't wrong. I was a shell of myself, but it was a choice I'd make again. "I came to negotiate."

"*Negotiate?*" His muscles tensed beneath his sleeveless shirt. "You want to negotiate. With me." He rolled his neck to the side and shivered. "You're about five years too late, *old friend.*"

"I know you might find it hard to trust me after—"

"Do you?" He wound the snarled string around his hand and balled it into a fist. "Your plea might be more effective if you weren't reaching for your precious sand as you said it."

I froze, unaware my hand had drifted in that direction, then snapped it away. "There was nothing for me to barter with last time. As you said, there's something else I want now."

"*Last time.*" He scoffed. "You have no idea what I was prepared to offer then. I didn't have the chance to extend the offer, did I?" The Weaver freed the marionette. It staggered on its feet, and he drew a slow breath. "But maybe I should thank you for that. I realize now how foolish it would've been to search for common ground with you."

"The binding is wearing thin," I pressed. Whatever his offer entailed, it wouldn't have been enough. No nightmares could be allowed out. "If you leave Nora alone, I won't seek to strengthen it. The gates will still be locked to your magic—I can't undo them without the dream Nora has, and I won't take it back—but you'll eventually be able to pass through if you're alone."

The offer felt heavy. I didn't want the Weaver roaming the Day World as he pleased any more than I wanted his creations to, but it might be the only way.

"So, your Dream Keeper will be safe, and I'll *eventually* be able to Day Walk?" He cocked an eyebrow. "It seems to me that you'll be getting everything you want while I only get a fraction. If I continue as I am, I *will* have everything. My freedom, now and forever, and open passage to the Day World. The ability to send whatever I want, to whomever I want, whenever I choose is my cost, but that's what you're denying me. There's no incentive for me to agree."

Sometimes wishes were only that. *Wishes.* And I couldn't let regret cloud my actions. There was no choice five years ago and there was no choice now. I had to rebind the Weaver before he could do more damage. To do that, I had to be close enough to steal a thread from his arm. Then I needed enough time to force my power into the unborn nightmare and tether the Weaver to this place.

That was all.

One tiny, impossible feat after another.

My humorless laugh was lost in another roll of thunder. I felt exposed here with only a satchel of sand to work with. Powerless. Useless. I should have been with Nora, helping her through the loss of her friends. My back arched against the thought of how much pain she was in. But this *was* helping her. This was *saving* her. Saving her from making a choice between her loved ones and the world as she knew it.

"How did you find her anyway?" I asked softly, buying myself more time.

"I followed your magic back from the beach. It wasn't hard." He gave me a bored scowl. "It was easy to keep track of her after that. But that doesn't really matter, does it?"

"No." I swallowed hard, forcing myself not to look at his arm and tip him off. "No, I suppose it doesn't."

When he glanced at his marionette, I took the opening, as small as it was, and lunged for the threads wrapped around his wrist. The Weaver threw an elbow into my nose. Blood trickled down my lips, and I landed in the mud with a grunt. He advanced, his fists tight, with the nightmare hobbling behind him. I climbed onto my knees to lunge again, but he kicked me onto my back before I found purchase. He slammed a boot down on my chest. His smile was cruel. Entitled. All traces of the friend I once knew, gone. He drew a thread from his wrist and dangled it over me.

"Is this what you want?" he asked. "Maybe I should give it shape and let you have it. Or," he shook it slightly, "let *it* have you."

"Do it," I dared him through my teeth. My satchel dug into my lower back, cutting off my access to the sand. I gripped his ankle and waited. "If you think the balance will right itself, then do it."

A flash of uncertainty crossed his face. There was a reason we stopped trying to kill each other eons ago, and it had nothing to do with the destruction of the only weapon capable of it. Hurting, tormenting, binding—those were another matter. But the balance did always right itself. Neither of us were brave enough to find out what would happen if the other ceased to exist.

The Weaver bent at the waist, his metallic breath skating over me. "You'll soon find out there are worse things than death."

My hand shot up toward the band of threads around his wrist. The Weaver straightened, snapping his arm away, and my fingertips grazed their target. The marionette, somehow tangled again, flopped into the mud and army-crawled toward me. I ground my teeth together. When I rebound the Weaver, it would be so tight he would never take a single step outside of his Keep.

"Now." The Weaver exhaled quickly. "Get out of my realm."

The heel of his boot ground into my chest. The world spun, and then I found myself at home. Stars twinkled in the sky, their light mirrored on the beach. I groaned and wiped the blood from my face without getting up. He was right there. The threads were *right there.* I lifted my head and let it thud back to the ground. *Useless.* I should have fought harder but…

Next time. Next time I wouldn't hold back. Wouldn't let our connection, our history, stand in the way. Nora was too important to allow it.

Hopefully, the Weaver didn't kill anyone else in the meantime.

I worked the ties holding my tunic tight against my chest until I had enough room to stretch the neck of my undershirt down to expose the mark on my breastbone—a navy blue crescent moon, nearly a semicircle, concave up. From the dip flowed a stream of silver and blue that broke off below the hollow of my throat, reaching toward each collarbone, and cascaded down my arms before reaching my fingertips. The epicenter of my power prickled. The starlight offered its strength, and, beneath me, the sand began to hum.

Chapter Ten

Nora

A frenzy charged the community as desperation to find the killer took root. Calls flooded the tip line, a curfew was set in town, and search parties combed through every surrounding park and forest. The one I joined spanned twenty-three people wide, inching across an empty field next to a new cul-de-sac. My mother trudged on my left with hollow eyes and Paul on my right, a line of sweat shining on his brow. Dry grass pricked my shins, the underbrush crunching beneath my sneakers, and I scanned the ground.

It felt like most people were hoping against hope to find some material clue instead of another body. I couldn't blame them given what had happened lately, and they weren't wrong thinking the killer had my sister. They were just wrong about what was going to save her.

The sun burned hot at my back, and the string holding the Sandman's bag chaffed against my sweaty neck. The bag itself clung to the skin beneath my shirt. I almost left it home, but the thought of ever taking it off sent my heart racing. It was proof—hard, undeniable proof—that none of this was in my head. Each painful rub of the knot against my skin was a reminder. All the murders they blamed on some mystery psychopath, the *suicide* they were now blaming on drugs—it was all the Weaver.

And he had my sister.

Cold fury swept up my body, starting at my feet, and turned my heart to ice. Images of a blood-soaked living room wavered in my mind. I slammed a lid over those haunted thoughts to focus on the one person I still had a chance of saving. My sister needed me—both here and in the other world. That was all that mattered. So, today I would search for where the Weaver hid her body, and tonight, her mind.

I skipped ahead to regain my place in line, fueled by my newfound resolve. I had to believe Katie was more useful to the Weaver alive than she was dead. She was leverage over me. A bargaining chip to get what he wanted. Only this time I knew what would happen if I denied him. Giving him the dream was the last thing I wanted to do, but I wanted my sister alive more.

I balled my hands into fists and glanced over at my mother's worn face. New lines seemed to appear overnight. Her hair frizzed out of its clip, and she still wore yesterday's clothes. She was so focused, so determined, I wasn't sure how to approach her. I wanted to shout that I would save Katie. That I knew what happened, and it would all be fine. I would make sure it was. But I couldn't promise any of that. Not really. And if I tried, I would be back in a psychiatrist's office faster than I could say *Sandman.*

But, while she watched me before, waiting for something to trigger another *episode*, she barely looked at me today. I would've been grateful under other circumstances, but something told me it wasn't only because she was worried about Katie's disappearance. It was that she was afraid to look at me and see the impending break. To her, it wasn't *if* I would fall to pieces anymore, it was *when*.

A police radio crackled from the end of the line where a young officer helped with our efforts. The sound fizzled in my ears, warping into a chant of *Dreamer, Dreamer*. I shook my head until the imagined voice disappeared, and I concentrated instead on the highway traffic zooming back and forth behind us. I listened for the different sounds the passing cars made and wiped sweat from my brow. Specks of white and grey siding peeked through a copse of trees. The newly built homes around the cul-de-sac had already been searched by the police.

The line narrowed along with the field until we were almost shoulder to shoulder. We continued into the trees. I shivered when the shade cut off the heat from the sun and again when the prickle of watchful eyes crawled across my shoulders. I glanced back but the field was empty save a row of cars parked just off the street. When I turned back, my mother and Paul had closed the gap between them, leaving me behind.

"Dreamer, Dreamer," whispered a familiar voice. This time there was no mistaking it as the real thing. It was too loud, too focused.

I froze, watching as everyone continued, not noticing I had fallen behind. There hadn't been time to find out from the Sandman exactly what the Weaver wanted from me or why. Yet, if something was important enough for the Sandman to hide, it was probably better that it stayed put. Especially since the

Weaver wanted it badly enough to go on a murder spree. Until I knew, I couldn't say yes.

But I couldn't say no either.

A human silhouette appeared between two oak trees and chuckled. "Come closer, my little Sun-Kissed Keeper."

I looked between him and the safety of my parents and crossed my arms. If I held onto the anger, let it overwhelm the fear, maybe, just maybe, I could walk away from this conversation without agreeing to his demands. The bloody words on Emery's window flashed through my mind, but I forced myself not to react. Anger. Not fear. I had to hold my ground.

"What do you want, Weaver?" I hissed.

He moved forward, and I got my first true look at my nemesis. His sculpted face was shrouded in black gossamer, his bright gold eyes gleaming. Halfway down his wide, muscular body, the gossamer tangled and cut him off mid-thigh as if he were floating.

He smirked. "Ah, he told you about me then."

"Give me back my sister, asshole." I strained to keep my voice low.

He lifted a hand and ran it down the cloth encasing him. Flecks of black and gold thread sparkled around his wrist, stretching up his arm to join his sleeveless shirt. The embroidery there moved among the weave of the fabric. "I'll give you what you want when you give me what I want. Say yes, and I swear no one else will die for this."

"For *this*," I snapped. He seemed to take pride in slaughtering people, and I imagined someone with that kind of insanity wouldn't stop. "But they will die, right?"

The Weaver quirked an eyebrow. "I wonder what assets you're hiding. The Sandman doesn't strike me as someone that would gravitate toward angry little sprites." He leaned toward me but came up short as a beam of sunlight broke through the branches. "Make no mistake. I will get the dream that's locked away in that pretty head of yours, one way or another, and everything will be as it should have been. If you cooperate, I can guarantee your safety."

He shifted to avoid another line of light and a slow, angry smile spread across my lips. He needed the shadows. I stepped into the sun, lifting my chin in what I hoped looked like confidence. "Like I would trust your word? My safety is guaranteed if I keep the dream hidden, not the other way around."

Rage flashed across his handsome features, disappearing as fast as it came. "*Yours,* perhaps."

"If you—"

"I see you need a little more time to mull things over," he said in a flat voice. His hand fell away from the gossamer and when he brought it back up, a clump of Katie's bright pink hair laid across his palm. "Think hard, Dream Keeper, and remember—tick tock."

Then he was gone.

I stared at the empty space, my heart thundering. He wouldn't murder Katie yet, but I hadn't said yes. *I didn't say no either.* It was a small victory. Or, it would have been if there wasn't a sinking feeling in the pit of my stomach. Someone I knew was on the chopping block. A wave of white-hot terror washed over me. Who did I fail this time?

"Mom." I bolted toward her narrow, hunched back. "Mom, I have to leave."

She and Paul stopped, the party continuing forward without them. "What do you mean you have to go? What could possibly be more important than finding your sister?"

"Please, Mom, I can't..." I couldn't watch someone else I loved die. I couldn't search a field I knew would be empty. "I can't deal with this right now."

"Nora—"

"Let her go, Val," Paul said. "She's been through a lot, and she's running on two hours sleep."

She held her breath and stared at my chin, refusing to make eye contact. I forced myself not to twitch under the scrutiny. What Paul said was mostly true. I felt everything my mother did—on top of losing Natalie and Emery—but getting two hours of sleep last night would have been a blessing. Even if I wasn't dealing with my delusions becoming real life, it would be too much for a lot of people. It was too much for *me*, but I wasn't going to allow myself to break down. One day I would, but not yet.

"Okay, you're right. I'm sorry." She pulled me into a careful hug. "Lock all the doors behind you and make sure you turn on the alarm. Do you remember the new code?"

I stepped back and nodded. "Call me if you find anything."

***

I barreled through the house to the bathroom attached to my parent's room. With frequent shift changes at the hospital, both my mother and Paul occasionally took pills to fall asleep. I couldn't risk being scared into waking up again, even if it was for my own protection. The Sandman was the only one who could give me answers, and I needed them now before anyone else got hurt.

I opened the medicine cabinet with shaking hands to reveal a row of orange prescription bottles. This was wrong. I knew it was, but there was too much on the line to care. I gently twisted each bottle to read the label. Old antibiotics, a few I didn't recognize, and finally, the one I was looking for. I swallowed hard and shook three white oval pills into my palm. One should do the trick, but if I needed to do this again, I would be ready.

I replaced the bottle exactly in its original spot, closed the cabinet, and hurried into my room to stuff the extra two pills in my sock drawer. The third sat on my palm, heavy with promise. It would give me hours, maybe. If I was lucky. But luck didn't have much to do with it. Natalie and Emery weren't lucky. Katie wasn't.

Hot tears splashed against my forearm before I knew I was crying. Time stopped then. I stared at the droplets as if they were something foreign. I supposed, to me, they were. More fell, scalding my skin. Without me, everyone would all still be alive. Still be here. Safe.

An agonizing sob ripped free of my chest, and I collapsed to the floor. I pressed my fists over my breastbone, praying for something, anything, to ease the sorrow as I curled in on myself. It felt as if my heart was made of tissue paper. Every second I wept disintegrated another piece of it until all that was left was a tattered mess. I laid there in a fetal position until I heaved. Until each breath was an absolute struggle.

And then I cried some more.

I cried until there were no tears left.

Until I was a husk.

Then I sat up, wiping my nose on the back of my hand. I blinked my swollen eyes until the room came back into clear focus, and climbed onto shaky legs. *Breathe*, I told myself. This wasn't going to help Katie. When she was home again—when I brought her back—there would be time to grieve. I clutched the pill in my hand tighter, and my stomach lurched.

What if the Weaver showed up again and I was stuck? If I was going to do this, if I was going to put myself at risk, I couldn't rely solely on the Sandman to protect me. I dropped the third pill into the top drawer and sprinted to the kitchen. A butcher knife was my first choice, but it came with the risk of stabbing myself in my sleep. I needed to think about getting a pocket knife or a taser tomorrow, but for now, I needed something else.

I dabbed at the raw corners of my eyes and stared into the utensil drawer. An apple corer. A cheese grater. A meat mallet.

Two hard knocks rattled the front door, and I jumped. Bile immediately filled my throat. I glared at the shape on the other side of the frosted glass, praying it wasn't a reporter, or, even worse, one of Natalie's relatives. Cars filled her driveway next door, spilling out onto the side of the road. I couldn't face any of them yet, especially not her parents. Not when I was the reason she was dead. Not when I was the only one to survive. To look at them after seeing... I tapped the heel of my hand on my head, fighting against the memory of the blood-soaked carpet beneath my feet. Something tugged in my chest. A threat. The sense of being buried alive.

The knocks came again.

I blinked the bleariness from my eyes again. I had to keep it together. "Coming," I called, and glanced at the meat mallet again before sliding the drawer shut.

When I cracked the door, my heart lurched. Ben stood on my stoop in khakis and a white dress shirt as if he just came from work. His curly hair drooped, and his eyes lacked a bit of their usual light.

"Hey," he said, a line forming between his brows. "I was worried when I couldn't get a hold of you. Are you okay?"

I scowled and drew my phone from my back pocket. Ten texts and two missed phone calls, all from him. He must have heard the news. Who hadn't? It was all over the television and social media was exploding with goodbye messages to Natalie and Emery. Right alongside them were a dozen different theories on who did it, and I was suspect number one.

"I'm..." *Far from okay.* But I wasn't going to say that. Admitting the truth out loud gave it purchase. It locked it into place and made it undeniable.

"Can I come in?" he asked, tugging at a curl near his temple.

I hesitated. I was home alone, for one thing, and about to grill the Sandman for information. But he heard the Weaver at Howell's. He *talked* to him in the back room like they knew each other. Whatever he knew, I wanted to know it too.

"I promise to be a perfect gentleman," he added when I stared silently at him.

"Okay." I shrugged and moved aside.

Ben stepped into the living room, and I shut the door behind him carefully. My pulse boomed. How did I bring the subject up? He probably wouldn't admit to anything without proof; maybe not even with actual evidence. I certainly wouldn't if I were in his shoes. I lifted a hand to my chest to feel the bag of sand tucked safely beneath the fabric.

"So," he started, gazing down at his shoes.

"So," I repeated.

"You're okay then?" he asked, looking me over, then amended, "You're not hurt?"

I shook my head. The movement sent a heaviness clanking through my skull. It felt as if I could sleep for a week. Despite that, I knew if I saw the nightmares again, answers or no answers, the pill would be the only thing keeping me there. I was out of time to be afraid.

His shoulders slumped forward, and he stuck his hands in his pockets. "I was hoping we could talk."

My eyes narrowed. I wanted to believe that my friends' deaths finally pushed him to come clean about whatever he knew, but, to anyone else, showing up with some crazy tale when I was grieving would make him look worse than crazy. It would make him look like an inconsiderate jerk. Treading carefully about this seemed to be an unwritten rule.

"If this is about what happened on the Ferris wheel—"

"Not about that," he said quietly, his cheeks turning pink.

"Then about the Weaver?" I asked before I could change my mind. There was more to Ben than met the eye, and not only because of the Weaver. He reminded me of the Sandman for a reason. What that reason was, I didn't know, but there had to be a connection somewhere. "Don't say you don't know what I'm talking about."

His eyes widened, his lips parting. "It's... Yes."

My breath caught. There were so many things I could ask next. How did he know the Weaver? What were they arguing about? Does he know how to contact him? Would he help me? If the Sandman helped me there, and Ben helped me here, maybe I could save Katie before the Weaver decided he was tired of waiting. I stared into his violet eyes, my heart thudding. How did Ben fit into everything?

I jumped at another sharp rap on the door.

"Nora, it's Detective Bell."

I ground my teeth together. "What now?" I told him everything. Twice. More than twice. I glanced at my phone again. My mother hadn't called which meant Katie was still missing. "One second," I called.

"What do you know about him?" I asked Ben in a rush.

"The answer to that is a lot longer than we have time for." Ben motioned to the door. "Should I call your parents?"

"Not yet, but..." I held my phone out to him and eyed Detective Bell's silhouette through the frosted glass on the door. If he dragged me out of here in handcuffs under some ridiculous pretense, I didn't want to wait for them to give me my phone call to let them know where I was. "Their numbers are in here, just in case."

Ben took it and slipped it in his back pocket. "Got it."

"This conversation isn't over," I promised.

He nodded and opened the door. Detective Bell stood on the porch in a mint green shirt with buttons in the wrong holes, his glasses resting on top of his head. An unmarked car idled in the driveway. His bloodshot eyes flicked to Ben. "I see you have company."

The way he said it grated against me. Like I was using the opportunity of an empty house to have my boyfriend sneak over. As if I would do something like that when my sister was in trouble. As if Ben was my boyfriend.

"Ben stopped by to see if we needed anything," I said, feigning complacency overtop my annoyance.

He pursed his lips. "There are search parties going on all over town that could use another pair of eyes."

Ben nodded. "I thought the family might need some groceries or errands done."

Detective Bell sniffed before turning back to me. "I hate to do this now, but we need you to come down to the station and finish your statement."

I glared at him. "Did my mom say it was all right?"

"We stopped by the search location you were supposed to be at. She plans to keep looking for your sister but gave us the go-ahead. Your step-father is waiting for us."

I paused. He wasn't really asking, and if I didn't cooperate, things would look bad. *Worse.* If they asked Paul to be there, it meant I wasn't simply considered a witness anymore. It meant the people online weren't the only ones to think of me as a suspect anymore. "All right."

Chapter Eleven

Nora

"I don't know what else you want from me," I said, avoiding my reflection in the two-way mirror behind Detective Bell. "I've told you everything."

My step-father was a steady presence at my side in the frigid interrogation room. The red light of a camera blinked down from a corner of the ceiling and the grey brick walls made the room feel like the dankest part of someone's basement. Paul spent the last forty-five minutes scratching the stubble on his chin, staring blankly at a dent in the metal table, but I knew he was absorbing every word. It was his focused face. The one he got when he didn't like what he was hearing but wasn't ready to make his case yet.

"None of this adds up. I want to be sure I understand everything correctly," Detective Bell said. "One murder is a travesty but when they start piling up, it sends people into a panic. It looks like we're dealing with a serial killer here, and we must figure this out before anyone else gets hurt. Right now, you're the only thing connecting all of the victims. And, of course, you were present for the incident at the mall."

I clenched my teeth. I did understand, and if anyone wanted the killer stopped, it was me. Telling him about the Weaver wouldn't do anyone any good, though. It would land me in a straitjacket, and then I would be a sitting duck. The Weaver could get to me anytime. Torture me. Kill people. I couldn't stop him from a locked ward.

"I can't tell you something I don't know," I said, sighing.

Detective Bell clicked his pen. "Is there a new drug you kids are doing? Something that wouldn't appear on the test but would make you do things you wouldn't normally do? Like stab yourself or hurt the people around you, for instance. I don't work in drug enforcement—you can tell me the truth."

"That's enough. Nora *passed* the drug test," Paul said in a low voice. "She's cooperated with you every step of the way and answered all your questions with more patience than I would have. I'm not going to let you harass her so if you want to talk to her again, you can contact our lawyer."

His eyes swiveled to my step-father. "We have to explore all our options."

"You think a girl that weighs one-ten sopping wet broke a man's neck? Can you honestly tell me that you think she looks capable of doing any of those things?"

"Mr. Thompson. With her history—" Detective Bell snapped his notebook shut and slid it off the table with calm fury. "Could we speak in the hall for a moment?" he asked in a strained voice.

Paul shoved up from his seat and stormed from the room. When the door clicked shut behind them, leaving me alone, I rested my head in my hands.

Deep breaths. In. Out.

My history. By now, they had to know about the psychologists I used to see, though the subject matter was confidential. I never threatened to hurt myself or anyone else, so unless my mother told them all the specifics, they had no reason to believe it was for anything other than my parents' divorce.

I scrubbed at my face. My mother may have been watching me like I would break, but she couldn't think… I slammed the door on the thought. My mother couldn't believe I had anything to do with this. Even if I was crazy, she had to know I wouldn't hurt anyone. Not like that. Not like anything.

"Dreamer, Dreamer," the Weaver whispered. "*Such* a schemer."

I jerked back, my spine perfectly straight. He hovered in the corner beneath the video camera. I couldn't reply without someone seeing me talk to an empty room, and I wasn't going to out myself as mentally unstable. A-plus for his effort though.

"Had a secret…" He inched around the shadowed perimeter of the room with a sly grin. "Couldn't keep it."

My hands balled into fists under the table. I couldn't take the bait. *Couldn't.* Even if I wanted to lunge across the table and strangle him with my bare hands.

"Ah, Sun-Kissed Keeper, does that piece of technology frighten you? Do you think they will lock you away if you're recorded talking to me?" His lips curled. "You do. I see it. Smell it. You fear they will assume you lost your mind and killed your friends during one of your episodes. That's the word your mother uses, yes? Episodes?"

I squinted at him. I didn't *think* they would. I knew they would. Doubt reared in the back of my mind. *Give it to him. Give him the dream, and he'll go away.* My family would be safe, and I could return to some semblance of sanity. But at what cost? The Sandman was going to give me answers tonight so I had to wait until then, at least. Besides, I still wanted justice.

Not justice.

Payback. I wanted payback.

"No? Perhaps I'm projecting. That's what the Sandman used to call my… Well, episodes." The Weaver leered at me over his shoulder, something human flitting across his eyes, gone as quickly as it came. "Before they began playing on an endless loop, that is. Who knew one teensy banishment would—" He cleared his throat. "Never mind."

Endless loop this. I tapped my middle finger on the table as casually as possible.

The Weaver cocked an eyebrow, amused, then rose into the air, a gossamer trail stretching behind him, tethering him to the floor. "Impressive," he said and stared into the camera lens. "Unable to capture my image, of course. The only reason you can see me is because of that tiny piece of my world residing in your brain."

Each taunt was gasoline on the fire, an inferno in place of a beating heart. Once Katie was back, I would unleash the heat building in my veins and burn him to the ground. I took a deep breath. He couldn't get to me when I was awake, or he would've had me strung up and tortured by now. I had to wait until I knew how to get the upper hand.

"You know." He lowered himself and turned to face me again. "If you don't wish to give me the dream, you could ask the Sandman to take it back. He could hide it in some other poor soul. As he's so torn up about putting you in danger, I'm sure he would honor the request."

The Weaver knew nothing of what the Sandman felt. He couldn't; he didn't *have* feelings. Besides, if someone else had the dream, he would do the same thing to them. More people would die. Not *my* people, but people nonetheless. And what if they caved? What if they gave him what he wanted? I couldn't take that risk.

"Ah, little Keeper, you look perturbed." He shifted back into the corner, his gold eyes gleaming, and crossed his arms. "We sense each other, you see. I know what the Sandman is feeling as he knows what I am. For example, I know right now, he is worried sick about what I'm doing. He feels it—the thrill of having you so close. Just as he felt my ecstasy this morning when I murdered your father."

I flew to my feet, the interview room echoing with the scrape of metal chair legs. "Wh—"

The door swung open. Detective Bell and Paul looked in with matching looks of confusion. "Everything okay?" my step-father asked.

"Cramp," I lied, clutching my calf. The Weaver chuckled.

"Maybe you should sit down," Paul said carefully. When I didn't listen, he rolled his shoulders. "Detective, I think we should wait for her mother before making a decision about this."

"About what?" I stammered and rubbed the imaginary cramp away to hide my shaking hands. The room tilted. My father wasn't dead. The Weaver was lying. He had to be because my dad was over a thousand miles away. How would the Weaver even connect us? It was impossible...

"A polygraph," the detective answered.

I plunked back into the chair. They would ask if I knew who was behind the murders. They would ask, and I would fail. Then what? They wouldn't let me leave until I told them everything. "A lie detector test? Is that really necessary?"

"No, it isn't," my mother snapped from the hallway. Relief washed over me. "I just talked to your partner, Detective, and you won't be speaking to my daughter again. You said there were a few things to clear up with her, not that you wanted to put her through an interrogation."

"Ma'am, as we've stated, your daughter isn't a suspect," Detective Bell said with an exasperated sigh.

"You're doing your damnedest to make sure she becomes one." My mother shouldered her way into the room and grabbed my hand. Her eyes were red and glassy with tears, the purple bruising beneath them stark against her ashen face. "We're going home."

I didn't argue; I wanted nothing to do with their investigation. The only way to solve this was to find Katie myself and stop the Weaver before anyone else could die. With the Sandman's help, I could do it. I had to.

When I murdered your father.

Nausea gripped my stomach. He couldn't be dead. Because he was all the way in New York City, like a mile off the ground in a penthouse or something. Or, if he was on a business trip, maybe he was even halfway around the world.

"Val, I think we should talk about this," Paul whispered on our way through the parking lot. The sun felt blistering after being in the air conditioning for so long. "It could put an end to their focus on Nora and let them concentrate on finding who really did this."

My mother pressed the unlock button and the SUV lights flashed. "This is a witch hunt, Paul. It's obvious Nora had nothing to do with what happened to those girls. Right now, all we have to do is find Katie."

Paul raised his hands in surrender. "All right. I'll call a lawyer first thing in the morning."

The leather seats burned my legs when I climbed into the back of the vehicle. To know who my father was, the Weaver would've needed to root around in my head, right? And have dug pretty deep while he was at it because I rarely thought of him these days.

"The *best* lawyer," my mother clarified in a stern voice.

No matter what else my mother thought of me, at least she believed I wasn't capable of *this*. I wrapped my arms around my waist and tried not to fidget. What would happen if the lawyer said I had to take the lie detector test? I absolutely couldn't do it but refusing would look terrible. I'm sure the court could find a way to force me anyway.

First thing's first, though. I had to dust off my father's telephone number. He was a sorry excuse for a dad, but I didn't want him dead. I needed to hear his voice. To know without a doubt that the Nightmare Lord was only waging mental warfare. That was all. *That's all.*

***

My mother went straight to the computer to read through Katie's social media for clues again, while Paul pried a boxed pizza from the freezer. I watched them from the living room as if they weren't real. As if this were a reality show, and I was a mere observer. But I wasn't. I did this; I ruined my family. Five years ago, and again now.

I gnawed on the inside of my cheek to stop the tears from forming and reached into my back pocket for my phone. Only it wasn't there. Because I gave it to Ben. I hung my head and groaned. "Have you told Dad about Katie?" I asked, weary.

"I sent him a text this morning," my mother said, exhausted with an edge of annoyance. "He didn't reply."

He was busy. That's why he didn't reply. He was *always* busy. He probably saw my mother's name pop up and ignored the message. "Can..." I wasn't sure how to phrase the next question. For however little I cared about my father, my mother cared less. Or maybe she cared more. She couldn't hate him and not care about him at the same time. "Can I call him?"

My mother paused mid-scroll and spun in the office chair beside the stairs. "Why?"

I looked to Paul for help, but he was studiously reading the pizza box. "He deserves to know about Katie."

"If he wanted to know, he would've gotten back to me." She spun back to the computer. "But you don't need my permission to call your father."

"Can I use your phone?" I asked quietly. "I don't have his number."

Her head bobbed, and I scooped it up off the computer desk before she could change her mind. I dialed, my heart thumping in my ears. The phone rang. Once. Twice. Four times. Then a woman answered with a warbled *hello*.

"Hi." I paused. "Is this Michael Gallagher's phone?"

"Yes." The woman sniffled. "Who's this?"

"Nora. His daughter," I added in case he never mentioned me to this woman. It wouldn't surprise me. There was a long pause. "Hello?"

"I'm here."

I stalked away from my mother. "Can I talk to him?"

"No. He's... Maybe I should speak with your mother. Is she there?"

I closed my eyes. The Weaver wasn't lying; he did something. I clutched the lump beneath my shirt that was the Sandman's bag. "Where is he?"

"Your father had a heart attack last night. He—" *Hiccup.* "He didn't make it."

"Oh." The phone almost slipped from my hand. "Okay."

She sniffled into the receiver again. "The doctors said he went to sleep and didn't wake up so there wasn't any pain."

"I see."

"Are you—all right?" she asked.

I eased onto a stool at the kitchen island. "I'm fine."

"Is there—"

I hung up and slid the phone across the counter. *Dead.* He was dead, and more people would be soon. I could protect my mother and Paul, but my father lived so far away when the Weaver got him. What could I have done? I tightened my grip on the Sandman's sand. It wasn't possible for me to save everyone, but that didn't stop the guilt from clawing at me with its thorny fingers.

"What's wrong?" Paul asked.

I opened my mouth, unable to find the words. The bag of sand weighed heavily against my breastbone. It should hurt more—losing a parent. But I felt nothing. Almost as if someone had jabbed a needle full of Novocain straight into my brain. As if I was made of stone. Maybe I was now. Maybe I had to be, in order for all the deaths not to utterly destroy me.

A quiet, hesitant knock broke the silence.

"I'll get it," I said, slipping off the stool. I half expected it to be Detective Bell standing on the other side of the front door with a warrant, but Ben stood there instead.

One side of his mouth lifted in a grin, but it didn't extend to the rest of his face. His skin was waxen, his expression pinched. "Hi," he said softly.

"What are you doing here?" My voice was raw.

Ben held out my phone. "You can't call for my expert advice without this."

Expert advice indeed. The screen was warm with his body heat, and I hurried to set it on the end table. There was no one left for me to call anyway.

"And you are?" Paul asked from directly behind me.

Ben looked over my shoulder, his violet eyes dull. "Ben, sir."

Paul glanced between us before stepping back. "Come in."

"I really shouldn't," Ben said, chewing his bottom lip.

His eyes met mine in a silent apology, and my chest ached. The thought of going up to my room, of being alone, crushed me. The weight of millions of lives threatened to snap my bones, the strain of my sister's fate choking me.

"Stay." The word was half statement, half question, and one hundred percent desperate. But I didn't care—I was.

He blinked once, slowly, heavily. "Okay."

"Paul, have you ever heard Katie mention *Zach* before?" my mother called.

"We'll be in my room." I took Ben's hand and lead him toward the stairs before they could object.

He followed silently, his fingers loose around mine. My brain might have felt as if it were in some suspended state, but my body certainly didn't. It was the first time I would have a boy in my room. A boy I kissed, no less. Even though I had no intention of going down that awkward path again, it didn't stop my nerves from remembering. From tingling.

I couldn't think about that now. I needed to not be alone. To be with someone who didn't think I was psychotic. Who wouldn't ask questions. Ben knew the Weaver, so he must have some idea of what I was up against. That's what I needed. *Understanding.* And his answers to a hundred questions, but not now. Not tonight. I waited five years for the Sandman's answers and Ben's only a matter of days.

"Are you okay, Nora?" he asked when I kicked my bedroom door closed.

"No," I admitted through gasps. "No, I'm not."

He wrapped an arm around my shoulders and gathered me close. I tucked my face into his shoulder and, for the first time since the night I sketched my friends, hot tears scalded my cheeks. They came as a flash flood, washing away my entire life. I cursed them, hated them. Hated *myself* for letting them fall. I couldn't give in to the sorrow yet; I had to be the stone. Now wasn't the time to lose myself in a vortex. Now was the time to fill the hole inside with something else: revenge. When that was complete, when the Weaver paid for everything he had done, the hole would be there, waiting, but so would Katie.

I balled my hands into fists against the threat of defeat. If all those years of pretending to be normal taught me anything, it was how to pull myself together when it felt like I would fall apart. I stepped away from Ben and turned my back to him to wipe my face. "My father had a heart attack today."

Ben eased down on the edge of the mattress with a small creak. "I'm sorry."

"At least they can't blame me for that one," I grumbled.

"They shouldn't blame you for any of it," he said. "You didn't do anything."

"You know it as well as I do." I bit the inside of my cheek. *The Sandman first.* I owed him a chance to explain as much as he owed me the explanation. I kicked off my sandals and sat down beside him. "Sorry, it's been a long day."

He patted my pillow. "You look exhausted. Why don't you try to get some sleep?"

It was more than exhaustion. Each cell in my body ached as if they wanted to cry as badly as I did. I sat down beside him, still in jean shorts and a loose T-shirt. I had no plans to change tonight; pajamas weren't my choice attire for greeting any enemies that might show up. I eyed the sandals I took off. They would have been helpful, but I couldn't put them back on now.

"Sleep isn't as relaxing as it used to be," I murmured.

Ben's eyes flashed, and he studied the string circling my neck as if he knew it held the pouch of sand beneath my shirt. His fingers trembled, and he slid the neck of my shirt up over my bare shoulder. A blush colored his pale cheeks. "I know."

I rubbed at the spot his fingers grazed, both savoring the warmth left behind and willing it away. That he could bring such a mix of feelings fluttering to the surface when I knew so little about him, made me want to run the other way. Instead, I inched closer and asked, "Will you stay?"

"The next time you open your eyes, I'll be there," he said with a small smile.

My mind struggled to understand his answer, but my eyelids lost the fight to stay open. I laid down. "We're going to finish our conversation tomorrow." The words were thick and slurred with sleep. "You're not getting out of it."

The mattress shifted against his weight. One of his arms slid beneath my head until my cheek rested on his chest. It felt sturdy. Safe. The quick *thump thump thump* of his heart pulsed against me. I snuggled against his side, letting his warmth lull me into slumber.

"Sleep well, Nora," he whispered, and I faded away.

Chapter Twelve

The Sandman

For the first time, it wasn't the humming along our cord that told me the exact moment Nora fell asleep. I felt it in the weight of her head against my chest and the slight change of her breath. Her hand slid down my side, limp. I slipped my arm out from beneath her and gently set her head on the pillow, brushing the hair from her face.

The next time she laid eyes on me, it would change everything about our relationship. The trust we built up over the last five years would shatter in a single instant. Every word I ever spoke, all the promises I ever made, each laugh, each smile, each kind gesture wouldn't make any difference. She would question it all, and she would be right to.

With a sigh, I closed my eyes and followed her consciousness back to the beach.

Sand shifted beneath my boots, my hood and gloves already in place, shielding me a moment longer than I deserved. Nora's eyes burned into my back. The thought of turning around and seeing the look on her face turned my blood to ice.

Before I found the courage to move, she said, "Off with the hood."

My nerves prickled, and I spun, peering at her from the safety of fabric. She crossed her arms, glaring at me from a few feet away. Her eyes were glassy with unshed tears, or maybe it was fear shining back at me. I couldn't tell. Either way, it was my own doing. My own stupid, stupid fault.

"Nora..."

"Sandman," she countered with raised brows.

I grimaced. But maybe if she understood first... Maybe if she knew... "Let me explain."

"Explain what?" she snapped, her arms dropping to her sides. "You said you would take it off tonight."

"I will... I just..." My voice caught in my throat. *I just what?* "Let me start at the beginning and when I'm finished, I'll remove the hood."

Her nostrils flared, but she gave a terse nod.

I stared at my gloved hands held out before me, curling my fingers before letting them drop to my sides. "I thought it was better if we didn't get attached. If a situation arose with the Weaver, I needed to keep the big picture in mind. I thought that if you didn't see me, or know me, or touch me, that it would be impossible to care about each other. But I was wrong. Very wrong."

Her green eyes narrowed. "I have no idea what you're talking about."

"You're right. That isn't the beginning." My voice was weary. Resigned. The first and possibly biggest lie had to come first. I closed my eyes, and said, "The Weaver is the Lord of Nightmares as I am the Lord of Dreams. Everything created from magic has a counter, and he's mine. But where dreams are holograms crafted from my sand, his creatures are living, breathing things that he inserts into people's minds."

"Five years ago, the Weaver found a way to release his nightmares into your world. They tortured and killed hundreds of people all over the world before I was able to bind him and seal the exits against his magic. It left me weak, and I had just enough power left to secure the knowledge of how I changed the fabric between our worlds. It was too dangerous to keep the information when I couldn't defend it, so the night you called to me, instead of giving you good dreams, I gave you something else."

She shook her head, rubbing the back of her neck. "What *did* you give me?"

Each of my breaths wavered, fighting their way into tight lungs. "A dream containing the secret to releasing the Weaver's nightmares into your world. I...I made you a Dream Keeper to save us all."

She stood straighter and took half a step toward me. "That's what a Dream Keeper is? *That's* what I'm keeping?" Her voice was harsh and constrained. "That's what the Weaver wants so much? To bring a cosmic-ton of monsters to my world and kill *more* people?"

I chomped down on the inside of my cheek and backed into my hood, relishing my last moments in shadow. "Yes." Then, riding a tiny wave of unwarranted defensiveness for my foe, I added, "I'm sure whatever his reasons are, they make sense to him."

Nora paled, the freckles stark against her face. Her fingers trembled, and she touched them to her chest. "You want to talk about reasons? *I'm* the reason everyone is dead right now."

My heart stopped. "No, Nora. *No.* It's my fault. Magic isn't infinite; it wears down and frays like well-worn cloth, but I didn't notice. If I had..." If I had, no one would be dead. But I thought there was more time. I stepped forward to touch her, to let her feel my sincerity, but stopped myself. "I wouldn't have done this to you if it weren't absolutely necessary at the time. You understand that, right?"

"I don't understand anything. Are you crazy? I was *twelve.*" Nora sucked in air and paused. She tilted her head, her brows lowering. When she exhaled, her whole body seemed to deflate. "You asked my permission the night we met, didn't you? You were hurt and said you needed my help with something important. And I agreed."

I nodded. It wasn't a fair question to ask her; she was young and didn't know the risks. How could she when I didn't explain any of the details? But I had no choice. It had only been a few hours since the battle, and it was all I could do to keep from bleeding out in front of her. I assumed she had forgotten that night.

"I've spent every night since making sure you didn't accidentally see it," I said. "I've protected you from the consequences of my mistake for the last five years, but it wasn't enough. *I* wasn't enough to keep him from finding you. If he kills you, the dream will be lost forever. By killing people around you, the Weaver is poisoning your dreams in hopes you'll become more susceptible to nightmares—so he can snatch you out of the Dream Realm."

"And if he does?" She dug her fingers into her hair and scanned the beach. "If he gets me?"

Dread oozed through my veins, thick and cold. If the Weaver ever broke through and managed to get his claws into Nora, that would be the end. Everything would have been for nothing. There were too many nightmares for me to take on alone, and if Nora was in his realm, every single one of them would be there. Safeguarding their master while he tortured his way into her mind. Helping him do it. I shuddered. He wouldn't let her go until he got what he wanted, then the entire world would be in peril.

"He may not be able to kill you until you allow him access to the dream, but he *can* keep you from waking up," I told her carefully.

Her head jerked side to side. "If he did that, and I still refused to give it to him…?"

I stepped forward, but my knees threatened to buckle. "You would," I said quietly. The Weaver had an endless supply of terror devices at his disposal. Things that got pleasure from pain. Things that would be more than happy to rip into her. "Trust me, Nora. You would give him anything he asked for."

She stumbled away from me. "This whole time I thought we were friends."

"We were." I reached for her hand and when she didn't pull away, I laced my fingers through hers. "We *are*."

She stared down at where we were joined and scowled. Her eyes flashed with a dozen emotions before she spoke. "I want to know everything." The words were so soft, I barely heard them. "All of it."

A smile tugged at my mouth. She wasn't running. She didn't hate me—at least not completely. Not yet. She was listening, trying to understand, so maybe there was a chance my identity wouldn't ruin us. *Maybe.*

So, I told her everything. I explained the barriers and what was really on the other side of the one around the beach. The Day World and the Night World. The Dream Realm and the Nightmare Realm. About the importance of maintaining the balance and how the universe would find a way to even things out if something disturbed it. About magic and Day Walking and why I was weaker now than I had ever been because of where I chose to allocate my magic. The Weaver and his threads. The connection I had to him and to her. The cords tying me to all the Dreamers who knew my legend. How I needed to find the Weaver to re-bind him, and how I would do it once I had.

I left nothing out while she stood there absorbing every word. Every detail. She didn't interrupt me once, but when I finished speaking, her eyes traveled up to my hood. I braced myself. There was still one thing we hadn't covered. *Me.*

She took her hand from mine, her face set. My feet were rooted in place while I watched the war wage within her. It went on for so long I nearly fell to my knees and begged for forgiveness. She deserved that much, but I might as well finish digging my grave first.

Finally, she whispered, "No more secrets, Sandman."

"No more secrets," I echoed.

Terror coiled through me, and I gripped the edges of my hood. I wasn't ready. I might never be, but there were so many more important things at stake than our friendship. I didn't come so far safeguarding the Day World only to fail because I was afraid of hurting someone I loved. Losing Nora would be the same as having my beating heart torn from my chest, but she was in this, for better or worse. I would rather she be alive and hate me than distrust me and perish for it.

With a steadying breath, I brushed the hood back, letting it fall between my shoulder blades. I felt naked as I slowly lifted my gaze from my boots. Nora's face was unreadable. Blank. Of all the reactions I was anticipating, *nothing* wasn't one of them.

"I didn't mean to lie," I said in a rush. "Not really. I wanted to tell you who I was, but you didn't believe I existed *here*, so I didn't think you would believe I existed *there*." I held my arms out to the side and shrugged. "But now you know."

She didn't take her gaze off me, her eyes locked on mine. "Now I know," she repeated slowly.

My heart pounded in my chest. I pried off my gloves one finger at a time, showing her the rest of what I kept hidden. The marks she saw in her world shifted around my hands, twisting and swirling with exposure to the sand.

"I knew it. *I knew it.* Your voice, something about the way you moved..." Nora reached out and grazed the back of my fingers. A jolt of energy rushed through my body. The marks fluttered, shifting toward her touch. She watched, transfixed, and her fingertips followed the specks up the back of my hand. "I recognized you."

I flipped my hand over and curled my fingers to hold hers. That she would let me... "You're not mad?"

"Are you kidding? I'm furious." She lunged, wrapping her arms around me, and buried her face in my neck. "But I'm relieved more than I'm angry. You're real. *Really* real. I mean, I believed it after you gave me the sand but... I'm not insane."

Her breath danced over my skin, and I brought my arms up to return the embrace. Having her against me felt surreal as if *I* were the one dreaming. I breathed her in, my body buzzing. I didn't know what it meant for us. If she forgave me. Trusted me. Cared for me. She was relieved, that much I could see without being told. Everything everyone told her was broken about herself was false. I was proof of that. Real, living proof. It didn't mean she loved me. It didn't mean she still wanted me here— outside of getting her sister back and stopping the Weaver. If she rejected me now, it would be so much worse. So much more personal. I swallowed hard. The truth was worth it.

"Oh, God." She leaned away.

I blinked at the sudden loss of contact. "What?"

"What do you mean *what?*" Her cheeks blazed. "I *kissed* you."

"You did." I grinned. I couldn't help it.

"Oh, my God." She gently shoved my chest. "I can't believe you let me do that. Are you crazy?"

I grinned wider.

"Sandman! Wipe that smug look off your face." She covered her face with a groan. "This is so embarrassing."

I cocked my head, the smirk fading. The rejection would be more personal, yes, but I had to know. It was already a secret kept too long, and we just agreed not to have any more. I carefully pried her hands away from her face. "If you knew it was me..." I cleared the lump from my throat. Hope I hadn't dared allow before bubbled to the surface. "Would it be so bad?"

"Would what be bad?" she asked, keeping her gaze down.

"If the person you kissed was me?" Her eyes snapped up to mine, silent and probing, and a flood of emotions broke free of their gate. "I've been in love with you for a year," I blurted before I could stop myself. The blood drained from my face. It was too soon to tell her that, but the words were out and there was no rewind.

"You have?" she asked, breathless and half-believing. Her gaze dropped to my chest.

My muscles burned against the strain of remaining upright. I had no regret about my feelings, only pain-laced terror. Her reaction held more power over me than the Weaver ever could. "Yes."

"Oh." Her fingers rose to her lips, her cheeks glowing red. Then slowly, her hand fell. Her blush faded. She met my gaze again, and my heart skipped a beat. "I think I have too."

I froze, not daring to breathe, while I waited for her to change her mind. To say she was kidding. But when she didn't, I leaned down to press my forehead to hers, our noses brushing. She was still there. In front of me. Close to me. Seeing me. *Me.* Not the hood. And she felt the same way. My vision spun. "I'm yours. I'll always be yours."

Her breath hitched, the same break she had before she kissed me on the Ferris wheel. My lips tingled at the reminder. Would she allow me to kiss her? If I asked her permission, whatever spell this was, might break.

Nora tilted her chin up as if sensing the unspoken question. I shifted closer, and her hands skimmed my shoulders. A tremor rolled through me, but I was too afraid to move. She placed a tender kiss at the corner of my mouth, and my fear shattered.

She wrapped her arms around my neck, and the hem of her shirt lifted. When my hands found her waist, they grazed bare skin. I tightened my grip and urged her closer. Our lips collided. My whole world exploded in that moment.

A soft sound escaped her, and we pressed closer. My hands moved to her back, sliding up until my fingers tangled in her hair. I breathed her in. Memorized the feel of her. The taste of her. How long I had wanted this. Wanted her. *This* with *her.*

But if we kept going, if her hands, now sliding down my chest, went any lower, I wouldn't want to stop. I would if she wanted me to, but if she didn't... I brought my hands to her shoulders. If she wanted to, we would. However, as much as I wanted it, it *definitely* wasn't the right time for that. Not with everything that was happening. When—*if*—it happened, I wanted to know it wasn't because she felt lost or lonely. I wanted it to be because she knew she loved me as much as I knew I loved her.

"Nora," I mumbled against her mouth.

She broke the kiss and rocked back off her toes. She watched me, studied me, with an expression I only dreamed about. "You're real," she said, closing her eyes. Her head pressed against my chest, over the epicenter of my power. "You're real."

I wrapped my arms around her and set my chin on top of her head, trying to calm my erratic pulse. "I'm real," I assured her.

***

I sat beside Nora, drawing circles over her kneecap with my finger, while she told me about her run-ins with the Weaver, the problems with the police, and her mother's wariness. Her head rested on my shoulder, and we sat on the beach, watching the luminescent waves lap the shore. There hadn't been a single nightmare in the sky. Part of me wanted to believe she was too content for the Weaver to pinpoint us. But, even if she was as happy as I was, fear still lurked beneath the surface. It had to; her life was falling apart.

"Don't you have questions?" I asked, breaking the quiet calm.

Nora sighed. "I wish I could say no, but I do. I have so many, Sandman—wait." She shifted her head to look up at me. "What do I call you?"

I nudged her forehead with my nose. "Whatever you want."

"But is Ben your real name?"

"I don't have a name," I said into her hair.

"Everyone should have a name." She set her head back on my shoulder. "Ralph? Sherwood?"

"*Sherwood?*"

"You don't like it? How about Mortimer?"

I wrinkled my nose. "I take it back. Don't call me whatever you want."

"It's a work in progress." She laughed, and we were both silent for a moment before she said, "Why me?"

"What do you mean?"

"Why did you choose me as Dream Keeper? You probably had a million people to choose from."

I hesitated, wondering if she was asking something more than her words. There was nothing special about Nora in the Dreamer sense—or there wasn't before, at least. Did she want there to be more? Would it hurt her to realize there was no special pull between us before I created one? "You called to me at the exact right time," I said, my voice strained. We promised no more lies. "That's all."

She nodded, accepting the truth as easily as she had everything else. "How old are you?"

"How old is the human race?" I asked with a shrug.

"Wow. You're such an old man," she joked, but her eyes widened in honest surprise. "Were you born or... Do you have parents?"

"No. Before humans, there was magic in your world too." I grinned at the awe on her face. "The Weaver and I were both born from it, in a way. The details are a bit fuzzy now, but I remember feeling the magic dying. I think we were its last effort to adapt and survive."

She made a low, contemplative noise in the back of her throat and something heavier clouded her expression. "If… If I asked you to take the dream back, could you do it?"

My heart plummeted. She couldn't know what that meant, but I wasn't sure knowing would change her mind. Too much was already lost to her because of it. Because of me. If she wanted to be free, I would let her go. It was the right thing to do.

"If that's what you want," I said carefully. "But, we wouldn't be able to see each other again. There wouldn't be time. I'd have to hide it in someone else and protect them as I've protected you."

She leaned into me and drew a deep breath. "I'll have to think about it after Katie is home."

"Of course." My hand stilled against her leg. The uncertainty I felt before Nora knew my feelings resurfaced. She cared for me but that didn't mean it would be enough. That *I* would be enough when the trade-off of our relationship was a lifetime of potential terror. "Are there any new leads?"

"No." Her muscles tensed. "The police want me to take a polygraph, and we both know I'll fail. I'm running out of time to stop the Weaver. I need your help."

Stop him. There was nothing she could do to stop him. We could save her sister, I could bind him again, but there was no *stopping* him. He would never give up. Thousands of years ruling the Nightmare Realm left him bored. He wanted to expand his territory. To feel something new. I felt it in him, but I also recognized the same desire in myself.

"I'm doing everything I can, Nora."

She sat up straight, her eyes heavy. "What can I do? There has to be something."

"Once I find Katie on this side, we can figure out how to wake her up. If we can get to her before her body is found, maybe she'll be able to find her own way home. All you can do is keep looking. The Weaver won't kill her while she's of any use to him."

Nora looked up. The stars, bright and endless, danced across her face. "Will she be okay when she wakes up?"

My stomach clenched. "It's best to concentrate on finding her."

"That means no," she said with a frown.

"I didn't say—"

"Sandman." Her gaze cut to me. "I know what you're saying when you don't say things."

"She might be okay again with time." After days of psychological torture, I wouldn't say it was likely. I dug the heels of my boots into the sand. "My associate is searching for her now."

She stared at me with one raised brow. "You have an associate? Since when?"

"Since always." I smirked. "Baku has a thing for nightmares, so we're sort of allies by default."

Her other eyebrow shot up. "By *thing* you mean...?"

I leaned forward, squinting playfully, and whispered, "He eats them."

She cringed. "That's not terrifying at all."

"Would you like to meet him?" I asked.

"I don't know." She paused and wrinkled her nose. "Do I?"

I chuckled, my lips quirking at her expression. "I'll introduce you next time."

"Okay," she said around a yawn.

"Would you like to rest now?"

Nora drew a slow, steady breath and a smile crept over her face. "Not yet."

"Then what—"

But she already shifted away from me. She hovered over the sand on her hands and knees and licked her lips. "I've wanted to do this since the first day I saw you at Howell's, but then everything happened and…" She shook her head slightly and peered at me over her shoulder with that perfectly wrinkled nose. "It's about time I got the chance to draw you."

I watched in awe as her fingers brushed through the sand in long, smooth strokes. Her back muscles shifted through her shirt with each movement, and she kept pausing to tuck her hair behind her ears. *Stars.* How I loved this talented, beautiful woman. The world began and ended with her. And there she was, delicately sketching my face with a gleam in her eyes that rivaled the one I imagined shone in my own.

"There," she said triumphantly. "What do you think?"

"It's perfect," I said in a hoarse voice.

"You're not just saying that?" She lifted her chin, glaring playfully.

"Never."

"The eyes are wrong." She sat back on her haunches and cocked her head to examine her work. "I guess it's hard to really capture them without my colored pencils."

"It's perfect," I repeated. "You're perfect."

She snorted, and I held my hand out to her, asking her silently to sit beside me again. When she shuffled back, I guided her head to my thigh and ran my fingers through her hair. She sighed, content, and my heart nearly burst.

"Close your eyes. You won't be of any help to your sister if you're exhausted. I'll watch over you while you rest."

She yawned again. "I didn't get to use your sand on my parents tonight."

"I'll take care of it when they're ready," I promised.

She tucked her knees to her chest. "Will you be in my room when I wake up tomorrow?"

"No. I need to save my strength for the battle that's coming."

"Will the Weaver try to kill you?" she asked, brushing bits of sand from my pants.

My fingers slowed. "I'm sure he would like to, but no."

She made a soft, skeptical sound in her throat, and her eyes fluttered shut.

***

The ache began as soon as Nora woke up for the day. A tight, weightlessness in my chest, as if I were trying to expel a helium balloon instead of magic. I was near empty, but the barrier had to be reinforced and Katie had to be found. I clawed at my chest through the layers of fabric, scratching an impossible itch. It would take too long to absorb power from the beach tonight. Time—I didn't have.

I closed my eyes and turned my attention inward. The cords tying me to my Dreamers stretched out before me. I ran my finger over them, feeling the person on the other end until I found a young Dreamer with a cache of dreams brimming in his queue. Gaining power this way hadn't been necessary since I bound the Weaver, but however much I didn't want it to be, it was again essential. I rubbed the space between my brows with my free hand and slowly exhaled.

Then I gripped the cord. My body hurdled down the unfamiliar path to a room I had never seen before and a boy who had never asked for my help. He slept beneath a set of Spiderman sheets, his dark hair mussed by the pillow. For me to find him, someone must have told him about me, but no one actually believed anymore. That didn't stop the sand full of my power from reaching him night after night. More importantly, it was full of his hopes, his innocence, his happiness—everything necessary to amplify the magic.

I leaned closer, my head hanging. "I'm sorry," I whispered.

With the last few drops of power within me, I held my hand over his head and called my power home. Silver and blue swirled from the boy's head, rising to greet my waiting palm. Glimpses of his dreams danced through the air. The wheel of a bicycle. The fall of a block tower. An old dog with a white peppered snout. They flashed against my skin and disappeared. The power shot up my arm and slammed into my chest like a bullet. I clutched my shirt and staggered into a wall, slumping against it. My lungs drew a haggard breath despite the rush of new energy.

The boy would sleep dreamlessly tonight, and in the morning, he would wake without realizing anything was stolen. He wouldn't know how much he missed these dreams. These answers to questions he didn't know he had. They gave him something his waking hours couldn't—endless possibilities without rules, a conversation with a deceased loved one... *anything.*

I would make up for it one day.

I would repay each child I visited tonight for the things I stole. But first, I had to save them. First, I had to get the Weaver under control.

***

When I returned to the beach hours later, I practically glowed with stolen dreams. I trudged toward the barrier to begin my work when the sound of racing steps reached my ears. I turned in time to see Baku skid to a halt behind me.

"You found something?" I dropped to my knees in front of him and scooped up handfuls of sand to read his dreams. "Show me."

Chapter Thirteen

Nora

An army of reporters stood below the podium. Cameras lined the back wall on tripods to record the news conference. For whatever reason, the scent of burnt rubber invaded the meeting room at the hotel, and the dry heat threatened to suffocate my last bit of patience. Or maybe it was the clingy capris and high-necked ruffle blouse with cap sleeves. It was too warm for stiff, restricting fabrics, but my mother insisted. People were watching, the police included, and I needed to project a certain degree of respectability. I tried not to take her words offensively since I didn't disagree with the thought behind them, but I also hoped passing out from heat stroke fell under my mother's opinion of acceptable behavior.

While Detective Bell addressed the news stations, I recounted every moment of last night's dream. Ben was the Sandman. The Sandman was Ben. He loved me. Pieces I hadn't realized were missing from the puzzle fell into place. How long had I loved him too? How long had I kept myself from acknowledging that because I didn't believe in him?

I believed now. The Sandman was in my corner. With his help, Katie would be back home soon. Maybe even today. Maybe before dinner. I clung to the thought and let it steel my nerves. The detective rattled off Katie's height and weight. He told the press about the scar on the back of her knee from a bike accident when she was seven. That she would likely be with someone armed and dangerous but as of yet, they had no suspect. Then he introduced me, my mother, and Paul.

We stepped up to the podium as a unit, hands clasped together. A united front. My mother choked back a sob, and Paul rubbed circles on her back. I wanted nothing more than to ease her fears, but the only way to do that was to find Katie. Surveillance proved she hadn't left town on public transportation which meant she was close. All her shoes were accounted for, so she couldn't have walked far.

"Katie, if you're watching this, we love you, we miss you, and we won't stop looking for you until you are home. If..." My mother paused. "If you have my daughter, please let her go. We..."

I stared at my black flats and tuned out the rest of her plea. I couldn't listen to it when I knew I was the reason the Weaver took Katie. When I was the reason my mother was in so much pain. Even knowing the truth about what the Weaver would do with the dream, a raw, aching part of me wanted to give it to him and be finished with all of this. But we would fix it. The Sandman and I would make things right again.

Paul tapped my shoulder when Detective Bell resumed the podium, and I stepped back. After what felt like forever, the reporters finished asking their questions and packed up their equipment.

When Detective Bell turned to speak with my mother, I nudged Paul. "Can I go hang up the posters I made this morning?"

He hesitated. "I don't know about that, kiddo. With everything going on it might not be good for you to be walking around on your own."

"It's the middle of the day, and I'll stay in town." When he didn't reply, I added, "Please?"

"All right, all right." He cleared his throat. "Be home before dinner or your mother will kill me."

"I will." Although I likely wouldn't eat again tonight. I needed to put on a show for my mother and the police, then fall asleep as soon as possible to see if the Sandman or Baku found any trace of my sister.

I ran to my car a block away and leaned into the back seat for the stack of fliers. The door on the other side clicked open. I jumped, slamming my head on the roof. The Sandman stared across the seat at me, his eyes full of life again, and my heart lurched. He said he was saving his strength...

"Who?" I breathed, squinting my eyes.

A small crease formed between his brows. "What?"

"The Weaver. Who did he kill this time?"

"That isn't why I'm here." He took the fliers and wall stapler from the back seat. "We're being watched so let's hang these while we talk."

I eased out of the car and glanced casually back at the hotel. Two police officers stood outside their vehicle, staring down the street in our direction. The Sandman and I walked around the corner in silence.

Tension crackled between us. It felt as if this were a dream with concrete under my feet instead of sand. A sky decorated with clouds instead of stars. But his presence at my side, that was the same. A smile spread across my lips before falling away. "If you're not here because of the Weaver, why are you here?"

"Baku heard a rumor about your sister when he was in the Nightmare Realm," he said, his face a perfect mask of calm.

My heart jumped. "Where is she?"

"I'm not sure." The Sandman glanced over his shoulder and shifted closer.

He stopped at a telephone pole and handed me the top flier. I held it against the wood while he stapled the corners down. Katie's smiling face stared at me, and I smoothed the paper so that he could attach the bottom edge.

My mother chose two photos—one from Katie's birthday six months ago with the rest of the family cropped out, and the other a candid of her smiling on the couch. Probably at something on one of her favorite reality shows. I trailed my fingers over her familiar cheek, so like my own yet freckle free, and a bit rounder.

"Baku doesn't speak so I have to read his dreams, but it looked like she was sleeping on a table or floor. There wasn't anything else in the room, and there weren't any windows to let light in. Do you know of any place like that?"

"Do I know a place with a table or a floor?" I raised an eyebrow at him, my hope plummeting. "You have to give me something more than *no windows.*"

He motioned for me to keep walking. "A shed, maybe?"

"Also, not helpful." I held up the next poster and struggled to keep the disappointment from swallowing me. There was still hope. It was *one thing* more than we knew this morning, as vague and unhelpful as it was. "But it would have to be close by."

His eyes shifted to the police again. "We'll lose them and then head to your neighborhood to see what we can find."

***

I led the way through the same field the search party and I combed through. My car was parked in a nearby parking lot to avoid suspicion, but I looked over my shoulder every few steps for flashing lights. What would the cops say if they found me sneaking around here? They already thought I had an accomplice and Sandman looked fit enough to have snapped a neck or killed two teenage girls.

The Sandman nudged me with his elbow. "You okay?"

"The police already looked here," I said. "They would have searched the sheds too."

"What if the Weaver moved her? You said he spoke with you during the search party which means this area would be safe to hide her. It's not far from your house so it's worth looking again."

I chewed on my lip. It was a valid point, but I hated wasting time double checking the same places. When we entered the trees near the new cul-de-sac where I spoke to the Weaver, I reached for the Sandman. He wove his fingers through mine. "None of this feels like real life," I whispered. "Not everyone being dead, not Katie, not the Weaver. Not *you*."

He was quiet for a long moment. "I'm sorry, Nora."

I knew he was; I was sorry too. Sorry to Lisa and that cashier's family. To everyone that loved Natalie and Emery, and to the woman who answered my father's cell phone. I wasn't sure

154

my mother would want to know about his heart attack, so I still hadn't told her. The numbness swept back in, erasing the pain that threatened to cripple me. After Katie came back, I would fill the family in.

We reached the edge of the woods, and I squinted toward the brand-new houses. With only two of them occupied, and only one with a visible shed, we shouldn't have much trouble getting in and out. It was the middle of a weekday so with any luck, no one would be home either.

We rushed up to the nearest building, and I plastered myself against the back porch. The Sandman smirked. "I don't think that's necessary," he said.

I stuck my tongue out at him. "Says you. If we get caught you can *magic* your way out of here." I waved a hand at the shed. "Check, please."

"Sure, let me get my invisibility cloak out first."

"Sandman," I growled.

He laughed. "Hold on, Nancy Drew."

He didn't bother hiding; he simply strode over and cracked the unlocked door of the tool shed. He shook his head.

I sighed and tilted my head toward the sun. The roof shielded me from most of it, but it beat down on me like a drum. Of course, Katie wasn't there. But she was under the same sky as me, breathing the same air, so it was only a matter of time. The Sandman brushed a stray piece of hair from my forehead. My heart lurched at the touch.

"We'll find her," he assured me.

I nodded, and a square vent caught my attention at the peak of the house. I shoved away from the siding, accidentally knocking his shoulder. "Do you see that?"

He followed my gaze. "The attic vents?"

"A vent isn't a window." I launched myself up the back porch and peered through the sliding glass door. "It's empty."

"Watch out." The Sandman removed a small pouch from beneath his T-shirt like the one beneath mine. With a grin, he pinched a bit of sand from inside and blew it at the latch. The sand sparkled in the bright light before disappearing into the creases of the frame. A moment later, he twisted the knob and stepped inside, holding the door for me. "Open Sesame."

"That's handy," I mumbled, hesitating before following him into the kitchen. I couldn't be caught breaking-and-entering right now. Detective Bell wanted nothing more than a pliable reason to lock me up—but I needed to see.

The stillness of the house raised the hair on the back of my neck. Each rustle of our clothes as we moved through the hallways scraped my eardrums. Each footstep, a stomp. When we found the hatch to the attic and the Sandman pulled it down, unfolding the ladder, I cringed against the squeak of hinges.

He stepped back and stared into the darkness above.

"You first," I whispered and followed him up the rungs.

The attic was broiling. It wouldn't be possible to survive up here long without overheating. That was the only consolation for finding the space empty. My shoulders drooped. If Katie wasn't in any of these attics, where else should we look? There were so many possibilities that it made knowing impossible. Baku needed to give us something more concrete.

"Did you hear that?" the Sandman asked.

I froze and strained my ears. "What?"

Then the distinct sound of a door opening drifted through the house. "I really think you'll like this one," a woman said. "It's a new build, of course, with all the upgrades."

"A realtor," I hissed. What were the odds?

The Sandman ushered me up the last rung of the ladder and tugged the folding stairs back in place as quietly as possible. "Squeeze into the back corner."

My eyebrows rose, but I shuffled into the narrow space where the floor met the slanted roof. "How is this going to help exactly?"

"Do you have the sand I gave you?" he asked.

I nodded.

"Good." He squeezed in beside me and removed the sack from around his neck. "I need it."

My fingers dove into the ruffles at the base of my throat, and I unfastened the top three buttons. The Sandman's eyes widened. "Relax," I said, and tugged the bag free from the tank top I wore beneath my blouse.

He opened and closed his mouth, the corners of his lips quirking. "If they come up here, pour it into my hands and be as quiet and still as you can."

"Again, how is this going to help?" I asked in a hushed, panicked voice. "You can't put people to sleep on a ladder. They'll fall and break their necks."

"I won't put them to sleep."

"Then what? And if you joke about an invisibility cloak again, I'll strangle you."

He raised an eyebrow, amused. "I'm going to create the illusion of empty space."

My eyes narrowed at the bag of fine, silvery sand. "Huh."

"One day, after this is all over, I'll show more to you than your own dreams," he said. A blush rose on the back of his neck. "I mean, if you want. If you decide you don't want me to take the dream back."

My heart dropped like ice against the floor, sending tiny chips scattering in every direction. It was selfish to want to keep him to myself when the dream put everyone around me in danger. Keeping the secret kept the entire world safe, but that wasn't why I hesitated. I was sure that I wanted no part of it. I wasn't up to a burden like this but... "I don't want you to take it. I can't lose you too."

The backs of his fingers caressed my cheek, leaving a flush in their wake. I inched closer, the voices continuing below our feet. "I promised I would always be yours," he said, earnest. "I will never break that oath."

His breath skated along my temple, and I shivered despite the overwhelming heat. "Sandman..."

He nudged my ear with his nose. "I swear it, Nora. Even if you change your mind later."

"I know." I clamped down on a moan as his lips danced across the edge of my jaw.

"We spent so long not touching that it seems like I'll never get enough. That I'll never get close enough to you. Not like I want to," he whispered. The next kiss was as light as his breath. "You should stop me."

"What if I don't want to?" I asked, surprising myself. My entire body screamed for more. If it weren't for the realtor downstairs, I might have said as much. *Might.* But I felt bold with him. Strong and safe. Secure.

His lips crashed against mine and his blue fingertips rested against the sides of my neck as if I were made of glass. His breathing quickened at the same moment mine did. He tasted like spring. I wanted more. I didn't want to be careful. Not anymore. I nudged his lips with the tip of my tongue and heard a groan catch in his throat. His hair was silken clouds between my fingers.

A creak broke through the attic followed by a bang. "It's a little warm up here right now, but the electrician should be back tomorrow to finish the central air."

The Sandman leaned away and cupped both hands together. "The sand," he rasped.

My fingers fumbled with the tie, and I poured the contents of both bags into his palms. The silver and blue tattoos on his arms came alive, and he turned and blew the contents into the air in front of us. It rippled in a sheet. He flipped his palms outward and the sand froze in place. It glowed for a moment before becoming a single translucent wall like the one around the beach.

A man crawled up first with a flashlight, followed by a woman's head. My pulse roared in my ears. This was it—we were doomed. The Sandman's jaw clenched, his fingers spread wide before him. I wanted to inch closer to his side but didn't for fear of making a sound.

The woman swung a look around and shrugged. "It's a lot of storage space."

"With such a spacious yard, there are some nice options for outdoor storage as well," the realtor said from below. "Or if you need something bigger, a storage facility is only a few minutes' drive."

"I don't think that's necessary," the man said. "This is plenty."

The beam of light swung back down the ladder. It seemed like forever before the ladder slammed shut, sealing us into darkness again.

"That was amazing," I breathed, my heart still racing. "It's like we weren't here at all."

The sheet of magic exploded into nothingness, and the Sandman sagged against the wall. "I can't stay much longer," he admitted. "It uses a lot of energy to be in your world."

I clenched my hands in fists. He couldn't leave; we hadn't found Katie yet. But I saw the tightness around his eyes and labored rise and fall of his chest. "You should go," I said. "I'll keep looking for a while."

He shifted onto his knees and searched my face. "Are you sure?"

No. I didn't want to do this alone, but if I wanted to find Katie, he needed to recharge. "I'm sure."

"I'll see you tonight then." He leaned over and kissed my forehead.

I gripped his shirt, holding him in place. Panic clawed through me, an irrational fear that if he left, I wouldn't see him again. "Sandman?"

"Yes?" he asked, his mouth hovering above my skin.

"If you're always mine, then I'm always yours," I said. Because that was the truth, no matter what happened.

His arms wrapped around me, pressing me against him. My fear withdrew until only a single tendril of it remained. "This will all be over soon," he whispered.

"I hope so."

"I hate to leave you here like this."

"We got in. How hard could getting out be?" I pulled away and shrugged. I couldn't finish the other empty houses without him, but that didn't mean I couldn't look somewhere else.

He glanced around the attic space. "Be careful in the dark."

"Where were you?" my mother asked the second I walked through the door. "You couldn't have been hanging up fliers this whole time."

I wrapped my arms around my mother's waist and hugged her. She stiffened for a moment, probably unsure if it was a tactic to get out of trouble, before hugging me back. I hated that pause. Hated that she didn't show me the same affection other mothers show their children. That she showed Katie. She was afraid of me; she hadn't stopped being afraid since the day I insisted the Sandman was real. I don't think she ever really believed that I stopped seeing him, but she *wanted* to. Every time I zoned out or chose sleep over an invitation from a friend, it reminded her of that year she spent dragging me to doctor after doctor. She loved me—I knew she did—but she didn't know how to show it anymore.

"I was driving around to see if I could find Katie," I answered. As fruitless as it was. I hadn't really expected to see her waltzing down a back road anyway, but after looking in all windows in the cul-de-sac homes, I didn't know where else to go.

She tapped my shoulders, and I let go. "Natalie's father called today to let us know that the funeral is going to be this Saturday," she said, ushering me into the kitchen.

Funeral. A hollow pit opened in my stomach. "Okay."

"I made spaghetti."

I nodded. I could force a few bites down to appease her, but not much more than that. "I'll go change. Be right back."

I ran to my room and shut the door. For a minute, I simply leaned against it with my eyes closed, forcing back the desperate sorrow clawing its way through me. *Funeral.* Because Natalie was gone. Forever. Just like Emery. A thousand memories stacked on top of each other. Building and building and building. I shoved away from the door, knocking over the tower of images, and peeled off my sweaty clothes. I barely had my running shorts and tank top on when warm air curled around my ankles.

"Sun-Kissed Keeper," crooned the Weaver. "Keep digging deeper."

"You've got to be kidding me," I said through clenched teeth. I didn't turn around to face him—I couldn't.

"Has the Sandman told you that the stronger your mind is, the stronger your nightmare is?" The warm air wrapped its way up my leg. "How strong do you think yours is?"

"Strong enough." I yanked my hair up into a ponytail. When I turned, the Weaver's gold eyes watched me carefully from the open closet. "Get out of my room."

"How strong do you think your sister's mind is?" he asked with a tilt of his head. "Some things a person can't come back from. Do you think you'll find her before my nightmares break her?"

"I think *I'll* break *you*," I growled.

He gave me a mock bow, lifting his upturned palm. "I welcome you to the Nightmare Realm, Dream Keeper. Please, do take me up on the invitation."

Break her. Katie was running out of time. I slammed the closet door in his face and bolted back to the kitchen before I could suggest an exchange.

***

Spaghetti churning in my stomach, I flopped down on my bed, sleep already dragging me under. I took a deep breath and rolled onto my side. The air conditioning blew directly on my legs. My skin prickled against it, but the idea of moving enough to crawl between the sheets seemed too daunting.

I felt myself slipping. Falling. Drifting. The dream was close, beckoning me forward, but something yanked me back. A sharp, terrifying sensation gripped my core, and my eyes flew open.

My mother stood in the hallway. The wall sconce glowed behind her, casting her face in shadow, but I knew she was looking at me. It wasn't an awestruck look a mother sometimes gives her child while they're asleep, nor was it one of concern. It radiated hate. A scathing anger that made the hair on my arms stand on end.

I hesitated. "Mom?"

She lunged into my room, her hands outstretched, and grabbed the pillow from beneath my head. There wasn't time to get out of the way before she slammed it over my face. I thrashed beneath her, clawing at her arms. I tried to scream but the pillow blocked my breath.

Then, as fast as my mother had flown into the room, she was back in the hall. I gasped for air and scrambled from the bed. My mother grinned. My heart stopped, my palms sweating. She threw the pillow at me and disappeared into her bedroom across the hall, slamming the door behind her.

The Weaver's laugh traveled from somewhere down the hall. I held my breath and charged around my bed to shut the door, blocking out the sound. The lock beside the doorknob clicked beneath my thumb, but I wasn't taking any chances. One bobby pin and it would pop open. So, propping myself between the wall and my dresser, I slid the heavy antique in front of the door.

I flung myself into bed a second time, adrenaline pumping, and watched the knob until I had calmed enough to fall asleep.

Chapter Fourteen

The Sandman

"My mother tried to smother me."

My eyes snapped away from the barrier overhead to find Nora stomping across the beach. "*What?*"

"Technically it was the Weaver," she clarified, her breath uneven. "Don't worry. I barricaded myself in my room."

I ground my teeth together. It was only a matter of time before he sent a sleepwalker after her, but he couldn't kill Nora. He needed her alive. It was a warning and a good one at that. Using her mother too…

"Have you found anything?"

"Not yet." I motioned her forward, not taking my eyes off the sky. A crack scarred the barrier. A mere hairline fracture, no longer than my little finger, smaller still from down here. It hadn't been there when I left to help Nora find her sister. "Do you see it?"

She squinted. "See what?"

"There." I moved behind her and held my arm out so that she could follow where I pointed. "A crack."

"I just see the sky," she said, shrugging.

I stepped around her. Maybe it was too far up, too small, for her to notice, but it wasn't too small for nightmares to sneak in. Some were tiny, slippery things. I did a sweep after I returned but came up empty-handed. With a quick flick of my wrist, I sent sand racing through the air to patch it.

"It isn't safe here tonight," I said.

She jerked, her eyes scanning for the imperfection again. "I thought those things from the other night couldn't get in."

"Those things couldn't. The barrier was solid then." I scooped sand into a pouch and handed it to her to replace what we used in the attic. She tossed the string over her neck.

Her sister disappeared three nights ago. Which meant for three nights and two days, she'd suffered torture at the hands of who knew what. If we didn't find her soon, there might not be anything left to save. My first concern had to be Nora though. If she wasn't safe, no one was. I took her face in my hands, my thumbs skimming the freckles along her cheekbone.

"How cozy," came a familiar voice. I spun, shoving Nora behind me, to find the Weaver walking from the sea. Water rolled off him as if he were made of wax. He glanced up at where the crack had been. "And how... lazy."

"You can't be here," I growled, tightening my grip on Nora.

He clucked his tongue. "It took me so long to find a way in." The Weaver circled us, and his heavy metallic scent turned my stomach. "Besides, let's not forget that you waltzed into my realm uninvited first—the least you could do is ask me to stay for tea."

I held my hands out, palms parallel to the ground, and sand shot up to greet them. "Nora, go."

"No," she hissed. "You can't keep telling me to leave every time he shows up. I have to face him sooner or later."

The Weaver grinned at her words. "She must."

"Shut up." Nora sidestepped me, her face red with fury. "Don't ever touch my mother again, and I want my sister back."

A black blur zoomed out from behind the Weaver. Something small and rodent-like, heading straight for her legs. I slammed my fingers into a fist, and the sand followed my movement. I flung my arm toward the nightmare, fingers splayed. A spray of tiny needles met the creature's side. It fell to the sand, black blood pooling beneath its bristly fur. Sharp tusks stuck straight out from its mouth, ready to impale. Yellow liquid oozed from tiny, bulging venom sacks beneath each one.

"Leave," I said again, both to the Weaver and Nora.

"What *is* that thing?" Nora breathed.

The Weaver frowned. "That *was*—"

"It doesn't matter what it was," I hissed, meeting the Weaver's glare. "Only what it could have done. The same goes for all his nightmares."

He shrugged, nonchalant. "You can't blame me for trying."

More sand rose around me, and the ground shifted beneath my boots. I blamed him, yes. For letting nightmares into the Day World. For forcing me to bind him. But, if he was anything, it was consistent. The Weaver relied too much on his minions and not enough on himself.

"Are you going to oust me? With all that overflowing magic?" He grinned. "Or are you going to sick Baku on me? He's causing quite the stir these days. I fear he will become rather obese after turning my realm into an all you can eat buffet."

"She's not giving you the dream," I said, rage coating each syllable.

"I rather think that's not up to you. A tough pill to swallow, I'm sure, after so many years of prancing around like someone dubbed you the Night Emperor." The Weaver leaned sideways to better peer at Nora. "Say yes, little Sun-Kissed Keeper. Give me access."

"Give me my sister," she countered with such calm fury that I shivered.

"Nora, go," I begged. "Please."

"I won't leave you alone with him, and I won't leave without Katie," she said, standing her ground.

The Weaver extracted a string from the band around his wrist. Gold filaments glinted against the black thread. With a flick, it stiffened. "Last chance, Keeper."

"Don't you dare release another one of your filthy creatures in here," I snarled.

He tossed the rigid thread, and it exploded midair in a cloud of black powder. A deep rumble tore across the beach a moment before a hairless, human-like creature with jagged fingers stood beside the Weaver. Grey skin clung to its ribs. The nightmare stared hungrily at Nora through hollow slits, and brown saliva dripped down its chin from between pointed, yellow teeth.

There wasn't time to think, no time to reason with Nora. I couldn't fight this thing and protect her at the same time. There was a chance I wasn't going to be able to protect myself. Sand whirled around us, and I jerked her close, trapping us in the center. "Don't be angry," I whispered. Then I did something I knew I would always regret; I dismissed her decision to stay, and shoved her, hard, from the dream.

Dagger-like fingers dug into my shoulder the moment she was gone, sending me to my knees. I swiped my free hand across the ground. A spray of sand swooped upward toward the nightmare as a blade. The metal sliced through the air with a piercing shriek and the gleaming edge severed its wrist. The hand fell to the ground with a soft thud. The sand faltered around me as the taint of the nightmare's presence grew. The infection crept deeper, the blood seeping beyond the surface of the beach.

I stood on unsteady feet and stumbled backward, away from the creature. Foam fell from its mouth in globs. The Weaver was no longer behind him—his presence registering far away. Anxious. Annoyed. He had left me alone with this *thing* to do his dirty work.

"What?" I snapped. "Is that all it takes to stop you?"

It roared, and spit rained across my face. My fingers twitched, rushing to turn the sand into something useful. But I wasn't fast enough, or maybe it was *too* fast, because in the next instant, razor sharp pain seared up my torso. Blood spilled from vertical claw marks on my chest. I barely drew breath before it raised its remaining hand for a second strike.

I leaned back to avoid the blow and fell, landing flat on my back. A whiff of decay hit me instead of claws. They passed through empty air and impaled the nightmare's own thigh. Its slit-eyes constricted in shock.

I tossed a handful of sand in its face and scrambled to my feet. My cuts screamed in protest when I raised a fist above my head. A curtain of sand rose up behind the creature. The shadow fell first, a grey blanket coating the beach. When I brought my arm down in one violent jerk, the wounds wailed, and the curtain fell. The sand encased the shrieking nightmare in a cyclone. Pulling it. Crushing it. Tearing it. I hated that move. Hated the screams mixing with cracks and crunches. Hated the soft clink of sand against sand that echoed through the pain.

Footsteps beat in my ears, a strange new note to the wretchedness before me. Baku skidded to a halt on the other side of the smaller dead nightmare. His eyes lifted to mine with a flash of hope, and I nodded once. Let him eat it. Let him eat the second one too, as soon as it was dead. It was one less mess I needed to clean.

My knees buckled, my arms falling limp at my sides. I looked away from the disaster playing out on my beach, blocked out the sounds, and pried the torn fabric from the middle gash. It had almost—*almost*—nicked the edge of the crescent moon there. It was hard to look at the wound and consider myself lucky, but I was. There wasn't time to heal from something like that. Not now. It would take months, at least.

I rolled my sleeves up and started the tedious task of drawing out each grain of contaminated sand. Baku swished his cow tail and made his way to my side. He lifted the severed hand with his trunk on his way by, and I cringed. "I hope you found something," I said.

The cyclone narrowed, and the screams reduced to tortured mewls. Baku flopped down beside me with a disgruntled huff, his side pressing against my leg. Then he unhinged his jaw and stuffed the entire hand into his mouth. I slammed my eyes shut. The sound of crunching bones set my nerves on edge.

"Nothing, then," I said, more to myself than him.

My energy faded, leaving me feeling empty and dull. I cracked my eyes open in time to see the sand fall around a mangled corpse. Baku lunged for it while I dug into my reserves again—so soon after stealing dreams.

Too soon.

Chapter Fifteen

Nora

I wrenched out of bed, gasping for air, and clutched the leather string around my neck. Those things... The nightmares... That was what the Weaver wanted to unleash on the world. That's what I was protecting humankind from. Not just the people I loved—but everyone. The Weaver could rot in his realm—there was no way was I giving him the dream. Not now, not ever. I still felt the creature's dead gaze crawling over my skin and the scent of rotting flesh lingered in my nostrils.

And I left the Sandman there alone. *No.* I didn't leave him. He kicked me out. Ejected me somehow. My blood fizzled in my veins. It was my dream—I held the power. I could have done something. Helped.

Don't be angry.

Well, I was. I crossed the room in two steps and yanked the top dresser drawer open. The white pills glared up at me from the bottom. They promised sleep. Sleep I couldn't wake from until morning, at least. There would be no shoving me out again. The Sandman and I were in this—all of this—together, and I needed to pull my own weight.

"Keeper." The voice came in a rushed hiss, hot against my ear.

I slammed the drawer shut and spun on my heel. "*You.*" I advanced one step for each one the Weaver took backward. He cocked his head and smirked. "I swear, if anything happens to him, I'll—"

"You'll what?" he drawled. "Boil me in oil? Dream Keeper, I turned torture into a fine art long before you were a twinkle in your father's eye."

I grabbed my hairbrush off the displaced dresser and threw it at him. Then a pen. A tube of mascara. A hand-mirror. It all bounced off his semi-solid form; the mirror shattered into a dozen pieces. I froze, panting, waiting to hear my mother's hurried footsteps in the hall, but there was only silence.

"Ouch," the Weaver deadpanned.

"Is he alive?" I growled.

"Naturally."

I balled my hands into fists. "If you're lying..."

"What reason do I have to lie? Do stop wasting my time; it grows irksome."

I narrowed my eyes. "I'm going to kill you."

"Yes, yes. Very scary." He smiled as if he was genuinely amused, and the beauty of it made me sick to my stomach. "At least one of you has the courage to try."

I opened my mouth to defend the Sandman, but the words stuck in my throat. He hadn't tried before? *Never?* Not even when the Weaver was letting nightmares loose? The binding had to be

Plan B. Weakening himself to keep the wards up, constantly fearing the day they broke. It had to be a last resort. But he'd only ever mentioned trapping the Weaver again. Not once had he said anything about a more permanent solution. About delivering the punishment the Weaver deserved.

"Even if he wanted to, the Sandman will never kill me," the Weaver said as if he knew where my thoughts had wandered. "Why do you think I'm here now? Do you think it's because he was incapable of bringing about my death five years ago? No. My life was in his hands when he did this to me, but we have a history, he and I." He casually waved a hand through the air as if it didn't matter, but the way his voice pitched betrayed him. "Besides, he believes in balance—a darkness to the light." He leaned closer, the amused glint fading from his features. "But I'm tired of being bound, Dream Keeper. Do you understand? We did something that needs undoing. This isn't how things are supposed to be."

I squared my shoulders. The Sandman said the balance always rights itself so what was stopping him? I shifted under the Weaver's scrutiny. "Sucks to be you."

"Give me the dream," he growled. "Enough games."

I folded my arms across my chest, my heart hammering against them. Yes. Enough games, indeed. "You might as well kill me because you're not getting it."

The Weaver rose to loom over me, blocking the moonlight from the window. His golden eyes glowed in the darkness, but I held my ground. He couldn't scare me anymore. There wasn't enough left in me to be afraid, and what did remain was too busy being pissed off.

"I've come to offer one last deal," he said after a long silence. "Give me what I want or everyone you know, everything you care about, will be swallowed by fear."

"Wow." I rolled my eyes, but a metallic tang coated my mouth. *Blood.* The only thing telling me that I chomped down on the inside of my cheek. "What an offer, Weaver. It's almost as if it isn't an offer at all."

His top lip lifted in disgust.

"I want Katie back, safe and sound," I said.

"I gathered as much."

Goosebumps dotted my arms at his tone, but I wasn't backing down. He had my mother smother me in my own bed, sent a nightmare straight for me on the beach, and created the most vulgar thing I'd ever seen to hurt the Sandman. *No.* I was finished letting people walk all over me. It got me nowhere. It got me *here.* To this place with him.

"I want to see her first," I said.

He narrowed his eyes. "I see trust is not your forte."

"Call me crazy." I glared at him, waiting, too nervous to breathe.

"I'll show you your sister." If trust wasn't my forte, bargaining wasn't his. "Then you'll give me the dream."

"*If* Katie is okay," I answered. She had to be. *She had to.*

"Tomorrow at dusk," he said slowly. "52 Maple Street. I'll know if you go looking before that. If you try anything, if you drive by or I see a single police officer near that address, I'll let my Blood Army devour your sister piece-by-piece."

Blood Army? I forced myself not to shiver. "I believe you."

Not that he should believe me. If there was ever the tiniest chance of me giving up the secret, seeing the threat he carried with my own eyes had crushed it. But I was tired of waiting for someone else to find Katie. Tired of fruitlessly searching. The Sandman didn't want me to help him fight nightmares—fine. He was probably right. That didn't mean I was going to sit around while there were things that needed to be done.

"A temporary truce, then. Do not think to cross me." The Weaver backed away, fading into the shadows.

I scrambled back into bed. Of course, I was going to cross the Weaver. He had to know I was.

***

The carcass of the nightmare that rushed me was gone from the beach, and blissfully, there was no sign of the other one. But the normally smooth sand was covered in divots. Blood so dark it was almost black filled the small pits, and a trail of it led away from the water, following deep drag marks.

Alive suddenly didn't feel as comforting as it did a moment ago. The Sandman could be unconscious. Bleeding out. Tortured. Alive meant nothing except that I wasn't too late *yet*.

The blood led past a tall hill to a part of the beach I had never seen before—and I had explored every nook and cranny over the years. My face fell, taking the color with it, and I ran. My bare feet dug into packed sand, and I scrambled up a foreign dune.

"Sandman," I whisper-yelled. It was lost in the endless stretch of sand. The ground was nearly untouched, the drag marks the only thing disturbing the smooth, glimmering grains. Drag marks and footprints. My feet slid back the way I came. Whatever did the dragging was distinctly not human. Four oval toes were spaced above the pad of an animal's foot—a foot nearly as big as my head.

175

My heart pounded. The open terrain suddenly felt too defenseless, like something would fall from the sky and leave me with nowhere to hide. A soft *thump* froze me in place. My muscles tightened until they ached. A tiny, familiar voice whispered doubts in the back of my mind, telling me I wasn't brave enough. Strong enough. Smart enough. It was probably right. I knew I was about to cross the Nightmare Lord, but I had no idea what exactly I was walking into. My plan sounded good in theory. Katie's life depended on my finding the Sandman though—I couldn't do this without his cooperation.

I jumped when another *thump* echoed off the invisible barrier. A stout creature appeared in the distance. It was too far away to see, but I knew it was watching me as closely as I was watching it. Then it moved. I locked my knees, bracing myself. Each footstep was another *thump*. My hands shook at my sides. I wouldn't run. Wouldn't. My right foot slid back a step. *Traitor.*

As the creature neared, he studied me through beady eyes. I fought against a scream, my breath rapid and shallow. He stopped in front of me and his elephant trunk reached out, sniffing my hair. A musk emanated from the thick, furry hide, not entirely disgusting but not something I wanted in my face. The black and yellow brindle fur at the base of his neck rose. If he was anything like a dog, that was a horrible sign. I stared at his curved tusks, tinged pink with what I only hoped wasn't blood, and my stomach dropped.

"Um." I took an involuntary step back and cringed. "Hey, there. Nice...nightmare."

He dropped his trunk and glared. I glared back, not daring to breathe. I could've sworn it frowned before scooping up a bit of sand and tossing it at my ankles. Then he turned and lumbered away. His skinny cow-like tail swished angrily back-and-forth as he followed the drag trail.

"Wait," I called. "Where is—"

He paused and glanced back at me. It was a look of understanding so deep I thought only humans were capable of. It shook my core, tethering me in place. When he moved again, I hurried after him, stepping carefully over each of his gigantic paw prints.

It could have been a trap, but what choice was there? I needed to make sure the Sandman was in one piece. So, I followed him and followed him. And followed him some more until the water was far behind us, endless glittering sand the only thing in sight. Then, finally, he stopped in front of an open structure. Two walls held a thatched roof over a wooden platform almost completely hidden under an array of pillows. On one wall was a series of built-in drawers, and on the other… I blinked to make sure it wasn't a mirage. But the three drawings I'd gifted him over the last six months didn't disappear. My self-portrait—the only one I'd ever done, per his request—and two landscapes of his world hung, evenly spaced, across the second interior wall. I swallowed hard.

The Sandman hid himself from me for five years; he hid this even longer. My visits were regulated to a one mile stretch of beach when there was so much more. My pulse roared, an angry thing. This… this was a secret. There weren't supposed to be any left. What else didn't I know?

The creature dug at the sand just outside the structure with his tiger paws until a groan came from beneath the ground. I slapped a hand over my mouth.

"Not yet," the Sandman croaked as his face appeared from under the sand. "I need more time."

"Sandman?" I asked, louder than I intended. "What are you doing?"

His eyes flew open. Silver flecks swirled around his violet pupils. "Nora? What are you doing here?"

"Looking for you."

"You shouldn't have." He closed his eyes again and sighed. "Things might not have ended well. It was dangerous for you to come back this soon."

"Apparently things didn't end very well, regardless," I said. "Are you okay?"

The creature huffed. I shot him a deadly look, and he strode away.

"Don't mind him," the Sandman said, and the footsteps thumped away.

I eyed the creature cresting a nearby dune. "What is that thing?"

"Baku."

I gaped. "*That* is your associate?"

He cracked his eyes open to look up at me. "He's going back out right now to look for Katie."

I bit my tongue, instantly sorry I called him a thing. He wasn't just the Sandman's associate anymore—he was mine. *By default*, as the Sandman had said, but helpful nonetheless. I squinted at him, following his movements, and he waltzed straight through the barrier.

My face fell. "The barriers are down?"

"Baku has been here as long as I have, perhaps longer, but he belongs to neither the Nightmare nor the Dream Realm. He goes where he pleases." His voice was low and tired.

I faced him again and repeated, "Are you okay?"

He paused. "I will be."

I kneeled beside him. His face was the only thing visible while the rest of him lay hidden, perfectly camouflaged, in the sand. I tucked my feet beneath me, then untucked them, and tucked them again. "Are you sure? Do you need help getting out of there?"

His lips quirked. "It's healing me."

"What?"

He sat up with a quiet grunt and ran a hand through his hair. His tunic was gone, and three long, jagged rips ran up the abdomen of his second shirt. I ran my eyes over him for other injuries before stopping at the gaping holes dotting his shoulder.

"The sand. It's—"

"Yes, yes." I waved my hand at him. "The sand heals you, but you never mentioned being buried in it." I dropped my gaze to scowl at the ground where his waist disappeared. Even after all the explanations, what did I really know about the Sandman? About his life or his abilities? I knew he could conjure up pretty illusions. I knew he could travel into my world and break into houses, but not the *how*. Maybe magic was one of those things that had no explanation, but for all the time I spent here, it felt like I knew absolutely nothing.

"Hey." The Sandman ran his thumb down my cheek. "It's faster this way. I'll be fine."

Of course, he would. Because the sand was healing him. My nostrils flared. *Later.* Later we would talk about this hidden oasis and everything I still didn't know. But right now, I was working on a deadline. "I need your help figuring out something specific."

The weight of his eyes made me twitch. I refused to look up. He said nothing for what felt like forever, but it couldn't have been more than thirty seconds. "I'm not going to like this, am I?"

I gave him a quick, fake smile. "That's a pretty safe assumption."

He released a breath. "All right, but first, would you mind?"

I looked up to find him gently tugging an arm from his sleeve.

"Direct contact will speed things up, and Baku doesn't exactly have opposable thumbs."

I hesitated. I wanted to help, to do something I knew was undoubtedly useful, but the crate holding all my doubt weighed heavy, dragging me deeper into uncertainty. And not just about my plan with the Weaver. The Sandman was so certain of his feelings for me—he'd had a year to be sure—but it was new to me. I felt the same way but what if it was my relief tricking me? What if I loved him as a friend? What if I did love him more than a friend but I could never trust him like I had before?

I leaned forward anyway, brushing the thoughts away. My feelings could wait in line. Right now, the Sandman needed to get better so that he could help me trick the Weaver and save my sister. My fingers grazed his stomach, and his breath caught. I pinched the hem of his shirt. The stretchy material clung to him, squelching as it separated from his bloodstained skin.

His abs flexed, and he shifted to lift his arms over his head. My eyes caught on the tattoo over his breastbone. Thousands of blue and silver specks blinked in and out, spilling from a thick, navy-blue crescent moon. My fingertips hovered over it, but I was too afraid to make contact. There had always been so many layers between us that touching bare skin still seemed forbidden.

The Sandman's fingers carefully circled my wrist, and he brought my hand forward. My palm almost covered the moon, only the pointed tips peeked out on either side of my knuckles.

Electricity zipped through my arm, leaving peace in its wake. I gasped, my eyelids drooping. I hadn't felt this calm in ages.

"My magic lives in you," he said in a hoarse voice. "The dream I gave you fused with your own power, but it remembers where it came from."

"I don't have power for it to fuse with." The pulsating rhythm beneath my hand was like a second heartbeat.

"Of course, you do." He released my wrist and placed his palm over my collarbone. "It lives here. In your heart." He trailed his fingers up the side of my neck and skimmed my temples. A blush burned my cheeks. "And here."

I wanted to tell him he was crazy, that what he said made no sense, but maybe he wasn't. Maybe it did. *Keep a true mind and a true heart.* I blinked slowly, watching the tattoo shimmer.

He sighed, his hand falling away. "I would love for you to stay, but it isn't safe yet."

"It is tonight," I said quietly. "I talked to the Weaver again."

His muscles stiffened beneath my hand. "Nora, no. Whatever you're thinking, the answer is no."

I broke contact, my skin tingling, and forced my eyes up to his. "Hear me out first."

"Do I have a choice?" he grumbled.

"Of course." I shrugged, one corner of my mouth lifting. "But only one of your options is *really* an option."

The Sandman's face grew tighter with every word as I explained my encounter with the Weaver and my intent to cross him, his chest barely moving with each shallow breath. "If I didn't know better, I'd ask if you had a death wish," he said when I finished.

I clenched my jaw. "My sister is wrapped up in this because of us, and we're going to get her out of it."

"Baku is still searching the—"

"There has to be another way." I inched closer. "There has to be a way for me to do something from my side other than search blindly for where he's hidden her."

The muscle in his jaw twitched. "If we could get one of the threads he wears on his arm, I could use it to track down Katie's subconscious in his realm but—"

"Great," I blurted, hope swelling. "How do we do that?"

"Nora." He leveled a serious look at me. "If it were that easy, I would have rebound him and none of this would be happening. He's not stupid. He knows I'll go for them if I'm close by."

"*You*. But not me." My voice wavered. I didn't want to be close enough to the Weaver to touch him, assuming I could when he wasn't completely in my world, but Katie needed me. "Tell me how to get one."

"If I gave you a…" He paused and clamped his mouth shut. "No. I won't let you risk it."

"Then I'll find a way into the Nightmare Realm and look for her myself." My heart raced at the idea, my palms sweating. No part of me wanted to go there. None. I would do it though.

"You really do have a death wish." He closed his eyes and scooped a handful of sand. The granules moved painfully slow across his palm. "You have to do *exactly* what I tell you. Once you get the thread, the Weaver will pull out all the stops. We'll have a little time before he recovers, but not forever."

Chapter Sixteen

A fog light illuminated the sign for MJ's U-Store It. I paused at the stop sign a hundred feet from the address the Weaver gave me and eyed the rows of grey steel boxes behind a chain-link fence. *A place with no windows.* The last remnants of sunlight glowed pink across the otherwise empty field, creating a dusk too beautiful to be spent double-crossing an evil lord.

I tugged the sleeve of my fleece sweater down over the heel of my hand. Four hair bands circled my left wrist and forearm beneath it, securing the box cutter the Sandman created. The warm metal dug into my skin—a promise of safety, a threat of failure. Really, the plan could go either way. However, as long as I saved Katie, I could deal with the consequences. I took a deep breath and eased the car forward.

The tires crunched against the gravel drive of the twenty-four-hour storage facility. I knew this was the right place thanks to the internet, but there were at least a hundred tan and green units. Katie was so close. *So close.* It took every ounce of willpower not to call the police the second I knew where she was, but for this plan to work, the Weaver couldn't sense my deceit.

My heart flopped, and I tugged at my sleeves again. If I was going to save Katie and move against the Weaver, I had to be braver than I felt. If I couldn't do that, then I had already lost.

I pulled into the center row, halfway down from where another aisle cut horizontally, and put the car in park. Easing out of the driver's seat, I slammed the door and willed away my nerves. The gentle purr of the engine felt reassuring, although the extra few seconds it would give me to escape wouldn't matter against someone like the Weaver. I rapped my fingers against the hood of the car and squinted into the shadows.

"You didn't back out." The Weaver stepped around the corner of the nearest row, the gossamer shroud still tying him down. "I admit to having my doubts."

"What choice did I have?" I snapped, the anger palpable.

He shrugged one shoulder. "There's always a choice."

I wiped sweaty palms on my grey leggings. What if I couldn't do it? What if I missed my mark? But it was too late for doubts. The ride had started and there was no getting off. "Which unit is she in?"

"Follow me," he said. I took one step toward him when he vanished. His voice drifted across the parking lot. "This way, Sun-Kissed Keeper."

I stomped toward the back of the units where his shadow flickered and strained to hear his voice again. "I have a name, you know," I shouted.

The Weaver popped up beside me. I jumped, hitting a unit door with a clang, and he grinned. "I care nothing for your name,

Keeper. Only what's behind that freckled forehead of yours." He bopped the air in front of my hairline with a finger.

I locked my knees, refusing to step away and show an ounce of the fear storming through me. "Where is she?"

His eyes narrowed, and he clucked his tongue. "Your Dreamer is here." He vanished, reappearing at the last door in the row.

My sneakers ground into the tiny stones beneath my feet, and I flexed my tingling fingers. *Okay.* Go in, make sure there's a clear path to the exit, check Katie's pulse, slide the box cutter out, open the blade, swing, grab the thread, run. *Easy.* Just like I practiced on the Sandman last night. I swallowed hard. I could do this. I had to.

When I stepped up to the Weaver, he grinned before disappearing, popping up a few units in the opposite direction. "Here, here." His voice bounced through my head. "She's so near."

"I'm going to kill you," I said under my breath.

He materialized an inch from me. "Now, now. Don't ruin the fun."

I scowled. "This isn't a game."

"Of course, it is." He stalked around me in a circle. "I let my nightmares out of the Night World. The Sandman bound me and slammed the doors shut. Now I do something to free myself, he comes running after me, etcetera, etcetera. The question is, who wins?"

"You were letting your monsters run loose through the Day World. What did you expect him to do?"

"People need something real to fear. They *crave* it." He tossed a hand at me. "How many horror movies have you seen? How many ghost stories have you enjoyed?"

"People like horror movies because they aren't real, not because they think being murdered is enjoyable." I pressed my arm against my hip, letting the cutter dig through my leggings and into my thigh. He had to believe I was going through with the deal. "Forget it. Do you remember your promise to ensure my safety?"

One of his eyebrows lifted. "If I want to torment the Sandman's favorite toy now and then, it's my prerogative, but yes, I recall what I said."

Comforting. "I want it extended to my family."

"You're hardly in a place to make demands."

I crossed my arms.

"Fine, fine." He dipped his head and flicked his fingers toward me. "Your family too."

"Good." If this were real, I would ask him for clarification, but his vague half-promise was enough. Let him think I was an idiot. It only helped my cause. "Then, Katie. Now."

"You'll take my word on the deal but not on your sister's wellbeing?"

I sneered, my muscles trembling. "If my sister isn't okay, the deal is off. Consider this proof of purchase."

He shrugged and lifted a long finger to point at the unit directly behind me. "The combination is 22-7-10."

I lunged for the silver lock and fumbled with the dial. "How did you even get a lock on this thing?" I grumbled to myself.

"Katie isn't the only sleepwalker in the world. I'd think that was obvious. How *is* your mother, by the way?" He hovered at my shoulder, and I jerked the arrow too far past the second number. "Seven."

"I know," I snapped. I wiped the sweat from my palms and spun the black knob to start over. It was too hot for this sweater.

Too stressful. But I had to hide the weapon and the leggings offered the best range of motion. Neither of which would matter if I passed out from nerves.

When the lock popped open, I yanked the overhead door up and rushed inside. Katie was still in her favorite pajamas—skull and crossbones shorts and a faded graphic T-shirt. Her hair was slick with grease, but her chest rose and fell in an even rhythm, her features smooth. No screaming, no tense muscles. Other than the fact that she was in the middle of a storage unit, she appeared to be having a regular nap.

"Don't worry. She received plenty of breaks to keep her heart ticking. I didn't want her to expire before I was ready—like your father did," he said reassuringly.

My heart twisted painfully. *Stay calm. Don't ruin the plan.*

"And now you see the proof," he added, a saccharine smile glittering on his features.

I dropped to my knees, my back to the Weaver, and pressed my fingers to her neck like I was taking her pulse. With my other hand, I slipped my fingers into my sleeve and slid the box cutter free. My fingers fumbled to grip the smooth surface. I sucked in a ragged breath and slid the blade from the tip. "Hang in there," I whispered to Katie. "It will all be over soon."

"Dream Keeper." The Weaver's voice was stern yet thick with anxiety. "It's time for you to keep your end of the bargain."

"How...?" I asked, stalling. I knew how. The Sandman told me I would have to fall asleep and reject the safety of the beach. Then the Weaver would snatch me away to his realm where I would allow him access. Like there was any chance of me letting him drag me off to his home turf. Deal or no deal, I had no doubt he would torture me if he had the chance. Once he had the dream, I was as good as dead.

"It's easy." He knelt on the other side of Katie. I shifted the box cutter so that it pressed between my knee and Katie's upper arm. "You go to sleep. I'll meet you on the other side and then you say yes."

"Will it hurt?" The black and gold band of threads on his wrist gleamed through the gossamer, stretching up his bicep to attach to his ever-moving shirt. I just needed one of them.

He trailed a finger over Katie's cheek without really touching her. "Not so very much."

"I see." I took a deep breath and fussed with my sister's shirt, smoothing the bottom down where the hem had flipped over. The Sandman sounded so sure this would work, and I trusted him with my life, but maybe whatever piece of his magic I carried wasn't enough to breach the barrier between our worlds. Maybe the dream didn't hold enough sway, even with the weapon made of sand to amplify it. *Be quick*, he warned. The binding would close itself almost immediately, and I didn't want to lose a hand when it did. I took a deep breath. "Well, then..."

I moved without thinking. The blade ripped through the fabric, tearing through the top layer of flesh below the Weaver's elbow. The threads floated away from him, squirming in an attempt to return to their master, and the blade slipped from my hand. I gripped the band around his wrist and yanked with every muscle I had. Three broke away, falling with me to the floor.

The gossamer flashed blue, and the Weaver's nails clawed against the resealed binding, his eyes darting wildly across its surface. "You," he bellowed.

"Yes." I scrambled off the floor, tying the three threads into a knot to keep them together. They twitched in my palm. "Me."

He bent, gasping over my sister's sleeping body. "I will personally peel the skin from her body while you watch."

My legs shook beneath me. I knew he would threaten Katie after I did this. I knew it, but I *also* knew it was the only way to save her in time. "Not if I skin you first."

"Foolish Keeper," he rasped. "You are no match for me."

"I appreciate being underestimated. It makes winning that much sweeter." I tucked my prize into the pocket of my fleece and zipped it shut. He would have more soon—apparently, all it took was a trip to his loom to replenish what was lost. Twenty-four hours until he had a full arsenal wrapped around his arm again.

I looped my elbows under Katie's armpits and dragged her toward the waiting car. The Weaver watched every step with fury blazing in his golden irises. Surely, he was imagining each way he would torture me for this betrayal, but I couldn't think about that now. I had to get Katie to the hospital, then find her in the Nightmare Realm before the Weaver paid her a visit.

***

A nurse in teal scrubs wheeled Katie back into the curtained area of the emergency room, an IV bag swaying from a metal pole. They planned to run every test to discover why she was in a coma, explore every avenue of possibilities, but so far, they'd come up empty-handed. Of course, they had, unless there was some sort of supernatural CT scan. My mother shuffled after them, speaking in a low voice to one of her coworkers from the maternity ward while I stood silently in the hall with Paul.

My eyelids threatened to slam shut where I stood, but I couldn't give in yet. When I finally fell asleep, it had to be somewhere safe. Somewhere no one would be tempted to wake me before the Sandman and I did what had to be done. He was waiting for me now, waiting for the strands of thread in my pocket, so we could follow one of them straight to Katie. Time was ticking. The Weaver wouldn't leave himself vulnerable by attacking her while weak, but there was nothing stopping him from telling his creatures to up their game. Nothing except some sort of sick satisfaction of doing it himself. The Sandman assured me that would be the case.

Katie still appeared calm. The heart monitor beeped in a regular, steady rhythm, and that had to count for something.

"She'll be fine," Paul whispered to me. "You did good."

But not good enough.

I pressed my lips together and nodded. By the way Detective Bell hovered near the nurses' station, casting suspicious looks in my direction, I guessed I was firmly up Shit Creek without a paddle. I could almost hear his questions now. How did I know where to find Katie? How did I know the combination to the lock? Why hadn't I called the police first? Was I hiding something? Did I turn on my hypothetical partner in crime? I couldn't handle it yet.

"It's going to be a long night." Paul fished the keys from his pocket. "Let's head home, huh? We could both use some rest."

I cast a glance at my mother. Her coworker held her up while another nurse went over Katie's chart, line by line. "What about Mom?"

"She won't leave until your sister does."

I knew he was right, but I just found Katie again. I didn't want to leave her, not even to save her, for fear she would disappear again. She was waiting though, stuck in the Night World. I had lost enough people to the Weaver for my sister to be next.

"Okay," I said. Twenty-four hours suddenly felt like minutes on the countdown, and I'd already wasted two of them. "Let's go."

Chapter Seventeen

Nora

An identical long-sleeved shirt replaced the Sandman's torn one, his old tunic gone. My pulse thundered in my ears, and I ran, my feet pumping nearly as fast as my heart. The Sandman moved toward me so fast I barely noticed him in front of me before he swept me into a crushing embrace. I closed my eyes, breathed in his light lilac scent. Allowed myself this moment of calm before venturing into the Nightmare Realm.

"I got it," I squeaked.

His breath shuddered against my hair. "Please, never ask me to help you do something that reckless again."

"It worked though," I said with defiant cheer and fisted the fabric of his shirt to hold him close.

"Should that make me feel better?" He stepped back and scanned my face. "We haven't even begun the dangerous part of this plan, and I feel as if I've died a thousand deaths. Are you sure you won't reconsider? Wait here or go be with your sister at the hospital while I wake her up?"

The idea was tempting. I had no idea what we would find in the Nightmare Realm, what we would face. If the things waiting for us were anything like the creatures that the Weaver brought here... I swallowed. "I have to go with you. Katie doesn't know who you are. I can get through to her and convince her to wake up. She might think you're one of them."

His eyes flashed. "I could never be mistaken for a nightmare, Nora."

"I didn't mean it like that."

"I know." He chewed on his bottom lip. "I know. Sorry, I'm a little tense."

I squeezed his forearm with one hand and opened the pocket of my fleece with the other. At least the weather here was always comfortable, so I wasn't dying of heat anymore. I hoped the same could be said about the Nightmare Realm. My stomach churned with a mix of hope and dread. I pinched the threads between my fingers and held them up. They wriggled weakly before falling limp. "Here."

"We just need one." He loosened the knot and plucked a single thread from my grip, wincing. "Put the other two away. It isn't enough to bind the Weaver but keep them safe in case we need to do this again."

"Will we?" I whispered, my brows lowered, watching him work.

"I hope not." A thin, almost invisible line of sand rose up to join the thread, surrounding it, then slowly sank into the fibers. The thread squirmed in the Sandman's palm.

"What are you doing?"

His eyes flicked up to mine, his head cocked. "I'm... giving it a lobotomy, I guess. Taking control of its mind."

"Its' mind?" I squinted at the piece of thread. The other two suddenly weighed down my pocket. "Are you saying they're alive?"

"It's an unborn nightmare." The Sandman picked it up between his index finger and thumb and shook it.

"You had me steal *nightmares?*" My jaw hung open, and I lightly punched his shoulder. "Are you crazy? Why would you let me do that?"

He raised his eyebrows. "I didn't *let you* do anything. As I recall, I explained what we would need, then tried talking you out of it."

"You could have warned me," I half shouted. "I've been carrying those...things...around with me for hours."

"If I warned you, you still would've done it." He gave me a knowing half-smile. "I'm sorry I didn't tell you, okay? I will next time."

"Next time," I grumbled. There had better not be a next time. I was lucky I didn't pee my pants in that storage unit. "Now what?"

The Sandman pinched the thread until it stiffened, as straight as a needle, and took my hand. "Now, we try not to be afraid."

I bit my lip. Even if I didn't want to be afraid, even if I somehow managed to talk myself into feeling safe, there were going to be things I couldn't shake. I remembered the small nightmare that ran at me and the one that followed. How many more were there? How many were worse? I shivered.

"We can find another way," he offered.

"*Is* there another way?" If there were, if it were preferable to this, I imagined we would have done it already. And now the Weaver was pissed. We were out of time and options.

He pressed his lips into a straight line and tightened his grip on my hand, giving me my answer. "I've linked the nightmare to Katie's cord. I'll use that connection to guide us through the Nightmare Realm to where the Weaver is keeping her mind."

Jealousy sparked in my chest at the mention of the other cords. I knew he helped other people in a vague sense, that he had a life outside the hours I spent with him, but I never realized how little I knew about it. He knew everything about me—my friends, my family, school, work. What did I know about him? A laundry list of how his world worked? I knew his morals though. His subtle movements, his habits, his likes and dislikes. That seemed like enough when I didn't believe he was real, but now I wasn't sure. "I'm ready to go."

He turned, looking down at me with an expression that rocked my resolve. It was a look full of knowledge and pity. He knew exactly what we would find outside of his Dream Realm. Not the specific nightmares, perhaps, but the scope of what waited for us. All the things I never faced because he had shielded me, and now he was leading me straight into the heart of their world. To where one wrong move could place me in the Weaver's hands.

"You're sure you won't stay?" he asked again.

"Positive."

He drew in a deep breath and kissed my temple. "Then don't let go."

Darkness swallowed the world, dragging us from beneath the bright starlit sky and into an inky black. It pulsed around us, a thousand times stronger than when I felt it the first time in

Katie's room. The familiar tang of metal coated my tongue, throwing me back to the first night I felt the brush of air and found Katie screaming in her bed. I reached my free hand out to grip the Sandman's shirt.

"I can't see anything," I whispered in a shaky voice.

"Wait," came his reply, soft, steady, and close.

Soon, shapes appeared in the lightening landscape. The sky faded to slate blue, the grass balsam. As more colors emerged, each maintaining a grey hue, I realized we were standing at the bottom of a jagged cliff. A smooth, silver lake reflected the peak. Low lying vines with pointed red and yellow thorns surrounded us. They scraped faintly at my ankles without drawing blood.

"Sandman?" I asked, needing to hear his voice again.

"This way." He tip-toed toward the lake. I followed in his exact footsteps. Each one was long and leaping until the thorns gave way to packed dirt. "Stay on this side of me," he said under his breath, moving to stand between me and the water.

I stared at the pond, and something broke the mirror-like surface. Two eyes protruded upward from a thick scaly forehead. The black orbs blinked, matching my stare. "What is that?"

"It would be impossible to know all their names. Don't stare," the Sandman warned. "It might take it as a sign of aggression."

Two more sets of eyes joined the first. I shifted so the Sandman's side blocked them from view. My heart was probably pounding, but I felt nothing. I was too numb, too stunned. I expected to enter a fiery cavern, complete with walls covered in shackles and echoing screams of tortured Dreamers. Not this. The stark setting was almost pretty in a macabre way, but I felt the danger hidden behind it. Lurking. Waiting. The unknown threat scraped against my skin, ached like a sickness in my bones. This was not a place to admire the scenery.

The thread in the Sandman's hand swiveled right, and he altered our course away from the water's edge. I breathed a sigh of relief, though I still felt the dark eyes of the water creatures at my back.

"They know who we are," he said. "They'll report our presence to the Weaver."

I shuffled closer. "Not what you want to tell me if I shouldn't be scared."

But of course, they would. Deep down I'd assumed as much, which was why we had to be quick. How far was the Weaver's Keep from this place? How close was he to finishing his new threads? I shouldn't have stayed at the hospital so long. Two and a half hours passed by the time I made it into my bed. Less than twenty-two left until he was undoubtedly ready to come for us. For me. Unless he decided to attack with his old nightmares.

The Sandman inched closer. "Katie isn't far."

I leaned into him, forcing myself to look straight ahead. "Is she okay? Did they hurt her?"

"I… don't know."

For as well as I knew him, I had no idea what his face revealed. I knew that pause though, so I studied him, concentrating on memorizing what his worried face looked like instead of the distant metal-on-stone scraping I heard to our left. The slight droop of his mouth. The strain around his eyes.

"What I told you before about holding all the power in your dreams?" He turned to follow the thread's direction again. "It doesn't hold true for nightmares. The creatures that live here are their own beings."

I discreetly patted the meat mallet I tucked in my waistband before bed. "I'll do whatever I need to do to save my sister."

"Good," the Sandman said. We slowed and approached the entrance to a cave. "Here's your chance."

The opening in the mountainside seemed to stretch forever into the darkness. A putrid odor wafted from the narrow crevice—rot and decay with an undercurrent of something sweeter. I slapped a hand over my mouth and nose. "What *is* that?" I asked without breathing.

"Your guess is as good as mine."

I gagged. "Katie's in there?"

"It seems so." He turned his head and hid a cough in his shoulder. "Any idea what she's afraid of?"

Nothing scared my sister. She rode every rollercoaster she found, went skydiving for her eighteenth birthday, and was the official killer-of-bugs in our house. She ate weird food. Got a tattoo. Katie faced life with a fearlessness that I had admired my entire life. "She isn't afraid of anything."

He wheezed. "Everyone is afraid of something."

My lungs screamed for air, and I forced myself to inhale. *Kettle corn.* The sweetness in the air was kettle corn. Like the kind Katie accidentally dumped on the woman in front of us at the circus when we were little. Right before she ran, screaming and crying, from the striped tent. "Clowns," I said. "She's afraid of clowns."

The Sandman paled, his jaw set. His hand dipped into the leather satchel at his hip. The sand was swirling together before he had it out of the bag. Once it stopped shifting, he held out a small gleaming knife and gave me the smallest wisp of a grin. "You can never have too many ways to defend yourself."

I tugged the meat mallet out of my waistband, holding a weapon in each hand. "Noticed this, did you?"

His grin widened a fraction. "It isn't exactly subtle."

I blushed. "So, should we...?"

"I can't." He scanned the rocky ledges above the opening. It wasn't until the scraping sound came again that I realized it had stopped. And now it was right on top of us. "It's planning to defend its territory."

"All the more reason to come inside." I followed where he was looking, then glanced at the opening again.

He shook his head. "We can't risk getting boxed in. If I'm wounded too severely by anything, I can't guarantee we'll get out before the Weaver finds us."

"But—"

"Go wake Katie up. I'll kill it and be right behind you." His hand dove into the satchel again. "Go, Nora."

A high-pitched laugh echoed from somewhere above our heads. My heart rammed against my chest, and I threw myself into the dark passage. The walls narrowed the further I went, scraping my arms through my sweater. Then, without warning, it widened again, opening into a vast cavern. The ground squished, sponge-like, beneath my feet, releasing a fresh wave of the pungent odor.

"Oh, my God." I breathed into the crook of my elbow and tightened my grip on the weapons.

I squinted into the darkness, blinking hard until my eyes adjusted enough to see Katie shackled to a hospital bed floating in thick pink goop. My pulse roared. There was no way to reach her, no bridge or rope to swing on. How did the nightmares reach her? Unless they didn't. My chest tightened. It wasn't the time for foolish wishes. Of course, they did, and there was no telling what state she would be in. If I didn't want anything worse to happen, I had to get over there and wake her up.

I nudged the goop with the toe of my sneaker. It wasn't as thick as it looked, and it didn't eat away at my shoe, but that didn't mean it was safe. If it was, there wouldn't be a point to floating Katie in its middle, but there was no other way to get to her.

With a deep, shaking breath, I waded into the reeking liquid. A spotlight on the ceiling flickered to life with the movement. "All right," I said both to myself and Katie. "No big deal, right?"

The sharp snap of popping bubbles was the only reply. *Bubbles*. Great. Bubbles meant air. Air below the surface of the pink goop meant... I didn't know what it meant in this place. Nothing good.

"Katie?" I sloshed the last few feet to the bed. "Can you hear me?" Her body remained still, the only sign she was alive was the shallow movement of her chest. I set the knife and mallet down on the mattress and worked the buckle of the brown leather cuff around her wrist. "It's me. Nora. You have to wake up, Katie. We have to go home."

The cuff splashed into the thick pink liquid, and I reached across the bed to free her other wrist.

A series of thuds resonated through the entrance to the cavern followed by a manic laugh. My stomach heaved. How long could the Sandman fight? He said he wasn't strong enough to beat the Weaver again, but he had to be strong enough to beat a nightmare or two otherwise we wouldn't be here.

"Wake up, wake up, wake up," I shouted in Katie's ear.

Katie stirred with a soft moan. I slapped her face so hard my palm stung. "No," she murmured. "No more."

"That's right. No more." I sloshed to the end of the bed to free her ankles. "Wake up so we can go home."

Her eyes fluttered open. "Nora?" Her voice cracked. "Is that you?"

"Yes. It's me." I smiled, laughing despite myself. She was conscious—a step in the right direction. My fingers fumbled with the last buckle. "Come on."

"No." She kicked out at my hands, one foot still tethered. "It's not you."

I hurried to her side and snatched the weapons up before they fell. "Katie—"

"Get away," she shrieked.

"It's me."

Katie shoved me, and I stumbled back, the goop splashing up to my shoulders.

"*Katie.*"

"Go away, go away, go away." She covered her face with both hands. A million angry red pinpricks covered her skin. "Please go away."

A large bubble *bloop*-ed between us. Ripples danced across the surface, and I froze mid-step. Fear swelled in my chest. I scrambled to shove the panic down before whatever lurked nearby noticed. *Clowns and...* I had no idea what else the Weaver would use to torment her. "We have to go," I said slowly. "Right now."

Katie sobbed on the bed, curling around herself.

More manic laughter floated down the tunnel, followed by the Sandman's roar. We didn't have long. I took wide steps toward Katie, twisting my body with each one, and something slithered against my kneecaps. I bolted onto the bed beside my sister and wrapped my arms around her shoulders. "It's me," I whispered. "Nora. Your sister. Your birthday is December Fifteenth. You have a scar on your knee from falling off your bike when you were nine, and I have one on the top of my foot from when you dropped the curling iron the day of mom's wedding. Our dog, Bear, was fourteen when we put him down. You slept with his collar for a month."

The longer I spoke, the less Katie's shoulders shook, but there wasn't time for a complete history of our childhood. A flash of white broke the surface before disappearing into the sludge again. I choked back a scream.

"Do you remember those hideous shoes you begged mom for?" Another flash of white. "The ones for homecoming?"

The head of a snake broke the water, rising up, up, up. Its underbelly was covered in pearly white scales, and the fur lining its back was sticky with the foul-smelling liquid. I met its yellow eyes and words froze in my throat. A thin black tongue sliced the air before its jaw unhinged to reveal several rows of razor-sharp teeth. Its hood flared, black and white speckled feathers spanning the width of the cavern, and a spray of pink splattered the walls. Its hiss filled the cave.

I dug my fingers into Katie's shoulders. "Wake up," I screamed.

The snake lunged.

"Katie!" I stood, straddling her legs, and slashed with the knife. Swung with the mallet. They both met nothing but air. "Open your damn eyes."

Chapter Eighteen

The Sandman

I didn't mind happy clowns with big hair and colorful clothes. Those were fine, but these... Clowns in the Nightmare Realm were the reason people had phobias. One glance had the potential to ruin someone for life. I shook out my hands. "Come on," I said under my breath.

There wasn't an infinite amount of sand here, only what I brought with me in my satchel. Each grain had to count. I scooped a healthy amount into my palm and formed a metal handle across my palm, with one end sharpened to a point. From the other, a heavy spiked ball hung at the bottom of a thick chain. I tested the flail, swinging it gently, and turned my attention to the opening Nora disappeared into.

The biggest danger lay outside, but that didn't mean the cave was safe. It was a risk—a horrible, stupid risk, but one we had to take. If too many nightmares found us, if I was too wounded to defend her, this would all have been for nothing. It was best if nothing followed Nora inside. She was strong and independent.

There was nothing I could do to stop her from going after her sister. Nothing I was willing to do, anyway, so I had to trust her the same way she trusted me. If there was anything in there with Katie, it would know better than to kill Nora when the Weaver needed her alive. If anything came out of the cave with her, I wouldn't let it take her, but she may have to fight. She would *likely* have to fight. Why hadn't I spent the last five years teaching her combat skills?

A small pebble bounced down the cliff. I squared my feet and scanned the area it fell from. A blur of white and red with a blip of yellow flashed against the dreary rock. I gripped the smooth handle of the flail as two grating honks sounded from behind me. My back prickled, and I knew without turning that the nightmare was there. In one swift motion, I bent, ducking, and spun while throwing the spiked ball at his knees. The clown leapt over it as if he were jumping rope, and his oversized shoes squeaked when he landed. I backed away to give myself more room to maneuver.

The clown watched me silently, and I tried not to shudder. His pasty white skin peeled away from his mouth and eyes, leaving exposed muscle and tendons in place of makeup. The red tip of his bulbous nose oozed pus and tufts of crimson hair dotted his head. The upturn of skin around his mouth made him appear like he was smiling, and in truth, he might have been. A twinkle filled his solid black eyes. On his black and white suit were three enormous mustard-colored pom-poms and a polka-dot bow tie with a black flower at its center.

"Sandman." His voice raked against my eardrums like nails on a chalkboard and his head bobbed erratically. "A pleasure to meet the legend."

I would waste no breath engaging the clown in conversation. We weren't there to chat but to tear each other apart. I smashed the spiked ball into his arm. Ruby blood seeped into the surrounding fabric. He laughed, a high-squeal. I struck again and again, hitting limbs, but the clown stood in place, taking each hit when he should have been writhing on the ground. His head continued to bob, growing faster by the second, until it seemed it would separate from his neck. The laugh rose and fell. I clutched the flail's handle and took a step closer, a bud of unease growing. If I could get close enough, I could stab the pointed end through his heart and end it.

But the clown's laugh grew and grew and grew. A spray of green acid shot from the flower at the base of his throat and hit my chin, searing a trail down my neck. I roared against the pain, and the flail fell to the ground in a rain of sand. I lifted the neck of my tunic and swiped at the liquid, but it only made it worse.

The clown darted into the mouth of the cave. I stumbled after him, gathering more sand into my hands, and let the darkness of the narrow crevice swallow me.

The acoustics carried Nora's voice toward me, and it gave me the incentive I needed to steel myself against the blazing pain of the clown's acid. He tapped my shoulder. I spun, but he was gone. Another tap, again from behind. I drew a shaky breath, the sound echoing in my head, and pretended to turn. Instead, I leapt back outside the cave. When the clown appeared again, his back was to me, facing the spot where I should have been.

I lunged, stretching my sand into a piece of wire between two blocks of wood, and wrapped it around his pale neck. He lurched forward but the wire sliced into his flesh. He gurgled a laugh. A splash of blood flew from his mouth, then his head turned slowly. Bit by bit, crack by crack, his face made the trek around to look me in the eye.

My muscles tensed, and I braced myself against the narrow walls.

With his body still facing away from me, the clown coughed. "Lord of Dreams." He grinned, his teeth red with blood. "Our master is coming for you."

I wrenched both blocks and his head thumped to the floor. *Our.* I dropped the wire and ran deeper into the cave. I knew it was a risk to send Nora in alone, just as my rushing in to help was, but none of that mattered. I had to wake her and her sister up before it was too late.

I sloshed into putrid pink liquid.

"Nor—" I tried, but it came out as a wheeze. I lifted a hand to the widening hole in my neck.

An enormous serpentine nightmare arched from the water. Nora screamed for her sister to wake up, and a hiss pierced the air. The snake lunged. Nora swung. I stepped forward, but it was too late. There wasn't time to reach them.

A flash of silver, another swing of the knife. The snake hissed again and knocked into the bed in the middle of the room. My heart dropped to my stomach. Nora gripped the edge of the mattress before she could fall backward. The knife I gave her was covered in slick, black blood. It ran down her hand, her arm, dripping on her thigh.

The snake flopped into the liquid, one feather of its hood hanging, half severed. Nora gasped. I moved toward her again, conscious of the danger swimming so close. She jerked at the sight of me, her fingers digging into Katie's arm. The meat mallet was gone.

"Go back," she called.

I shook my head.

"Go. Back. It's not safe." She turned to her sister. "Wake up, Katie. I swear if any of us die saving you, I will haunt you for all eternity."

"I can't wake up." Her voice cracked. "I can't."

Nora said something to her sister, but the roaring in my head prevented me from hearing. She was still talking when Katie vanished. Nora fell forward without her sister's body there to lean into. I tried to speak again but my vocal cords were too damaged. I had to get back to the beach and heal. The Weaver wasn't going to take this lying down. We had to be ready.

Nora pushed up onto her elbows and scanned me from head to toe. Her eyes widened at the sight of my neck, then again when they reached my knees. A series of bubbles popped a foot away. "Run!" When I hesitated, she said, "Sandman, go. I'll see you soon."

Then she vanished.

The snake shot out from the pink goop, straight at the empty hospital bed. Its jaws clamped down on the metal frame, and it shrieked in fury. I shifted back toward the crevice, where the decapitated clown lay across the entrance to the cave. The nightmare paused, watching me with a flick of clear eyelids. It inched forward. Once it decided to lunge at me, it would be over. I eased out of the liquid, watching each subtle movement the serpent made, then spun and darted back into the passageway. The snake slammed into the narrow crevice a mere second after I slid safely inside.

I reached deep inside myself, focusing on the beach, and shuffled sideways toward the opening. Darkness faded. My center shifted, then sand was beneath my feet instead of stone. I stumbled backward, hitting the ground. There was barely enough time to register the familiar sky above me before the sand swathed my wounds, burying me, knitting me back together. I closed my eyes and let the hum of it fill me.

We did it. Nora did it.

A faint smile spread across my lips, and I faded into unconsciousness.

Chapter Nineteen

Nora

I woke in a pool of sweat. My heart pounded in my ears, and I stared at the ceiling, gasping for air. The scent of rot lingered, but there was no mistaking where I was. Moonlight filtered into my bedroom and Paul's snores traveled through the door over the purr of the air conditioning. *I did it.* I woke up before the snake could strike again, and Katie woke up before me. Safe from the Weaver.

I kicked free of the tangled sheet and grabbed my phone from the dresser. My mom's cell went straight to voicemail. I shoved my dresser away from the door—a permanently necessary precaution—and bolted from the room. "Paul," I shouted, banging on his door. "Paul, we have to go back to the hospital." His snoring stopped, but there was no reply. I pounded on the wood again. "I'm taking the car."

There was a thud inside his room followed by a series of footsteps. When the door swung open, my step-father blinked the sleep from his eyes. "What's going on?"

Every second I stood there was torture. I had to know it worked. I had to be sure that I didn't go through all of that for nothing. That the Sandman and I hadn't risked our lives and failed. The blood drained from my face. *Sandman.* He got out—he had to. But his face. The skin on his chin and neck was gone, leaving a red blistering wound. I gripped the door frame. I had to get back, but first I had to know Katie was safe because the next time I went to the Night World, I wasn't leaving without the Weaver's head on a platter. "Hurry. We have to go back to the hospital."

He stood straighter. "What happened?"

"I don't know." I couldn't tell him I thought my sister might be awake or why. "Probably nothing, but I need to see Katie."

He grabbed a clean shirt off the top of the folded laundry in a basket. "Have you talked to your mother?"

"She's not picking up," I answered, barely keeping the jitters at bay.

He nodded. "Give me a second. I'll drive."

With that, I ran outside to wait in the car, my head pounding.

***

My muscles strained with the effort to not race to the elevator, but I didn't want to call unwanted attention to myself. I already had enough of that between my mother and Detective Bell. Finding Katie on my own was going to lead back to an interrogation room. Unless Katie cleared me. Unless she remembered something. I'm not sure which would be worse for her though—remembering or forgetting. *Remembering.*

When the doors pinged open on the third floor, I jumped. Paul scowled at me but thankfully said nothing. He led the way past the officer standing outside Katie's room and into a whirl of activity. Machines beeped steadily while two nurses stood beside the bed, checking tubes and screens. A doctor on the far side of the room was deep in a hushed conversation with my mother but paused in his speech when we entered the room. "Can I help you?" he asked with a thick accent.

My mother started. "What are you two doing here?"

My vision tunneled to the bed. Katie's feet and legs were hidden beneath a white blanket, unmoving. I bulldozed into the room, knocking into the nurse standing at a laptop on a rolling podium. "Katie?"

"Nora?" My sister sat up. Her big, bright, beautiful eyes were wide open. Haunted, but open. "Nora!"

I flung myself at her to a chorus of shocked complaints, but Katie latched onto me, sobbing into my shoulder. Her hands shook against my back, and I tightened my embrace. This was real life, not a dream. She was here. She was safe. The pit in my stomach filled with relief. "Thank God," I breathed.

"Thank you," Katie said. Her voice was dry. Broken. "Thank you, thank you, thank you."

I held so tightly it felt as if her ribs would crack. Hushed voices resumed behind us, rushed and confused. "I'm sorry." I shivered. "This is my fault."

"I had this awful dream," she said quietly so only I heard.

I buried my face in her hair and nodded.

"You were there," she said, half questioning the idea.

"I was there."

She sniffled. "But how?"

A shadow flickered near the closet. Gold eyes blinked in and out, and I tensed. He was less present than before—a flat image against the gossamer screen. I glanced at the clock. We should have another eighteen hours before he was ready, yet he was strong enough to press against the barrier between Day and Night. My elation drained away, dread taking its place. But my sister was back, and she was never going there again.

My mother's hand landed on my shoulder. "We should let the staff finish their tests."

"No. I want to talk to Nora," Katie said. When no one moved, she added, "*Alone.*"

I clasped Katie's hands, begging her with a look not to make me discuss everything then and there. Now that I knew she was awake, I had to make sure the Sandman made it out of that cave. The pit in my stomach yawned open. He was hurt when I saw him last—what if it was too much? What if he couldn't escape? That would be my fault too. I pressed a hand over the ache in my chest.

"Now," Katie insisted, her nostrils flared.

The room fell silent, a million unanswered questions pressing down on us. What happened the night she went missing? Who took her? Had she been in the storage unit the whole time? Why was she unconscious? Was anything physically wrong? Emotionally, there was going to be a plethora. I knew it, the doctors knew it, and the Weaver lurking in the corner knew it. The only one that might be in denial was our mother. She already had one crazy daughter, after all. But hopefully talking to professionals would help my sister come to terms with whatever it was she needed. Not that it had for me.

The doctor, an older man, moved first, ushering the nurses from the room. Paul practically dragged our mother out after them, whispering to her. When the door clicked shut, the officer stationed outside shifted in front of the small window.

"Tell me," she demanded.

"There's too much to tell." I glanced at the Weaver who grinned back. My heart slammed against my ribcage. I wouldn't give him the reaction he was looking for. Wouldn't let him see my panic or my fear. "All the deaths… They're because I have something someone wants. He took you to get to me."

"Oh, please," she hissed. "What could you possibly have that someone would want that bad? I mean, what the hell, Nora? It was like I was transported to some sort of alternate reality."

"You wouldn't believe me if I told you." *Breathe.* I had the same questions she did once. She deserved answers, but not with the Weaver listening in. Not before I made sure the Sandman was okay.

"You just waltzed into my head. I didn't imagine you there. It was real."

If anyone understood the feeling that something was real when everyone else thought it was imaginary, I did. There was a difference in someone being part of your dream and someone actually being in your head. I couldn't remember what the former felt like, not really, but I distinctly remembered how the first night with the Sandman jarred me. How different it felt.

"No, you didn't imagine anything," I agreed. The Weaver shifted closer. *Ignore him. Ignore him. Ignore him.* "The Sandman and I came to wake you up before the Weaver could destroy you."

Katie blinked puffy eyes. "*The Sandman?* Are you talking about that freak you used to dream about? God, Nora, seriously?"

"Don't call him a freak," I snapped. "We just risked everything for you. After what you saw over there, you still don't believe me? You just admitted my presence there was real, so why couldn't he be real too?"

"So... You've seen him this whole time?" She narrowed her eyes, head tilted in disbelief. "He never went away?"

"I don't have time to explain." I launched off the bed to pace between my sister and the Nightmare Lord. My hands shook at my sides. *Don't look at him.* "The Weaver is here, and he's pissed."

"Keeper," the Weaver chimed in. "*Pissed* doesn't come close to describing what I am."

Katie didn't react. Surviving the nightmare hadn't given her the ability to see him now that she was awake. I didn't know why I expected it to. Her gaze darted around the room, the machine beeping faster, and climbed to her knees. "The clown? It's here?"

"The clown is dead," the Weaver said.

"Not the clown. The clown is dead," I relayed before I could stop myself.

My sister slumped against the pillows and covered her face. "He was... Nora, he did so many things."

"I know." I turned to glare at the Weaver. "I saw the marks."

"Needles," she said with a shiver.

I glanced over my shoulder at the tattoo on her inner wrist. "Since when are you afraid of needles?"

"Since always." When she saw me staring, she lifted her wrist, exposing her tattoo. "I was trying to face my fears or whatever."

"Do you want to know what else they did in the cave?" the Weaver asked.

I whirred back to the shadowed corner. "Shut up," I snapped, spittle flying.

"Who are you talking to?" Katie asked.

The Weaver shifted, his face straining with the effort to get closer to me. "I must say, I admire you for leaving the Sandman to die alone."

My knees wobbled. "What?"

"*What?*" Katie parroted. "Nora, are you having a meltdown?"

"I'm not talking to you," I said to my sister. Then to the Weaver, "Repeat what you just said."

"Winning is a subjective thing, is it not?" he asked.

My heart dropped. Exploded. Shattered. "You're lying."

"You would know what a liar looked like, wouldn't you? But when have *I* ever lied to *you*, Dream Keeper? Why would I need to when I have so many of your people left to toy with?"

I fell onto the edge of the bed. Katie shook my arm, her voice droning in my ears. "You can't kill each other. He said so."

"Half true." He pressed against the fabric holding him back. "Technically, I suppose." He sighed dramatically. "But I did not lay a hand on your precious Dream Lord. I didn't need to."

"*Liar.*"

"Nora!" Katie yanked my hair. "What are you doing?"

I ripped the bag of sand from around my neck and pressed it into her hand. "Sprinkle this in your eyes if you're going to sleep and you'll be safe. Don't let them see it. Don't go to sleep without it."

"Please," she begged. "Stop. You're scaring me. Tell me what's going on."

I kissed her forehead. "Trust me. I'll fix everything."

She gripped my wrist. "You're always running away from things, but you can't run away from this. I need to know what happened to me."

"I'm not running," I promised. *Not anymore.*

The door swung open and Detective Bell stood in the doorway, the knot of his tie loose, his shirt wrinkled. Energy jolted my body, not because I was worried about another line of questioning but because I needed to get home to sleep. The Sandman wasn't dead. He couldn't be dead. *He couldn't.*

"I'm glad to see you awake," the detective said. He glanced at me, then back to my sister. "Are you feeling up to a few questions?"

"I..."

Our mother bustled into the room. "Is this really necessary right now?" she demanded. "She only woke up an hour ago."

"We need to know what happened," he replied. "It could help us locate the killer."

"Killer?" Katie asked.

I tore my wrist from Katie's grip, unable to listen to them explain what happened the night she disappeared, and ran. I nearly slammed into Paul on my way around the corner. He juggled two cups of coffee, nearly spilling one all over himself. "Where are you headed?" he asked.

"Home." I forced a smile. "Katie asked me to get some of her things from the house. Her phone and toothbrush, stuff like that. Can I have the keys?" He glared at me. I could see the wheels turning in his head. *Maybe her mother is right,* he was thinking. *Maybe she is crazy. Maybe she* did *have something to do with everything.* A whole list of maybes I didn't care to know. He could question my sanity all he wanted if he gave me the keys. "Please? I'll be right back. I swear."

For a moment I thought he would say no, or he would insist on driving me again, but then he handed me his coffee so he could dig through his pocket.

***

I hurried upstairs to my bedroom with unsteady steps, my breath equally so. Putting nothing past the Weaver, I shoved my dresser in front of the door. I yanked open the top drawer and fished through my socks until I found the three white pills at the bottom. Opening wide, I tossed them to the back of my throat and swallowed. I took a deep, shuddering breath. He wasn't dead. *He was not.* If this was a trick by the Weaver to force me to return, it worked.

I tossed a grey bag from the local WalMart Supercenter on my desk and dumped out the Swiss Army knife I picked up on my way home. I pried the plastic away from the cardboard, my teeth chattering. The meat mallet was gone, lost somewhere in the cave, and I wasn't going back empty-handed. After fiddling with the attachments—five different blades, a corkscrew, and a screwdriver—I stuffed it into the pocket of my fleece and froze.

The Weaver's threads were still there. Still shifting with life. I held them up and glared at them through narrowed eyes. Without the Sandman, they weren't of any use to me; I couldn't control the sand. Besides, the only person I needed to track down after finding the Sandman was the Nightmare Lord, and together we could do that without help.

I didn't relish the idea of carrying nightmares around in my pocket any longer than I had to, so I opened the top drawer of the desk and rifled through crumpled post-its, white-out, and paperclips until I found a narrow tin pencil case. Dumping the pens out into the mess, I set the threads inside and stashed the case at the back of the drawer. My fingers drummed on the desktop. We could destroy them later if we didn't need them. After I found the Sandman. After we stopped the Weaver.

Seventeen hours and counting.

I took a deep breath, letting it out through my mouth, and climbed into bed.

True heart.

True mind.

I closed my eyes.

I'm coming. I pushed the thought toward the Sandman. *Please be okay.*

Chapter Twenty

Nora

I blinked into the darkness. *Darkness*. Not the beach. The Sandman wasn't there to make sure I went straight to a safe place. My chest tightened, fear weighing me down, locking my joints. I couldn't let what the Weaver said get to me; the Sandman was alive. He was hiding maybe or lost. Healing—he definitely needed it. The last time he was hurt, he had healed enough for his magic to catch me but this time…

There could be a million reasons his magic wasn't here to greet me.

For the first time in five years.

After we ventured into the Nightmare Realm, and he fought whatever horrible thing was outside the cave… I winced. This train of thought wasn't helping.

As my eyes adjusted, I found myself amid low swooping vines. Thin, willowy trees dotted the landscape, and my feet sunk into the mossy ground, releasing a whiff of stagnant water with each step. Insects buzzed, and frogs croaked. Dim lights flickered in the distance, floating, swooping. I rubbed the chill from my upper arms.

"Sandman?" I whispered.

Everything fell silent and still the instant the word left my tongue. My pulse revved. This was not the place to invoke his name, to draw unnecessary attention to myself. The Weaver was real here, and if he found me first, it was all over. I would never be able to withstand the torture my sister had. The Sandman had sheltered me from my nightmares, so I didn't know what my subconscious feared, but I knew I feared drowning. Small spaces. The monkeys from the Wizard of Oz. Whatever waited for me here, it would break me. Maybe not right away, but it would.

My feet squished the entire way around the outskirts of the swamp, cool water leaking into my sneakers. Eyes burned down at me from treetops, but I kept mine forward. Looking would make the fear worse. Other things peered from behind fallen logs or boulders, the creatures they belong to mostly hidden. I shivered. How many enemies surrounded me? I hugged myself tighter, my fingers digging into my sweater, and walked faster.

The lights flashed again in hypnotic irregularity, and a drone like a distant jet roared overhead. I bit back a scream and flung my arms over my ears, ducking. The buzzing stayed steady, warring with my booming pulse. Six legs hovered over me. Translucent wings with cobwebbed lines kicked up fragments of God-knows-what. Two long antennae twitched, smelling, tasting, and domed black eyes seemed to look at nothing and everything. Its abdomen flashed. I let out a breath. A lightning bug. I could handle bugs. Not spiders though. Or those things with a million legs. My lips parted, and I watched it hover. My parents used to drive Katie and me miles to find and catch them on early summer nights.

The giant bug surged forward, its light flickering lazily, and the noise exploded around me. Chirps and whistles, growls and snaps. Buzzing. Splashing. I ran. My arms pumped furiously, and I gasped for air. I wasn't afraid exactly, but I didn't want to stick around and find out if there was something nearby that would change that.

The outline of a mountain loomed in the distance. If I made it there, I could get an aerial view. Maybe find that cave again. I shuddered. But the clown was dead, and I didn't have to go back inside the cavern. Those things watching me from the lake... Well, I wouldn't get close enough to find out what they were, but that's where I last saw the Sandman.

The ground shifted beneath me. My shoulder rammed hard into a tree trunk, and I tripped over a log hidden beneath ferns. A pair of milky-white, lifeless eyes popped open on a tree root, staring skyward. A woman's face shifted, emerging slowly, the pattern of lines on her brown skin camouflaging her to blend with the bark. A sliver of skull peeked through a crack in her forehead and, when her jaw stretched open, maggots wriggled in place of a tongue. I scrambled to my feet and swerved right, then left.

Something large crashed through the brush behind me, but I was almost free. The trees thinned. A brighter shade of grey filtered down, showing the end of the swamp. A low, confidant growl rumbled from somewhere nearby. Too near. I propelled myself harder, my lungs sucking in stale air, and emerged on the other side of the tree line.

Only there was nowhere to go because the ground wasn't the ground at all, but the thick, bumpy hide of an alligator. I was twenty feet in the air, trapped. The trees creaked behind me, and I looked. I didn't mean to. I shouldn't have. Birds—what I assumed were birds—with giant wingspans and clawed feet took to the air. Something shifted in the trees. Something large and orange. *Nope.* I wasn't facing whatever that was. I wouldn't win, but more importantly, I couldn't fail, especially not so soon. I turned and barreled along the alligator's neck. One gigantic reptilian eye blinked, and I inched toward its left flank.

I couldn't go back, and I couldn't go forward either. Not without going down. I grabbed onto one of the smaller ridges lining the alligator's back and swung to the outer side, peering down at the hard, rocky ground. "Oh, this is a bad idea," I mumbled.

Heights themselves weren't a problem, but that gut-twisting sensation of falling was. I could climb a mountain or fly on a plane without a second thought, but bungee-jumping was out of the question. And doing this... There was a ninety-percent chance I would fall to my death but under the circumstances, it was my only choice.

I cracked my knuckles and got down on my stomach. The alligator's head swung in my direction. "Don't mind me," I said as if I were talking to an angry dog. Its mouth cracked into a grin like it knew what would happen: I would fall, and my body would be his dinner, which was probably the same thing that would happen if I made it down in one piece.

My dreams are only as strong as I am.

Dreams. Not nightmares.

I blew out a breath and skidded down until the toe of my sneaker found a groove between scales. The alligator kept walking. Kept watching, waiting, while I worked my way down to the next edge. The growl above turned to a low whine. I bit my lip. This had to work. But each lumbering step jarred my hold. The alligator dragged its toes, flinging its foot out. The front and back feet on opposite sides moved together. The back leg slammed down beside me.

One. Two. Three. I took a breath. *Four. Five. Six.*

The front leg moved. I dug my fingers into the crevice and closed my eyes to wait for the impact. *Thud.* I moved as fast as I dared, sliding more than climbing, and counted again. Every time I missed my mark, each time I didn't catch a scale with my hands or feet, my stomach rose to my throat.

I was halfway there.

Halfway.

And the giant animal stopped.

Steam curled off the surface of a pond in front of us. If I didn't get down now, I would be in that water. Dragged to the bottom where I would either drown or be eaten. Or worse. There wasn't a doubt in my mind that other things lived in there. Snakes, fish, leeches, plants to catch my ankles and anchor me in the murky depths. Without thinking, I maneuvered around to the front of the leg. The farther I went, the faster I went, the scales scraping against my palms like razors.

I had to slow down, to stop and start again. My jaw ached from clenching. I curled my fingers to catch a groove, but the friction tore my nails back. I hissed. Then my foot struck something solid and the impact rattled my brain. I pressed myself against the cool leg. It moved again. Another drag, and slam of its front leg.

"Crap," I squeaked.

Five feet from safety. I held my breath and let go, free-falling. Pinpricks covered my body. I forced my eyes open until they burned, but I wouldn't be blindsided. My teeth slammed together when I hit the ground—the sweet, beautiful ground—and I swore a molar cracked. But I was alive.

My body screamed when I launched myself up. Muscles I didn't know existed cried out in protest, but I had to keep moving. Had to. I shook a wave of dizziness from my head. Without giving myself time to object, I bolted, staying beneath the alligator's soft belly where I wouldn't be seen.

I had to figure out where to go next. Nowhere was safe, but I couldn't stay out in the open. There wasn't much time left before I reached the alligator's tail; I would have to run straight for the mountain in the distance.

A splash sounded behind me. The alligator shifted violently and the things living on its back shrieked in unison. The squelching sound popped against my eardrums. I covered my ears and darted out from beneath the gigantic nightmare before it could crush me. Running, I looked back and my blood ran cold. Large maroon tentacles reached from the water, wrapping around the alligator's nose. It attempted to gnash at the bits skimming too close to its teeth. More sticky, rubber-like suction cups crawled over the ground toward the enormous clawed feet. Nightmares leapt from the alligator's back, some making the drop and others hitting with a sickening crunch. The ones that flew blotted out the grey sky.

I pushed myself harder, as hard as my body would allow. Away from the things fleeing whatever occupied that water. Away before they could decide to pursue me, to offer me to their Nightmare Lord.

Yellow fireflies blinked here and there among the black silhouettes. It was as if I were inside an engine with all the hums and clicks. The mountain suddenly seemed even farther away. Too far. I would never make it in time—I needed somewhere else to hide. A flutter of legs grazed my skin. I jerked forward, lowering my head.

Then I was off the ground. Two spindly black legs held me, veering away from the swarm of escaping nightmares, and I choked back a scream before I attracted more attention. I twisted and turned to loosen the bug's grip. Pushed and pulled at the legs. Pounded my fists against them. The bug dipped in response and dropped me in a field of dry, cracked dirt. It landed on a boulder beside me, glaring before taking off.

Thanks a lot, I growled in my head. Although, I was strangely certain it meant to help and positive it did just that. Whatever danger lurked in the swamp was now running loose. It was good I was nowhere near it, but he could have taken me toward my destination instead of away from it. The boulder was the only thing in the surrounding landscape. I was helpless; a rod in a thunderstorm, waiting to be struck.

Sandman? I thought toward him. Nothing. And I didn't dare speak his name out loud again.

I gathered my hair back with a rubber band from my wrist and took a steadying breath. "Okay." *I can do this.* A laugh bubbled from my chest before I could stop it. Who was I kidding? This was the worst idea I'd ever had. A death wish. But if I didn't do something, if I didn't try, these creatures would be in my world. I trudged across the scarred earth and trained my eyes on my target. Walking. Marching. Keeping a straight path to the mountain.

"Nora," something whispered. "Noraaa."

I froze. Not some*thing.* Someone. Natalie. My heart slammed into my chest. I spun, and there she was. Her dark curly hair hung loose down her back, her tan arms relaxed at her side. She wasn't alone—Emery was beside her. My mother. My father.

Paul. Katie. They stood in a line, a few feet from each other, each facing the same direction: away from me.

"What..." I licked my lips. "What are you doing here?"

Silence.

"Guys?"

I took one step forward, and they mirrored the movement. Again. Three times.

Goosebumps raised on my arms and my chin quivered slightly. "This isn't funny."

More silence. I breathed into my hands. This wasn't real. It couldn't be real. I ran toward them, and they vanished in a swirl of smoke. The landscape widened. Deepened. For as far as I could see, there was nothing. The mountain was a mere hill in the distance. I spun, my mind racing, and when I faced the mountain again, a familiar hooded figure stood a few yards away. My heart leapt in relief.

"Sandman!"

He was okay. Alive. I took one step forward, and he dashed away, disappearing like the others had. A hollow space cracked inside me. Emptying me. Swallowing me into its depths. I was alone; no one was coming to help me. This was a trick. A nightmare.

"This isn't happening," I said, my voice cracking.

But it was. So, I took a step, my limbs heavy, and lumbered away from the emptiness, toward the only thing that existed. That tiny blip of a mountain on the horizon.

Chapter Twenty-One

The Sandman

I bent over Nora in her bedroom and placed two fingers against her throat. Her pulse slammed against my fingertips, her eyes moving frantically beneath their lids. I should have known she wasn't going to wait. If things were reversed, I wouldn't have. I wasn't conscious to catch her when she fell asleep. My power was tapped, leaving only enough to heal me, which meant she fell smack dab into enemy territory.

"Nora?" I whispered in her ear. I repeated it again, a little louder.

She wasn't screaming or thrashing about which had to be a good sign. Maybe the Weaver hadn't found her yet. Maybe there was still time to extract her from whatever nightmare she found herself in.

"Wake up, Nora. Please." I needed to shout, but footsteps pounded on the stairs. Nora's step-father called her name. I shook her shoulders. "*Please.*"

When she didn't stir, I gripped her headboard until my knuckles turned white. She was in too deep. Something had found her, and they weren't letting her go. My stomach twisted. "Hold on." I placed a soft kiss on each of her temples. "I'm coming."

***

Thunder rumbled over the beach. This time it wasn't the Weaver coming for me, not when what he really wanted was in his own backyard. The thunder was anger, my determination. I would tear down the walls of the entire Night World if I had to, and I would do it happily. I would run my power dry to save her. Anything. Whatever I had to do.

Baku paced the water's edge, his pupils dilated. I ran to his side and fell to my knees. "Nora is stuck in the Nightmare Realm." I ground my bare knuckles into the sand. If the Weaver touched her… But of course, he would; it's what he promised. I winced. "I don't know where. Will you find her? Bring her here?"

Baku's trunk reached out to rub the soft skin that healed over my acid burns.

I brushed him off. "I'm fine. I need to steal more dreams first, but I'll be right behind you."

He flicked some sand at me. *Don't do anything you'll regret*, he seemed to say.

"Don't worry," I assured him. What I was about to do was reckless, but I would never regret it. "I'm going to raze the ground they walk on."

Baku's wide lips curled ever so slightly before he leapt from the beach.

If I found Nora before the Weaver did, I wouldn't let her out of my sight until this was finished and she was safe. The nightmare she was living would never become part of her reality.

Chapter Twenty-Two

The mountain was a mere pinprick through the tears spilling freely down my face. The longer I walked, the smaller it became. The chasm in my chest deepened with every step. I would never make it. Never survive. Never find the Sandman. Never stop the Weaver.

Never. Never. Never.

I wasn't good enough. Strong enough. Smart enough.

Not enough. Not enough. Not enough.

It was all my fault Katie was hurt. People had died. The world would soon be doomed.

All my fault. All my fault. All my fault.

The guilt gnawed from the inside out until each cell in my body ached. I lacked in every way that mattered. Why had I ever thought this was a good idea? Who was I to save anyone, let alone an immortal, unearthly *magical* being like the Sandman?

Who did I think I was that I could stop someone like the Weaver? I was a Dream Keeper. A container. A custodian. Not a warrior. My entire life, I hadn't taken so much as a self-defense class, and it wasn't for lack of trying on my father's part. He was a black belt. A lot of good it did him in the end.

My knees gave out, and I plopped to the parched earth with a sob. "I'm sorry," I said to the emptiness. I wasn't sure what I was sorry for exactly—maybe everything. Maybe nothing. What did my apology mean to the people who lost their loved ones? *Nothing.* Another sob wracked my shoulders. *I* was nothing.

"That's her?" snapped a male's voice. "Look at her. She's pitiful."

I didn't move. My fate had come, and I was ready for this to end. They would take me to their lord and master where he would repay me for my treachery. In pain and blood and death. The exact things I had planned to repay him in. It was everything I deserved.

"Shh," urged a feminine voice.

I sighed and closed my eyes. Cold palms cupped my cheeks, injecting prickling pain down into my marrow. My eyes flew open again, my jaw hanging open in a silent scream. The agony was too much to muster a real one, stealing my breath, solidifying my body.

The woman kneeling before me removed her hands from my skin, taking most of the pain with her, and stood. She wore a red silk ball gown with strings of beads that draped off her shoulders. Large black wings jutted from her back like branches from a winter tree, breaking off in a million jagged directions. Her skin was so pale I could practically see through it, and long, pin-straight black hair fell to her waist with a crown of raven beaks perched on her head. Red flecked eyes roamed my face.

"Hello, child," she said. Her voice was surprisingly soft. "You do not fear touch, so you must not fear me."

The pain her hands caused lingered, but I said nothing about her blatant lie. Instead, I stared at the beautiful woman, feeling as if I were nothing more than a husk, and what did pain matter to an empty thing anyway?

"I am Rowan." She motioned behind her. "Kail."

A man with golden brown skin stepped forward wearing a white half-mask with a long-pointed beak that curled away from his nose. Black hair fell out of place, skimming just above his left eye, and his lips pressed into a straight line. Black lace-like designs ran over the shoulders and waist of a black trench coat. "Leave her, Ro."

"You do not fear the unknown, so you must not fear him," she continued in a light voice.

"Rowan."

She bent and grabbed the back of my sweater, forcing me to my feet. "She will be fine once she leaves this place."

"But *we* won't be," he snarled.

Rowan nudged my back, the pressure of her hands through my sweater a dull warning, until my feet moved of their own accord. I managed to stumble three feet before stopping dead. Two black horses with clawed feet and spiked tails snorted steam. Behind them stretched a mass of people hidden beneath black cloaks. Red mist coiled around their ankles, hissing against the flowing fabric. A collective moan rose to fill the air, and I scanned the line of nightmares.

"You do not fear blood," Rowan said. "So, you must not fear the Blood Army."

Kail lifted me onto the smaller horse and swung himself onto the larger. Being hauled away by a horde of nightmares should've terrified me, but the edges of fear were dull. As we marched away from the parched ground, part of my brain responded, a spark of something igniting deep in my brain. Feeling crept back into my mind and body, bit by bit. It seemed like it took forever but couldn't have been more than five minutes before we reached the foot of the mountain. I blinked back my surprise.

"See?" Rowan walked between the two horses, smug. "She's coming back already."

Kail harrumphed.

"What—" I clamped my mouth shut. The world slowly came back to me, falling in place like pieces of a puzzle. *What happened?* I wanted to ask but ignorance was a weakness I couldn't afford to display. Everything was a weakness here. Everything but me. I wasn't empty. I wasn't nothing. This wasn't my fault, and I *would* find the Sandman. I *would* fix things.

"You fear many things." Rowan smiled kindly. "All humans do. That was one of your plagues."

"The lightning bug," I said before I could stop myself. "He brought me there."

"If you do not fear a thing, it will not see you as other. It likely misread your fear of the Barren as a longing for it when you fled. Not all nightmares are highly intelligent. It thought it was doing you a service, I'm sure."

How long had they been watching me? And the Blood Army… The Weaver mentioned them once. Mentioned letting them devour my sister. I shifted in the saddle made of bone— *bone*—and the horse whipped his head around to nip at my ankle.

"You fear horses." A small smirk curled on Kail's lips. "In case that was unclear."

"Do I?" I sneered. I wanted to point out that this wasn't a horse. Horses had hooves, unlike this beast, but I had bigger problems.

We fell into silence, the only sound, the sizzling of blood droplets hitting the ground and fueling the mist that traveled around the army. *The Barren*, she called it. The place that sucked me dry, made me feel worthless and alone, had a name. If that was only one of the things I feared, I had no interest in meeting the others. I needed to escape sooner rather than later, but I was lucky to have survived as long as I had. These people were going to take me right to the Weaver. Why else wouldn't they hurt me? Another touch from Rowan would be enough to send me tumbling to the ground. I rubbed at my tingling cheeks. There had to be a way out of this.

Kail whispered to Rowan. She replied, but I couldn't hear well enough to understand over the surge of wailing from the Blood Army. I took the reins and gave the horse a small, steady tug. His claws dug into the ground, and he wheeled on me. A single fang shot out from his top gums. He arched his head, aiming for my thigh.

Rowan tsked, and the creature froze. "Do not try to escape, Dream Keeper. This is our realm." She rubbed the horse's velvety nose until the fang disappeared. "Even if Poz cooperated in carrying you away from us, there are eyes and ears everywhere. It would do you no good."

"Does *he* know I'm here?" I spat, sure if the Weaver saw everything, he would come to get me himself. Unless he wanted the will tortured out of me before I was dropped at his feet to save himself the trouble

"The Weaver? He awaits your arrival."

Of course, he does. I leapt from the ivory saddle and landed in the middle of the Blood Army. Their crimson mist instantly boiled me, turning the blood in my veins to a river of fire. A scream ripped from my throat, and I flailed, reaching desperately for the stirrup. The horse sidestepped me.

"Kail," Rowan ordered.

He jumped down beside me and lifted me from the ground. A dusting of the mist clung to my clothes. Itching. Burning. I was going to die. I clung to Kail's neck and gasped for breath. The faint hint of cloves calmed my scream. Called my mind forward. *It isn't real. None of this is real. It's all happening in my head.* But it was real. Terrifyingly real. The truth was like being dunked in an ice bath. I shuddered. I should never have taken those pills. Never.

Kail tossed me into the saddle of his own horse. "Brainless girl." He swung up behind me and gathered the reins. "I bet you won't be trying that again."

"Shut it," I grumbled, my voice scratchy.

"You..." He smiled wryly down at me. His eyes flashed through an array of colors—blue, yellow, red, green, brown—never settling on one for more than a second. "You *are* afraid of me. Just a little."

"Am not," I wheezed.

"Don't lie."

He jabbed his heels into the horse and, with Rowan back on her own steed, we galloped toward a stone tower with flowing blood taking the place of mortar. My breath caught. I would never get out of there. Not with the hundreds of soldiers stoking the mist around the base. I pinched my arm until I broke the skin. The pain was real, as real as it was in the mist, but it did nothing to pull me from sleep.

Kail chuckled. "Nice try."

"No one asked you."

He stared down at me, his eye color changing faster. "Better." He looked over at Rowan. "But not enough."

"It will be," she said, completely confident in her words.

I pretended to fidget and reached for the knife in the pocket of my fleece. "What will be what?" I asked.

"You will be." Rowan slid gracefully from her horse, her skirts puffing around her, and waved the army away. They moved in unison, turning around, seemingly floating along the mist on their way around the tower. "Come. It's safe to talk inside."

I cast another glance at the moving unit of cloaked nightmares. Their moans changed to a dull murmur. "Let me guess." I motioned to where the cloaked figures disappeared. Kail practically tossed me to the ground. I stumbled and scowled back at him, blowing the hair from my face. "Zombies?"

"The Blood Army is the Blood Army." Rowan's eyes narrowed. "Pray you don't run into a zombie."

Kail landed on his feet beside me, too close. He grinned. "After you."

Rowan opened the door and disappeared inside. I planted my feet. No way. I wasn't going in there. Not in a million years. No.

"Problem?" Kail asked.

I jumped sideways away from him, but his hand shot out and gripped my upper arm. I glowered at him, anger replacing the fear, and brought my knee up, hard, between his legs. With my free hand, I flicked opened one of the attachments on the knife. "I don't know, Kail. Is there?"

He groaned, his teeth bared under the hooked nose of his mask and tightened his grip on my arm. I would have a bruise later.

"You…"

My pulse throbbed in my temples, the rest of his sentence lost to the ringing in my ears. Sweat beaded on my upper lip, and I swung my arm up in an arch, driving the corkscrew into his left eye with a pop. There was no blood, but his remaining eye flashed so fast I couldn't catch any single color. The world slowed. I forgot how to breathe. To move.

He released my arm and staggered back, his steps uneven. "I will *gut* you," he howled. There wasn't time to decide if it was a legitimate threat before razor sharp agony blasted through my skull.

I knew nothing then. Only the spinning darkness of the fall.

Chapter Twenty-Three

The Sandman

Fire exploded from the mouth of the cave where Nora's sister was tortured. The heat from my magic curled over my shoulders and blew my hood around my face. Flames snapped and popped, spreading over the thorny brush, drowning out the screech from the serpent inside. I strode through it untouched. One person's dream was another person's nightmare, after all, and I was the sand's master no matter what form it took.

I had hoped Nora would return to the only place that was familiar to look for a way into my realm, but there was no trace of her. Cold dread filled my veins. If I had to draw the attention of every nightmare in this realm to find someone who knew her whereabouts, I would do it. Let the Weaver come for me. I had the power of a thousand dreams while he had broken threads.

Three of the scaled creatures living in the lake broke the surface, watching the blaze with hungry black eyes.

"Where is she?" I roared.

Two dove back into the depths. The third smiled.

Smiled.

Fury rumbled in my chest. The crack in my heart widened, the fissures racing throughout my body. If this creature wouldn't tell me where Nora was, it was of no use to me.

I flung a handful of sand at the water's surface and bubbles emerged from the bottom. Boiling. Scalding. I drew in a steady, satisfied breath. The scent of charred meat from behind me mingled with the wave of rancid seafood in front of me. I held my breath. The bodies of two dozen hidden nightmares bobbed to the surface, rocking between bubbles.

I turned my back on the pond, on the destruction, and walked away, my shoulders squared, with another handful of sand in my fist.

Chapter Twenty-Four

Nora

When I regained consciousness, it was in a bed of heavy silks. Sweeping sheer curtains rustled around the wooden bedposts in a nonexistent breeze. A dozen candles glowed on scrolled stands inside a corner fireplace. Their light flickered across deep red walls—the color of freshly dried blood—and danced across the dark wooden floor. Through the window, the grey skies had turned charcoal.

How long had I been out? More importantly, how long did I have left?

I flung back the warm blankets and pain seared its way through my skull. I pressed the heels of my hands against my temples with a hiss. *Rowan.* I took a steadying breath and pieced together what happened. The Barren already felt like a distant memory, but the blistering misery of the red mist was clear as day. So was what happened just before my head exploded.

I lowered my hands, flexing the one I used to stab Kail in the eye. It was a small consolation considering I was now trapped in enemy territory without a way to defend myself. I shifted to the edge of the mattress and peered over it. Cliché or not, I wasn't willing to bet on there being a literal monster under the bed. I snagged one of the six feather pillows and tossed it on the ground. When nothing lunged out to attack, I eased my feet down to the ground, my sneakers still tied tight, and leapt across the room to the single window.

My heart struck the ground. The Blood Army that followed Rowan and Kail wasn't the entire army; it was a mere fraction. A single drop of water in a deep well. There were thousands of them. Their mist coiled and rose, the steady hiss reaching me three stories up. Luckily their moaning had stopped.

"Crap." My breath fogged the window pane.

I was doomed. There was no way I was sneaking out. Not with so many of those things out there waiting. My blood pulsed in my ears, warning me. Telling me to remember what the mist could do and not to do anything stupid, but I didn't need a reminder. Still... If Rowan and Kail were handing me to the Weaver, I had to be in one piece. They couldn't allow me to boil alive if they heard my escape attempt end in agonizing screams. I swallowed hard. Either way, if I was going down, I would do it fighting. I ripped a sheet from the bed and wrapped it around my shoulders, knotting the fabric. Maybe it would help shield me from the mist once I got outside. The cloaks seemed to work for the nightmares anyway.

There was no door to the room, simply an archway into a hall lit with wall torches that burned green fire. The brown and black wallpaper boasted large medallions and between wide planks of hardwood floor oozed a bit of black sludge. "Crap," I muttered again, and gingerly eased onto my tip-toes.

My fingers skimmed the wall to keep my balance and the wallpaper shifted beneath my touch. I froze, squinting. It moved again. Bile rose to the back of my throat. The medallions weren't a design at all, but black tarantulas with their legs pressed tightly against their bodies. What I thought to be an off-white design at the center turned out to be a single unblinking eye on their abdomen. "*Crap, crap, crap.*"

Something cool licked my ankle. I leapt back, leaving tiny strands of the sludge reaching up from the floor, patting the ground in search of the foot they just touched.

A door swung open behind me and the goo darted back below the floor. Kail stood in the doorway, dangling my knife between his index finger and thumb. "Hello, again."

I ran as fast and hard as I could. My heartbeat drummed against the lingering pain in my temples, nearly blinding me. I swerved right, following the green lights, and thundered down a set of stairs. Three identical doors appeared at the landing where a moment ago there was another hallway. My knife whizzed past my head, pinning a tarantula to the wall with a tiny squeal.

"Perhaps I was wrong about you being completely pathetic," Kail said, sauntering down the last few steps. He smelled of rich spices with an undercurrent of cedar now instead of cloves. He approached slowly, carefully, like a tiger stalking its prey, and my feet slid back. He chuckled. "Perhaps not."

I spun to rip the knife from the wall, but he got there first. The arachnid hit the floor with a tiny *plop*. Another morphed from the wall, and my stomach flopped. "That's mine," I said, determined not to let him see how he affected me.

"Not anymore, Dream Keeper." His eyes were cold behind his mask. The one I stabbed had healed but remained steady on blue while his right eye flashed between colors.

I grabbed the long-pointed beak and tugged. The mask didn't budge. Curiosity prodded against a flash of fear. Was the mask actually part of his face or was it well secured? What did he look like underneath?

He swatted my hands away. "Excuse you."

"Let me out of here," I growled, refusing to acknowledge the blush that swept up the back of my neck.

"Oh, of course," he drawled. "Since you asked so nicely, let me show you the front door. Never mind all the trouble we went through to find you first. Never mind the risk we took bringing you here. That's all irrelevant."

I balled my hands into fists, ready to strike. More than ready.

"Save your strength, human. You'll need it."

He wasn't wrong, but all the strength in my body wouldn't do me any good if I was forever trapped here. So, I swung. My fist met only air, the momentum nearly throwing my body to the ground. I pressed my lips together and straightened myself. He was on guard against me now. My next attack would have to be subtle and well-timed.

"Rowan is waiting." He flicked the knotted sheet at my throat, and his top lip lifted into a sneer. "She has a tonic for your head. If you behave, I won't smash the cup before you have a chance to drink it."

I snorted. "Like I'd drink anything either of you offered me."

His lips turned down into a sarcastic frown. He raised a calloused brown hand up to my ear. And snapped his fingers. The sound crashed through my head. My stomach bottomed out, and every drop of blood drained from my face. I wouldn't give him the satisfaction of collapsing to the floor. *I wouldn't.*

He smirked. "Follow me." He started up the stairs, his black trench coat flaring with each step, but I stayed firmly planted in front of the three doors. "Pick the middle one," he drawled over his shoulder. "The endless free-fall is a particular favorite of mine, although the other two aren't half bad."

I stared at the doors again, weighing his words. It could be a lie. One of them could be the way out, and he was just trying to scare me into walking away, but somehow, I didn't think he would need to trick me. Judging by the size of his arms, he could toss me over his shoulder and carry me to Rowan without breaking a sweat. *He needs me alive.* I didn't doubt there were worse things here than the wall decor so if I wanted to stay in one piece, I had little choice but to go with him. At least for now.

"Asshole."

"Oh stop. You're going to hurt my feelings," he said, raising the pitch of his voice.

"I'll hurt *something*, but it won't be your feelings," I muttered.

He stopped and turned back to glare at me. "Are you coming?"

I slowly placed a foot on the bottom step without looking away from his flashing iris and gave him the finger. He huffed but said nothing.

***

We didn't speak as we passed through hallway after hallway. Each was identical, but I still got the feeling he was walking me in circles. If he was trying to make me lose my bearings, he succeeded. I wasn't even sure what floor we were on anymore, let alone which passageway. Not that it mattered—the Blood Army was still outside.

Think, Nora. Think.

Kail stopped so fast I rammed into him, his back solid as concrete. I rubbed my nose expecting to find blood, but the back of my hand came away clean.

"Inside." He pressed open a narrow panel in the wall.

I peered around him to find the warm glow of a regular fire lighting a richly decorated den. A brown leather sofa sat across from two matching chairs, a thick red throw rug beneath all three. The mantel above the fire shelved a massive clock. The hands shifted backward and forward, not pointing to numbers but strange symbols. "I'll pass, thanks."

He grunted and gripped my arm, shoving me into the room. Rowan stood in the corner, thumbing through a book. "How are you feeling?" she asked.

"Super."

"Drink that." She motioned to a clay cup with steaming liquid. "I need to speak to you with a clear mind."

I folded my arms. "Trust me, it's clear."

She set the book down and crossed the room with rustling skirts, her strange wings scraping the ceiling. She lifted the cup and held it out. "I don't need to poison you, Dream Keeper. If I wanted you dead, you would be."

I pursed my lips. The pain in my head wasn't *that* bad. It had already receded to a dull, aching pressure—nothing a couple Tylenol couldn't cure. Or maybe something a little stronger than Tylenol. *A lot stronger.*

Still, there was no way I was drinking anything they offered me. Maybe it wasn't poisonous, but that didn't mean it wouldn't have other side effects. Like sprouting gills or stealing my willpower. Plus, it was probably made from the liver of some sort of creepy crawly creature.

"Pass," I insisted in a flat voice.

Her eyes narrowed slightly before she set the cup back down and smoothed her features. "Sit. Please. We mean you no harm."

My eyebrows shot up but before I could contradict her, Kail snapped, "You stabbed me in the eye! You deserved what happened outside. And you leapt into the mist yourself so don't try pinning that on us."

"I thought I didn't need to fear you or the Blood Army," I accused Rowan. "You said I didn't fear being touched or blood, so I didn't need to be afraid."

"Without your fear, we have no desire to harm you, and we certainly get nothing from it, but that doesn't mean we can't." She pointed to the sofa again. "Sit."

I adjusted the sheet around my shoulders. "No."

"We just want to talk."

Kail barked a laugh from the doorway. "We can't trust her, Ro. Forget it."

"*You* can't trust *me?*" I shouted. "Are you joking? Everyone here wants to crack my head open like a walnut to find the dream the Sandman hid there. Then whatever's left of me will be tossed away or fed to something with a lot of pointy teeth."

Rowan hovered beside me, and I held my breath against the scent of black licorice wafting from her body. "We saved you from the Barren and brought you safely here. You tried to run twice now." She glared at the fabric tied at my neck with unspoken accusations of a third attempt. "And you stabbed my friend with your tiny knife. I rather think we're being quite accommodating."

Kail poked the area between my shoulder blades, and I stumbled to the center of the room. *Fine.* I would sit, I would listen to them, but my eyes scanned the room for potential weapons. Anything I could use to free myself before the Weaver arrived. If I was going to escape him, I needed the element of surprise. Given Rowan's ability, the Weaver would probably walk in and expect to see me sitting, resigned to my fate, on their couch. I had to be part of the shadow. To use his world against him.

Rowan perched on the edge of a chair across from me. "We want to work with you."

"What?" Books lined shelves, but nothing sharp. Nothing I could wield in a fight. "Me?"

"The Weaver..." Rowan glanced at Kail. "He forces us to do things."

"To kill people," Kail clarified.

"Most of us don't want to. Killing is unnecessary; it culls our source of energy and serves no purpose other than to be cruel." She ran her hands down the hair that cascaded over her shoulders. "We are not all evil."

I very much doubted that, but Rowan had my attention. "Did you kill my friends? Any of the people I knew?"

They exchanged a glance before shaking their heads.

My eyes narrowed. "But you know who did?"

"The Weaver killed them himself, except your two friends. He was busy with the Sandman at the time, so he delegated."

"I want names." As soon as the Weaver was dealt with, they would be next. It wouldn't be painless either. They would feel each twinge of pain I locked away. Each unshed tear.

"We want to make a deal with you." Rowan shifted, her hands folded neatly in her lap. "We all want the same thing."

"*We* is an overstatement," Kail grumbled.

My nostrils flared. *Focus.* "How would you know what I want?"

"You want the Weaver gone." Kail flung himself in the empty chair and rapped his fingers on the arm. "If he's dead, your friends and family will be safe. Your world. There would be no more waiting around for bindings to wear down and barriers to break. For the rest of your life, you could live free of this place."

I looked between them. Kail with the lower half of his face set, his shoulders squared and tight. Rowan, sitting as if she came straight from a finishing school two hundred years ago, her face blank. Waiting. Patient. What did they want me to say? It wasn't exactly a secret I wanted the Weaver dead or that I would try my hardest to make that happen, but if I was being honest with myself, I knew it was impossible. It was the idea that kept me going. Pushed me forward. Not the hope of it coming true.

"And?" I asked suspiciously.

"And." Rowan paused. "The Weaver would expect an assassination attempt from us. His defenses would be up and when we failed, he would kill us. But you? He wouldn't think twice about turning his back on you."

I blinked. Once. Twice. They were serious. A harsh laugh flew from my throat. "*Me?* You're asking *me* to kill him when you're the ones with the power here? This is a joke, right?"

Silence. Thick, suffocating silence.

Finally, Kail said, "I told you this wouldn't work. Now what? We can't kill her, but if he digs through her head, he'll find out we tried to betray him."

"She hasn't said no." Rowan wiped her hands on her skirt. "If she does this, so many people would be spared. *We* would be."

I gaped at them while they discussed me like I wasn't right in front of them. "Why would I want to spare either of you?"

"Because." Kail stood and strode to the mantle over the fireplace. He pressed a brick. A hole opened in the wall, and he removed a blade. It was no bigger than a hunting knife with glowing red liquid embedded in a long crystal that ran down the center. The metal handle was woven from black and gold, blue and silver, a patchwork of dreams and nightmares. The power sucked the air from the room. "We have this, and you do not. Without it, you may be able to bind him again, but we would be back in this position a few years from now."

Rowan nodded, smiling. "In exchange, we will take care of the nightmares that killed your friends."

I could do it; I could kill the Weaver. Avenge the people that died. Live without fear of more death. I could stop watching the shadows. The Sandman didn't think we should because of the balance, but with this, I could do it alone. But did I trust them? Enough to betray someone I *did* trust? Cold sweat trickled down my spine.

"I can't do anything without the Sandman," I said. *And he might be dead.* I balled my hands into fists.

Rowan quirked an eyebrow. "Then what did you come here for?"

Nerves prickled beneath my skin. She was right. Why did I come if it wasn't to do something about the Weaver? After I found the Sandman, what did I think we would do together? It wasn't enough to find him alive and prove the Weaver a liar. To stop this, I was going to have to help the Sandman put an end to the threat. But what if the Weaver hadn't been lying? I couldn't walk away from this chance.

"She thinks her boyfriend is dead," Kail said with a smirk.

The room spun. "He's not?" My extremities went numb, my vision blurring behind a lens of unshed tears.

"The Sandman is not dead," Rowan said slowly, her head cocked. "He left the cave for the Dream World. I don't know precisely where he is now, but it would be easy enough to track him down."

The lightness in my chest made me feel as if I were floating away, out of this horrible place toward something better. I gripped the couch cushion so hard my knuckles turned white. I wasn't floating anywhere. I was trapped here until they decided to let me go. Or not let me go, depending on how this conversation went.

Kail snorted and flipped my knife into the air, catching it.

I ground my teeth together. If he wanted my help, he had a strange way of showing it. Were the offer not so tempting, I would pry that ridiculous mask off his face and beat him over the head with it. But it *was* tempting. And they could get me back to the Sandman—something I was apparently unable to do for myself.

"What do you want me to do, exactly?" I asked.

Rowan's red-stained lips turned up. "With the Sandman at your side, it won't be impossible for you to reach the Weaver's Keep. Get the Weaver alone—that shouldn't be overly difficult either considering it's exactly what he wants—and use the blade. It contains both Dream and Nightmare magic, so it can kill both lords."

I glared at the blade. It could kill the Sandman, yet they hadn't used it. Why? Surely, they hated him as much as their lord did. Had they tried and failed? If so, I imagine they would be dead, or at the very least the Weaver would have heard of the attempt and confiscated the blade. Or killed them. Maybe both. If he would expect Rowan and Kail to try killing him, he had to know they would use such a weapon against him eventually.

But the answers scared me more than those questions did. This was my chance to take the Weaver down. Probably my only one since the Sandman was so adamant about rebinding him. I needed to believe they never tried using this against the Sandman if I was going to accept their help.

"The Sandman can't know about this plan," Rowan added.

"Why not?" I asked. I knew my own answer but if *they* didn't want the Sandman to know, there was a good chance I shouldn't be doing it. There was so much I didn't know about this place, about the creatures here... I could be walking into something I couldn't walk out of.

"He believes everything needs a counter," Kail explained. "That his mirror image must exist for things to work, but we are capable of ruling ourselves."

So, for the same reason I wouldn't tell him. I rapped my fingers on my thigh. "This plan doesn't seem like much of a plan."

"You'll figure it out if you want your revenge." Kail's voice was cool. Flippant.

I would do anything to spare my remaining loved ones the same fate as the others but lying to the Sandman didn't feel right. I wasn't sure I could lead him into the heart of the Nightmare Realm and go behind his back. He risked everything to help me bring Katie back. He would risk everything again to protect me and the Day World.

But, if the Weaver was gone... Really and truly gone...

"Is there even time for me to get to the Weaver before he's finished weaving?" I asked. All sense of time was lost to me, but it felt like an eternity since I crawled into my bed.

Rowan's wings scraped loudly against the back of the chair. "He's strong enough to fight, but he's still working. If he's going to face the Sandman and win, he'll want an overflow."

I nodded. He was still occupied then. "You'll take me to the Sandman?"

Kail laughed and Rowan leveled a look in his direction. "We cannot be seen helping you, of course. But we'll provide a guide tasked with taking you to the Weaver. He won't know that isn't your true destination. You'll know when it's time to part ways; listen to the Sandman's magic inside you. It will lead you in the right direction, and then an ally will locate you."

Listen to the magic? I didn't even know how to begin to find it. I narrowed my eyes. "That's ridiculously non-informative. How am I supposed to get away from this guide?"

"I'll return your knife before you go," Kail said, tossing a hand in my direction.

I narrowed my eyes at him. "You can't be serious."

"Do I look like I'm kidding?"

"Will you do this?" Rowan asked quickly. "Will you kill him?"

"I..." Would I? I couldn't promise anything, but I could try. I wanted the Weaver dead. Deciding what to tell the Sandman could happen later, after I saw he was okay with my own eyes. I took a deep breath and let it out slowly. "Give me that thing."

Rowan smiled. "Excellent."

Kail turned back to the strange clock and collected a sheath. "Don't take the blade out until it's time to use it, or the Weaver will know you have it."

"You'll need better clothes before you go too," Rowan said.

Kail dropped the light knife on my lap and strode from the room without another word.

"Ignore him," Rowan whispered. "He thinks this is too dangerous."

"He's not the only one," I grumbled. But it didn't matter. Battles weren't won by cowards.

Chapter Twenty-Five

The Sandman

My footsteps echoed through the narrow canyon. Dull yellow stone rose a hundred stories on both sides, the sky nothing more than a shard of grey, yet its light reached all the way to the bits of crumbling boulders littering the path. I surveyed the walls from beneath my hood and ground my teeth. Seventy-one nightmares dead, nearly half my power depleted, and still no sign of Nora.

Rocks tumbled down the canyon walls, kicking up a cloud of dust. My heart lurched, and I fisted sand from my satchel. "I know you're there," I called, and broke into a jog. "Show yourself."

Heavy silence rang while the debris settled. The hair on the back of my neck stood on end, and I screeched to a halt. Cracks rent the air. The ground lurched, nearly knocking me to my feet, and the mountainside trembled. Pebbles rained down, and I flung myself behind a boulder. They pelted me one after another like nails on wood, puncturing and gouging through my clothes. I tugged my hood down to protect my face, dropping the sand. A dust storm devoured me. Blinded me. I held my breath and waited with strained ears.

Forever passed before the canyon finally cleared again. I wiped away the blood beading on my hands and cracked my neck. A grinding swelled in the canyon, plucking at my nerves. The sand I held when I took shelter was now scattered at my feet under a layer of powder. I leaned forward to rest on my knees and grabbed another handful from my sack. Whatever nightmare was on the other side of the boulder had one chance to tell me where Nora was. *One.* Just like the others.

But when I stood, my blood froze. A twenty-foot man made of solid yellow rock glared down at me with molten eyes. He staggered toward me and more gravel flew from his joints. I planted my feet. The sand hummed in my hand, and I squeezed it tight. When I opened my fingers, it spilled to the ground, forming a wooden crate with a black fuse poking through the wooden slats.

"Where is the Dream Keeper?" I bellowed.

He bent, ready to tackle, and took a deep, gasping breath. The crevices in his abdomen glowed, steam leaking out from between his lips. It didn't matter what came next. I wouldn't ask him again.

I flicked a pinch of sand at the crate and snapped my fingers. Sparks flew from the fuse. I planted my feet, locked my knees, and lowered my head. The creature gurgled and took another step forward. *Good.* The closer the better.

The fuse disappeared. Sand burst from my satchel and wrapped itself tightly around my body in protection. A moment of calm vengeance filled my heart.

Then the canyon ignited into fiery chaos.

Seventy-two nightmares dead.

Chapter Twenty-Six

Nora

Rowan led me back through the tarantula lined walls. Now that I met her approval, dressed in a form-fitting black T-shirt with a leather vest, tight cotton pants, and boots that came halfway to my knee, it was time to leave. The blade rested against my spine, the handle an inch from the bottom hem of the vest. When the time came, I would simply need to flick a clasp and unsheathe the weapon.

Already I was questioning my decision to go along with this disaster of a plan. The idea of killing the Weaver was appealing but to risk my life to do it? Hadn't I given enough?

But the entire world was at stake. How could I turn away from that? I was only one person. If I failed, millions upon millions would be affected. Including me, if I managed to get out of here alive. I forced my muscles to relax. This was this right thing to do. So, after I found the Sandman, we would go to the

Weaver's Keep with a plan to bind him. A plan I would deviate from. The lies I would need to tell curdled in my stomach like sour milk.

Rowan opened a side door at the back of their bloody tower. An icy wind blasted me in the face, and an explosion rumbled somewhere in the distance. I shivered at the smoke pluming in the distance.

"Follow Elkmar and no other," Rowan said.

Something clicked and clomped toward us. A solid shadow, faded in parts and darker in others, lumbered forward. It had a humanoid body with cow hooves for feet and long, frog-like fingers. The head was that of a gazelle, complete with two ribbed horns and empty eye sockets. With knees that bent backward, it didn't walk so much as creep.

I shook my head. "Tell me that's not Elkmar."

"He won't touch you," she assured me with a casual wave of her hand.

The creature opened its mouth and made a series of clicks. I winced at the stale, musty odor wafting off of him. "Comforting."

"Take the advice—follow no one else." Kail bumped against my back, the point of his mask grazing my shoulder. "There will be others that want to take credit for finding you. Don't listen to them, no matter how friendly they appear on the surface."

I snorted. It was good advice, except I would add them to the list of nightmares that wanted to use me. The others to gain favor with the Weaver, Rowan and Kail to kill him. Although it was completely possible they would betray me. What could they tell him that he didn't already know though? That I wanted him dead? That I planned on trying? He wasn't stupid. The only thing they could tell him was that I had the blade, but I saw no advantage to that.

Unless their plan was to turn the Sandman against me.

Let them try. If he learned I was keeping a secret from him, he would forgive me just as I forgave him. Hopefully. Worst case scenario, he would never forget my betrayal, but even then, he would never actively work against me.

Kail twisted me around and draped the knotted sheet back around my shoulders. "Don't forget your cape."

I flung my fist into his stomach and, when he doubled over, I grinned, tossing the fabric back at him. It wasn't as damaging as I had hoped my next assault to be, but it would do. Rowan ran her red-flecked eyes up and down my body. A cold sweat broke out against her examination. "What?" I snapped.

She shrugged, her skeletal wing shifting. "Nothing."

"I don't trust you," I said slowly, enunciating each syllable, and narrowed my eyes.

Another shrug.

Kail straightened. His blue eye fixed on me, his other flashing so fast the colors blurred together. He grabbed my hand, slammed the Swiss Army knife into my palm, and shoved me out the door. "Prove me wrong. Be braver than I think you are."

Elkmar clicked again, and the Blood Army parted. My muscles burned with tension, and I followed him away from the bleeding tower. Away from Rowan and Kail and their penetrating gazes. I knew then, with their eyes like daggers on my back, that they wanted something other than the Weaver's death, that they were using me to get more than they let on, but as long as the Weaver was dead and the dream inside me was safe, I couldn't care less what hellish plan they wanted to unleash on their brethren. Let this realm implode—I would never be back.

***

Elkmar walked a single step ahead of me. If I slowed to put space between us, he slowed with me. If I inched to the side, so did he. The proximity filled me with tension. It balled in my center, a twisting, aching thing. Pricks of cold broke through the heat radiating from his body, but at least he didn't have fangs or rotting flesh like the other nightmares I'd seen.

I didn't know how long ago we left the tower. The mist of the Blood Army had long since disappeared from the horizon, and my feet threatened to cramp inside my boots. The scenery hadn't changed. I was positive that was the same rock we passed five times now, but Elkmar continued with purpose. So, I followed. And I waited. Rowan said I would know when to run, but I didn't see how. And if I wasn't to trust anyone, how would I know the ally they mentioned? Maybe if I was a nightmare I could sense it, but I wasn't. I was just a human, a Dreamer, with no special abilities to my name. I crossed my arms, rubbing away a chill.

The blade they had given me wasn't heavy enough to weigh down the back of my vest, but it was sturdy enough to scrape against my spine when I moved the wrong way. I practiced masking my discomfort as we traveled. The leather was stiff yet flexible, hiding the blade in its decoratively sewn lines. The fabric smelled like *them* though. Bitter, and a little bit sweet. Like the bargain I struck. For all the Weaver had done and all he planned to do, I would gladly shove the dagger into his chest. Even if it cost me everything.

But Rowan and Kail were right about something else too. The Sandman wouldn't like it. He explained how he and the Weaver shouldn't kill each other because the universe wouldn't like it or some nonsense, but he never mentioned whether they were vulnerable to others. Maybe it was because he didn't know about the blade or he assumed no one else would be strong enough to get the job done, but I doubted that. On this account, the nightmares were more honest than he was. I dug my fingers into my upper arms. This once, I was going to do something I knew deep down was wrong. Something that was also right.

Elkmar screeched to a halt, and I slammed into him, flying backward. I caught myself on my palms, but the impact still sent pain racing up my tailbone. "What the—"

My voice stuck in my throat, and Elkmar leaned awkwardly over my outstretched legs. Silver flashed overhead, the source hidden behind my guide's form. The air rang with the sound of slicing metal. Glowing orange sparks rained down on us, and I ducked my head.

Elkmar let out a single low click and lowered into a crouch. That's when I saw it. A woman's naked torso connected to two scissor blades at the hip and another at each wrist. She stepped forward, steady on the pointed ends, and Elkmar lunged. I stayed frozen on the ground as they collided. The scissor woman fell sideways, stabbing at my shadow guide, and they rolled with each other.

I scrambled to my feet. Was this it? Should I run? Elkmar was distracted, but I was no closer to finding the Sandman than I was when I first fell asleep. His magic wasn't calling me in any specific direction. My head was void of everything but the rapid thud of my pulse.

I couldn't chance missing my moment though. With no idea where I was headed, I bolted toward the distant forest. It didn't matter what I was running toward as long as it bought me enough time to gain my bearings and catch my breath.

The sound of scraping metal faded last, but even then, the memory of it grated against my ears like rusted gears trying to turn. I kept going over the rocky landscape until I tripped over my own feet and skidded across the ground into a shallow puddle of oily blue liquid. Gagging on the scent of rotten eggs, I charged to my feet, my body screaming in protest.

A drip fell in front of my face, sending ripples across the surface of the puddle. Then another and another. I knew I shouldn't look up, but my eyes lifted anyway. A thin rope nailed to a tree held a giant, translucent pod aloft. Red veins snaked across the surface. Inside, a school of goldfish swam in circles, their mouths open wide in silent screams. Their scales fell off one at a time and floated to the surface where they bubbled and foamed over the lip.

I winced and backed away, straight into something solid. Elkmar glowered down at me, a puff of smoke flying from his nostrils. "Hey," I said in a light tone. "I... got lost."

The empty eye sockets narrowed, and he flung his head back the way we came. No doubt he expected me to follow when he turned, but I inched toward the blue puddle. Pulling the Swiss Army knife from my pocket, I sawed at the rope holding the pod up. I leaned my weight into the tree, and the coarse rope burned my raw, scraped hands. If the water inside was as slippery as it looked, maybe it would trip up Elkmar long enough for me to hide. I gritted my teeth against the guttural scream building in my chest.

A shadow fell over me from above, and I sawed faster. Hooves clacked against the stone. Elkmar must have noticed I wasn't behind him. I wasn't brave enough to look. Abandoning the rope with a single strand intact, I ran again. There was another set of clicks followed by a squelch which I could only assume was the pod, but still, I didn't glance back.

I ran until my calves cramped and my lungs begged for air. Until the endless rocky scenery gave way to a grassy plain dotted with an array of colorful wildflowers. Insects buzzed harmlessly from one to another. At first glance, they weren't any different than the ones in the Day World, and I wasn't about to get close enough to discover their differences. Every few feet, tall metal posts rose into the air, disappearing into a cover of grey clouds.

I slipped between them and collapsed on a patch of bare dirt. *Think*, I told myself. There was a way out somewhere—I just had to find it. Unless... Dread slithered into my limbs, making a home for itself beside the quivering muscles. Unless the sand was the only way into the Dream Realm, and I gave it all to Katie. Not that I could have wielded it anyway. My eyes closed for the briefest moment, and I grappled with my fate. Why had I taken those pills? *Why?* When would they wear off?

A breeze kicked up around me paired with a soft fluttering. My eyes popped open in time to see a wave of bees flee from the pink and yellow flowers nearby. *Now what?* I was careful not to move in case whatever it was hadn't noticed me yet. Something cooed. A soft, happy sound, and I pressed myself into the ground. A stronger breeze skated over the field, the flowers trembling. Then a hooked beak nuzzled the top of my head. My breath caught. Another coo. Above me, a green parrot the size of an ostrich tilted its head back and forth. Black eyes reflected my disheveled appearance.

Don't eat me, I urged silently, not daring to speak.

Its clawed feet scraped lazily across the ground, tearing up a row of flowers. It seemed to have no interest in me other than curiosity, but that could be part of its charm. A lure. I eased up onto my elbows and looked harder at my surroundings while keeping the bird in my peripheral vision. All around me, more metal posts rose, forming a circle. A shifting in the clouds revealed a swinging perch. *A cage.* I was in its cage.

Something black and yellow galloped around the outer limits of the bars. The parrot squawked. Its wings beat furiously, and it soared into the air, the wind blowing dirt in my eyes. "Wake up, wake up, wake up," I begged myself. I could try again. I could get the Sandman's pouch back from Katie and pray there was enough left for me to get to the beach.

The blur halted on the other side of the cage and stared at me. I blinked. "Baku?" Relief washed over me so quickly I was sure I would faint.

The chimera motioned me toward him with a bob of his head. I struggled to my feet, feeling every tiny scrape and bruise. My legs wobbled with each step toward the Sandman's friend. The bird's eyes burned into my back in what felt like a warning. Perhaps it was—perhaps the bird expected I would be eaten like it would have been.

"Where is he?" I slipped through the cage bars beside him. "Is he okay?"

Baku nodded.

A breath fell from deep in my chest, taking a slice of anxiety with it. "Where is he? How do I get there?"

Baku turned slowly, his trunk reaching over to skim each bar as we passed. The bird flew into a frenzy of beating wings and high-pitched cries. I bit the inside of my cheek. There was no choice but to trust Baku as the Sandman did if I wanted to escape, but I couldn't forget what he was. A predator. I might not have been on the menu but letting myself become too comfortable seemed dangerous.

Chapter Twenty-Seven

The Sandman

The hollowness in my chest ached, a dull, throbbing pain, begging for relief. I sat on the edge of my two-walled pavilion and shrugged out of my tunic. It smelled of iron and death. Remnants from 164 nightmares decorated the fabric, but I was still no closer to finding Nora. My muscles ached, and I kicked off my boots, contorting this way and that to remove the rest of my soiled clothes. I would cleanse the sand later. There wasn't time to waste washing myself, let alone the beach. As soon as I recharged enough to steal more dreams, I had to go back.

I leaned across the pillows and dragged a clean pair of pants from a built-in drawer on the wall. I tugged them on without standing up. The pillows cradled me, and sand crept up to my chest. The magic murmured against my tattoo. My eyes fluttered shut but flew open again when my imagination threw pictures of Nora's face skewed in agony across my lids. If I could, I would take the dream from her now. Turn their attention to someone else, *anyone* else, long enough for me to rescue her. But she would have to give me permission. She had asked if I would be willing to, not if I would, and as small as it was, there was a difference. Besides, she was clear that day in the attic when she said she wanted to keep it. Even if there was the hint of consent before, she recanted it.

"Sandman!"

And now I was hearing Nora's voice. I winced, pressing further into the pillows.

"Sandman?"

I jerked into a sitting position. Nora ran toward me clad completely in black, her blond hair pulled back in a loose braid. It had to be an illusion. A nightmare disguised as my deepest wish. The barriers around the beach must've worn down when I was busy in the Nightmare Realm, but finding Nora was more important. If the barriers to the Day World were in working order, she would be safe when I woke her.

I called the sand up to my hand and closed my fingers around the handle of a whip. The light-weight thong coiled beside me. The nightmare was two feet away when she lunged. I braced myself for the attack. For claws or teeth. But none came. My grip loosened on the handle, and Nora's arms wrapped around me. She buried her face in my neck, her shoulders shaking. She must have been crying because her cheeks were slick against my skin.

It was really her. I dropped the whip and pressed her to me. "Nora?"

"The Weaver said you were dead," she whispered. "I didn't want to believe him but when I fell asleep, you weren't there."

"I was unconscious. Why didn't you wait for me?"

She paused, and her arms tightened around me. "What if you never came?"

"I'll always come. You know that." I leaned back and smoothed the tears from her cheeks with my thumbs. She nodded but doubt still lingered in her eyes. A dull worry. "You're okay? Nothing hurt you?"

"I'm still in one piece." She hesitated, then recounted her journey so fast I had trouble keeping up. "Then Rowan and Kail came with the Blood Army—"

"The Blood Army?" I blurted. I scanned her over for wounds, but her fingers dug into my biceps, drawing my attention back to her face. To the dirt smudged against her freckles and the pieces of hair falling out of place. My heart cracked. "Why didn't you wake up?"

She pressed her lips into a straight line. "I'm fine."

I wanted to demand to know what happened, to know which nightmares I had to kill first for trapping her, but that wasn't us. Nora and I had never forced the other to talk. Pushed maybe, but never demanded, so I bit my tongue. *Later.* After we were finished binding the Weaver. "Where did you get these?" I plucked at the sleeve of her leather vest.

"Rowan."

My eyes narrowed. "Why would she give you clothes?"

"She and Kail helped me escape the Barren." Nora looked behind me, the moonlight reflected in her green eyes. "I wasn't sure I would see this place again."

Neither was I. My hands ran up and down her arms. Feeling her. Memorizing her. Her legs straddled mine, the heat from her hands now warming my neck. *Rowan and Kail helped her escape.* Why? I opened my mouth to find out, but she spoke first.

"Why did you keep this place hidden?"

Because I didn't want to share this place with her or anyone else. At first because I knew I shouldn't get too close to the Dream Keeper but, when I realized I already had, I needed this sanctuary more than ever. I came here every time my chest ached with want of someone I would never have. The one person I shouldn't want. But I couldn't admit that, so instead I shrugged.

"We have to finish this," she said in a flat, quiet voice. "Now. Before it's too late."

"There's time to regroup."

"No." The word was sharp as a nail.

I blinked, my heart squeezing. "Nora, are you sure you're okay? I can bind the Weaver alone. I've done it before."

"Your energy wasn't spread all over the Night World before," she said matter-of-factly.

She wasn't wrong. I was stronger the first time. Without warding every entrance to the Day World and protecting her dreams, I might've been able to rebind the Weaver a long time ago. If I had bothered to check in with him before now, I wouldn't have to. "I'm sorry I brought you into this," I said. "I didn't know things would end like this."

"I'm sorry too." Her forehead *thunk*-ed on my shoulder.

I stroked her hair. "What do you possibly have to be sorry for?"

"Lying by omission?" She tensed against me. "I wasn't trapped here because of a nightmare. I took three of my mother's sleeping pills tonight to make sure I didn't wake up before I had time to find you."

"Nora." My hand stilled, my fingers twined in the base of her braid. "You shouldn't have done that. What if you needed to wake up to survive? What if the pills hurt your body?"

"I know, okay?" She shuddered. "Trust me, I know."

There wasn't a doubt in my mind that she did. Or that she would wake up right then if she could, and maybe never come back. I rested my chin on her head. The bittersweet scent of nightmares clung to her, and I kissed her hair.

"You said Rowan and Kail helped you escape," I said gently, trying not to think of what they could have done to her.

She nodded.

That didn't make any sense. They were the head of the Weaver's largest force. They should have taken the Blood Army and marched her straight to his doorstep. The only person more powerful than Rowan was the Weaver himself—she would never risk her life to betray him.

And Kail.

I never really understood his role in things. Rowan's second, her friend, maybe her lover. They were a team, but when I faced them before binding the Weaver, he seemed almost hesitant to fight me. The unknown was his forte, however. If I spent a hundred years studying him, he would still remain a mystery.

But one thing I knew, whatever happened to Nora in the Nightmare Realm, Rowan and Kail would never risk losing her. Delivering the most wanted person to the Weaver would earn them an express ticket to the Day World once the gates were open or grant them creatures to torture. Whatever struck their fancy. But to let her go? It was impossible.

"When can we go back?" Nora asked, glancing at my tattoo. "Are you ready now or do you need more time to recharge?"

"Slow down." I understood her anxiety but rushing into things would only lead to failure. Her mind would crack wide open for the Weaver if we were caught, but not before he made sure I was far away, unable to help. "I'm not sure if it's a good idea for you to come with me."

She tensed on top of me. "You can't stop me."

"No," I agreed. She was her own person; I wouldn't force her to stay, even if I thought it was for her own good. Even if I wanted to, she would probably find a way to go on her own. It was safer if we stuck together.

"Then what's your plan?"

There was only one plan—the one where I went alone. What could I ask her to do that I wouldn't hate myself for later? How much risk could I expect her to take on? "First we'll have to break into the Weaver's Keep and steal more thread."

"I still have the other two," she said.

I shook my head. "We'll need more—whatever he's woven. Then, once the Weaver's inside his Keep, I'll wrap the thread around the building to trap him inside his own nightmare. It won't take him long to break out of it, but it should buy enough time for me to get close to him and reinforce the binding."

She stilled. "I'll get the thread then. If I'm inside, we know he will be too."

"Absolutely not," I said. Her fingers pressed into the tender muscle at the back of my neck. In a softer tone, I added, "I won't use you as bait."

"Why not? It makes sense."

I shook my head. "I'm not trapping you in the nightmare with him. What do you think the Lord of Nightmares could possibly fear that wouldn't destroy you? Besides, if he gets you, this whole thing will have been for nothing."

"I'll get out. Don't worry."

"Don't worry?" I laughed, mirthless. "You're asking the impossible of me."

Nora lifted her head from my shoulder and looked me in the eyes. A clear, determined expression steeled her face. "Don't think I'm not just as worried about you. The Weaver won't kill you but that doesn't mean he can't do something worse. Besides, what else do you want me to do?"

Stay away. But I knew she wouldn't. She had lost too much and come too far to turn back now. My gaze fell to her mouth. Neither of us spoke, and the air thickened with panic-fueled urgency. This could be our last moment together—the eye of our hurricane. On the other side waited a storm capable of destroying everything and everyone.

Nora shifted, bringing her calves closer to my thighs. Her hands trailed down the edges of my chest. My breath hitched. She lowered her lips to mine, and I leaned in to better meet them, clutching her waist. I drank in the taste of her, the feel of her, savoring each moment. Committing it to memory.

Her fingers blazed a path lower and lower. My grip tightened, and she arched into me. A groan escaped my throat before I could stop myself. She reached the edge of my waistband, and my heart threatened to explode, but it still wasn't the right time. She was nervous and afraid of our return to the Nightmare Realm. If we weren't about to face our enemy, I doubt she would want to move so fast. Not when we hadn't talked about a relationship. I didn't want right now with her—I wanted always. And I wouldn't get that by messing things up right out of the starting gate.

I stilled her hands. "We can't."

Her brows lowered, her breath uneven. "I thought..."

"It's not that I don't want to." *How I wanted to.*

She brushed the hair from my forehead. "If you're worried because I've never been with anyone before, I'm not afraid. And if things don't go well, we might never—"

"Nora." I winced. She wasn't going to make this easy. "It has nothing to do with that. But… we can't. Not yet. Things won't go wrong; we have time."

You terrify me, I wanted to say. *What you could do to me if you woke up a day, a week, a month from now and realized you were confused. That it was all an awful mistake.*

"Besides, you might change your mind about having the dream taken away," I skimmed my knuckles down her cheek. "Even if you decide to keep it, there's a chance you'll never want to see me again. After you've had time to process everything and realize what I did to you by making you a Dream Keeper, you could very well hate me."

She took my hand before I could pull it back, keeping it against her cheek. "You're not the only one with feelings on the line, Sandman. If my only choice was between my sanity and losing you, I would keep this dream until the day I died. It's other people's lives that are in danger because of what I am, but I already told you, I want to keep it. Do you think I don't love you? Do you think I kissed Ben for any reason other than that he reminded me of you? That he *was* you? You may have realized it first but that doesn't make my feelings any less true now. I'll never be able to break your heart without breaking my own. Why do you think I'm going through all of this? To save people, yes, but also to make it safe for us to stay together."

My heart soared, only to slam against an invisible ceiling and crash back down around me. She loved me, but she shouldn't risk herself like this to be with me. My future was a lot longer than hers, and if I regretted any part of tonight, I would never forgive myself.

I leaned forward and nuzzled her neck, placing a soft kiss at the hollow of her throat. "After we take care of the Weaver, I'll do whatever you want. I'll take the dream if you ask me to. I'll disappear or stay. We can go back to the way things were or we can finish this." I laid my forehead on her collarbone. "All I want is for you to be happy and safe again."

Her hands landed gently on my back, tracing lines up and down the sides of my shoulder blades. It warmed me from the inside out, drawing out my worries until I felt boneless. I leaned away from her. She needed an outlet for her anxiety as much as I did, and just because we weren't going to take our relationship to another level, that didn't mean my body couldn't offer her some comfort.

Her eyes widened when I pressed her palm against my tattoo. The bit of my magic within her stirred with recognition and rose to meet mine. She sagged against me, her breath skating over my shoulders and down my back. "Lay down with me," she said in my ear, shifting from my lap.

I eased back into the pillows and did as she asked. We faced each other, and her hand found my chest again. Her head came to rest in the dip near my shoulder, her nose against my neck. I rested a hand carefully on her hip, my other rising to play with her hair. A sneakered foot slipped between my ankles. I sighed silently, my heart both calm and frantic. I would gladly stay cocooned together like this until the sky fell around us, but that wasn't possible.

"Tell me where to find the loom," she said against my skin.

My eyes slid shut. I told her everything I knew about the Weaver's Keep and what we might expect to find when we got there, but even I didn't know the extent of what awaited us. A lot could change in five years.

Chapter Twenty-Eight

The Sandman asked me to keep my eyes closed for the trip to the Weaver's Keep. The less afraid I was, the less attention we would attract, but each sound that reached my ears sent fear rushing to the surface. Clicks and scrapes, hisses and growls. I was glad I couldn't see what was making them. Gladder still that nothing decided to risk an attack as he led me blindly over the ever-changing terrain. It didn't help that our plan was riddled with holes we couldn't fill without knowing exactly what we would find when we arrived.

There would be sentries, of course. With the Weaver working, he would need extra protection, especially if he sensed the Sandman coming. *When* he sensed him.

Really, our success hinged on how well the Sandman stalled him, so I could get inside through the basement window. There, I would work my way up the hidden staircase to the top of the tower where the loom was. *Do not use the outer stairs*, he warned. The Weaver might notice and go after me instead of him. The same for the patrols. I pressed a hand against my back pocket where I tucked the skeleton key the Sandman made in case of locked doors.

The skin on my back was raw where the knife chaffed through my shirt. It was a good thing the Sandman stopped us from going too far. What had I been thinking? If my clothes started to come off along with his and he saw it, everything would have fallen apart. But I *hadn't* been thinking. My mind completely shut down and the urge to be close to him took over. It still lingered in the pit of my belly. He was right to stop me, and not just because of the knife.

My treachery seemed so much worse beside him. The sensation his touch created, the way my heart flopped, I was risking it all. I hadn't realized I was doing all this, in part, for us until I said it. If nothing else, the panic made my real feelings for him crystal clear. Protection for the Day World mattered, but I would have it whether I went with his plan or stuck with mine. The chances of the Sandman forgiving me for killing the Weaver seemed smaller the longer I spent with him. Smaller and deadlier. After losing so much already, losing him would destroy me.

"We're almost there," he said in a soft, reassuring voice, his breath warm against my temple.

I nodded, sweat beading on my upper lip. *Almost there.* The odds of surviving this wasn't in our favor; these could be my last few moments with the Sandman. I inched closer until my arm pressed against his. "Is that supposed to be comforting?"

"That depends. Was it?"

I laughed dryly. "Not particularly."

"Then I lied. We're so far away that our feet will probably fall off before we make it to the Keep."

I nudged him with my side. "Oh, good. I was worried this would be too easy, but if we're going to fight the Weaver without feet…"

He chuckled. "I'm glad I could clear that up for you."

I smiled, but it didn't last long. I tightened my grip on his arm. "In case this doesn't work, can you promise me something?"

He paused for a moment before asking, "What?"

"Two things, actually." I swallowed. "If the Weaver gets me, take the dream. After seeing Katie and… and learning what's out there… I don't want to be responsible for destroying my world. Take it somewhere safe."

"He's not going to get you," he said in a sure, solid voice. "I won't let him."

I opened my eyes and focused on him, ignoring the dark swirling storm clouds surrounding us. "Promise me anyway."

He pressed his lips into a tight line. "What's the second thing?"

"Take care of my family."

"No." He squeezed my hand so hard that my fingers straightened. "I won't promise you either of those things because it won't come to that. We'll bind him, and you'll wake up safe in your bed."

"Sandman—"

"You will." His voice was hard. Final.

I blew a frustrated breath through flared nostrils. "Wouldn't it be easier to kill him?"

"You know I can't." He looked straight ahead, his eyes glazing over.

"But I can," I said quietly.

His mouth opened, and he paused. A thought flashed through his eyes, harsh and unspoken, before he shook his head. "Don't get any crazy ideas. We're going to bind him. It's safer for everyone that way."

I studied the grim lines on his face. That was as close as I would come to asking permission. I would obviously never get it, but I didn't need his blessing. He said himself the balance would find a way to compensate. Kail was right when he said the nightmares could govern themselves. I was sure someone else could step up as their leader, and on the plus side, there would be no new creatures.

The Sandman stopped at the edge of an empty moat and crouched in the tall grass. I followed suit, batting a cattail from my face. On the other side of the ditch rose a black marble building veined with gold. Half of the rectangular third floor was domed, while the other half was surrounded by glassless arched openings. A simple wooden staircase ran up both ends to allow access to the upper floors from the outside. Going through the basement seemed a waste of time when there was such a direct route. I bit my lip. It was important to stick to the plan. At least this part of it.

"I thought it would be bigger," I whispered.

"It was. A lot of it was destroyed during our last battle." The Sandman's gaze swept over the other side of the ditch. There was no sign of nightmares, large or small. "The loom is in the dome. I'm going to distract them over there." He nodded to the far end. "The basement window is there." He pointed to a small window just big enough for me to fit through at the base of the building. "Hurry inside as soon as you think it's safe. I'll keep them away long enough for you to get in and get the thread, then I'll meet you in the open tower."

Just like we said an hour ago. "But there aren't any nightmares."

"They're here," he promised.

Hiding. Waiting. A chill ran over me. What would I do when the moment came? Kill the Weaver? Help bind him? The chance may not present itself to use the knife Kail and Rowan gave me. Then I wouldn't have to decide. But if it did... I cleared my throat. "How am I supposed to get to the tower from the dome?"

"There's a hatch. You can't miss it once you're inside."

"Okay." I eyed the path to my destination, and ice prickled along my skin.

The Sandman hooked my chin with his finger and turned me toward him. Looking at him hurt. It made me question everything. Doubt it all. Was I a murderer? Could I do this and not lose myself? Lose us?

"Be careful," he said, his voice soft, wistful.

"You too." His eyes traveled over my face, drinking me in like he would never get another chance. The threat of tears burned, but I blinked them away. I would see him again. *I would.* And one way or the other, we would sort things out. "I love you."

He drew a sharp breath before pressing his lips to mine. It was a hard, desperate kiss that was over as quickly as it came. "I love you too."

Then he was gone, running away from me with a satchel of sand at his hip.

I crouched in the grass and held my breath. The moment he disappeared around the corner, the world felt as if it stopped. My ears strained against the silence, the hair on the back of my neck lifting. Nothing. I shifted to the balls of my feet. Was he wrong? Was nothing waiting? Or, more likely, was there an ambush? My lungs ached, and I released the breath I forgot I was holding. We never agreed on a signal and if I waited for one, I might not make it on time. I crept from my hiding spot.

A series of popping clicks raked the air, and a shadow moved in the open tower. Four long finger bones reached up over the sill. The nightmare launched itself over the edge, and I slammed a hand over my mouth before I could scream. Both two-fingered hands were attached to straight ivory bones held together at the elbow with a swiveling joint. The head was distinctly human but four times the size with a mass of flowing brown hair. She slithered down the side of the brick, her body nothing but an exposed spine, proportionate to her skull. It sliced through the air, sliding back and forth like a snake, and hit the ground with a crunch. She shot around the corner of the building where the Sandman disappeared, using her bony, pronged fingers to hurtle forward.

The moment she was out of sight, I raced headlong through the ditch and across the open lawn. My heart hammered, my pulse thundering in my ears. The basement window was two hundred feet away. One hundred. Fifty. A light flashed through the glass. Once. Twice. I dug my heels into the soft dirt, nearly falling forward. The light came again, this time stopping on the other side of the glass. Two bright eyes swayed gently from side to side. Then the bat-like nightmare flew straight at the window, slamming its body against the glass. A shrill cry rattled the frame. Leathery wings slapped against the pane and pointed white teeth snapped together below a wrinkled snout.

That there might be something inside was a given after being in Rowan and Kail's tower, but I didn't expect anything to try attacking me before I was in and able to find a place to hide. There wasn't time to deal with it. Even if I killed it, it was likely already drawing the attention of other things.

The clacking bones of the creature the Sandman fought echoed around me. I looked up at the outer staircase, then back to the trapped creature. A gamble to remain unseen versus a sure thing. I clenched my jaw shut and bolted to the outer stairs.

The railing was rough beneath my palm, splinters impaling my skin. Each step felt heavier than the last, each taking me farther and farther away from where I needed to be, until I barreled through an unlocked door at the top. I kicked it shut behind me and leaned my back against the smooth metal, gasping for air. The overwhelming scent of burned cotton strangled me, but I made it without being seen or followed.

A nervous laugh bubbled from my chest, and I straightened to find a loom taking up nearly the entire space. Black threads passed over the beams, casting the room in an eerie glow. Wood creaked, parts of the loom moving, guiding new threads through from an invisible source. I stepped toward it, and the smile fell from my face. The Weaver had to infuse the thread with his power to make his nightmares which meant...

A bench scraped the floor, clattering as it toppled, and the machine came to an abrupt stop. My heart sputtered. I didn't see the Weaver, didn't hear his footsteps, until he was right in front of me, his hands around my throat. "Hello, Dream Keeper." He beamed.

My mouth dried, my tongue sandpaper in my mouth. His grip was tight enough to keep me from speaking but not hard enough to prevent air from reaching my lungs.

"How brave you are," he continued, unruffled. "How stupid *he* is."

I gripped his arm, the solid muscle flexing beneath my hand. Thin, wispy filaments hung limp at his shoulder where he must have ripped the cut threads from his sleeve. The embroidery on his vest, missing. I drew a shallow breath, refusing to meet his stare. A pile of thread pooled at the corner of the loom, a single piece running into the machine four feet away, gold-filaments twined throughout.

"Don't even think about it," he growled. I forced my eyes up to his, and he dragged me away from the machine until my back slammed into the wall. The knife jammed into my spine, and I cringed. "You were right; I underestimated you. It won't happen again."

Except you already have. I opened my mouth to tell him to go to Hell but only a wheeze came out.

He gave me a crooked grin. "The Sandman is foolish enough to expect me outside right now, isn't he? Why else would he send you in here alone? But I am not so vain as to need to take him down personally. What good is an army if they don't fight for you, hmm?"

My heart leapt to my throat. I dug my nails into his arm, but his grip was steel. He stepped forward, leaving no space between us. His breath tickled my cheek. "I am faster than you, stronger than you. Did you think you could steal my thread again without being caught? That I would let anyone bind me a second time?" He forced my chin up and smoothed the hair from my forehead, staring at the space between my eyes. "Give me the dream."

"No," I squeaked.

The muscles in his jaw jumped. "You don't want to play this game with me, Keeper. You're in my house now."

Of course, I didn't want to. I wasn't giving up yet though. If things went wrong, the Sandman would do as I asked and take the dream, even if he hadn't made the promise.

Be braver than I think you are, Kail had said.

With my body screaming in fear, I didn't feel very brave. The Weaver was in front of me, choking me, promising to torture me, yet I hesitated because the Sandman wouldn't like it. Because the balance was so important to him.

But I knew I couldn't go through this again. Even if the Sandman took the dream from me after rebinding the Weaver, I wouldn't be safe. Not really. The next time he broke free, I would be first on his list. *No.* Not first. He would kill the little family I had left before he got around to me, but he *would* get to me for everything I've done. It wouldn't be a quick death either. My stomach rolled, and I wedged a hand between my back and the wall, gripping the knife. The handle was icy against my palm.

"Listen." The Weaver pushed the hatch open overhead and a dozen different horrifying cries bounced off the domed ceiling. "He can't save you. Give me the dream now, and I'll allow you to return to your regular life. Keep testing me, and you won't be the only one to suffer."

"Why?" I croaked. I was stalling, biding time before I made the switch from prison guard to executioner. His death wasn't necessary. Not for the rest of the world anyway. He could be rebound, live his life here until the next time the magic wore down, but this was personal. And it was time I did something to save myself instead of worrying about everyone else. "Why do you want to let them out?"

His gold eyes glimmered. "This place is suffocating me, Dream Keeper. Can you imagine being trapped in a single room for your entire life? Watching millennium pass by while your four walls stay the same? I want more from life, and so do my nightmares. Things were never supposed to be like this—I told you that." His grip loosened ever so slightly. "The Sandman and I… we did this to ourselves, you know? But this is going to fix everything."

His words were a lightning bolt to my chest. A twist to my gut. Randy was dead. The cashier. Natalie. Emery. My father. All of them murdered on his order, my sister trapped and tortured in a cave, because he had a severe case of cabin fever. Because he thought bloodshed would fix something.

"What are you talking about?" I rasped.

I flicked the snap holding the knife in place. The hurt and anger I'd kept locked away boiled over, the flames licking through my body. Burning my veins. Scarring my heart. I tightened my grip on the handle. The Weaver tipped his head toward the hatch and closed his eyes, inhaling the acrid scent of metal and decay that wafted from the opening.

"Smell that, Keeper?" he asked, ignoring my question. "Death is coming."

The world slowed. My arm moved as if detached. As if I had no control. A brief flicker of recognition lit the Weaver's face as he sensed the knife's magic, but it was too late. I rammed the blade into his chest. It tore through flesh. Ripped past muscle. Scraped against bone. Sunk into his heart. I stood immobile. His gold eye dimmed, his mouth hanging open. It might have been my imagination, but I swore I felt every flutter of his pulse echo through the weapon.

He stumbled away from me then. Air whooshed into my lungs, and I nearly collapsed. The Weaver tumbled into the loom, his boots crushing the pile of thread. It bucked and coiled beneath him until he fell to the ground. Blood oozed from the corner of his mouth, and a cough sent it flying at my knees.

I knelt beside him and gripped the gleaming handle. "You're right." My voice was low and scratchy, and I yanked the blade free. "Death *is* coming."

A bittersweet grin played at his crimson lips. His hand snapped out, gripping my wrist. "You have no idea what you've done to yourself, Dream Keeper."

Stars danced in my vision. I shook my head, blinking hard. "What...?"

"Dreamer, Dreamer. Couldn't redeem her." The Weaver's half-cough, half-laugh splashed hot blood across my cheek. "You stupid, stupid girl. I wish—" Another cough. "I wish I could be here to see the Sandman's face."

A whistle rose up from nowhere, growing louder and louder until I was sure my eardrums would explode. I tried to tug myself free of the Weaver's grip, but he held tight. His lips were moving. Speaking. Saying something. My body seized. I couldn't breathe. Couldn't think. Feel. See.

Then the Weaver's hand fell away.

My senses returned one by one.

The Weaver's body slumped against the loom. His blood pooled around us on the black and gold marble, soaking through my pants. I took a single shaking breath, and a burst of agonizing pain sent me flying backward. My skull cracked against the wall, my brain rattling. It was as if I were on fire. As if every bone was breaking. Every vein collapsing. The room blinked in and out. I struggled to my hands and knees. I had to get out. To run before any of his creatures found me like this and tried to avenge their leader. I needed the Sandman.

The woven thread snapped up, circling the same wrist the Weaver held moments ago. I gripped the coil, yanking it, but it only tightened. The blood flow ceased, and my fingers tingled. I screamed then. An angry, tormented sound rising from the depths of my soul. Waves of pain rocked my body. My muscles tightened and cramped. I was going to die here. Alone. In a puddle of the Weaver's blood.

I fell to the cool, slick marble. My legs convulsed, splashing blood across the floor. With my last burst of strength, I screamed again. This time a name. The only name I ever loved. The one I had just betrayed.

"Sandman!"

Chapter Twenty-Nine

The Sandman

The field was stained red and black with blood, both mine and the nightmares'. Mostly theirs. It weighed down my sleeves and dripped from my fingers. I stood in the middle of the carnage, panting. Each breath was tight against my broken ribs. Giant cats, humanoid beings, and a prehistoric creature littered the yard. At least fifty different nightmares, some powerful, some not. But Despina was different.

I held little hope of truly defeating her before my power ran out. For a spine with two forked hands and a giant skull, she was clever. There wasn't much to aim at. She had no vital organs, she felt no pain. I wasn't sure who I hated facing more—her or the Weaver. I needed to hurry though. Nora should've made it to the tower by now, and the Weaver was nowhere to be seen.

I stepped around and over lifeless forms, my boots sloshing against the blood-soaked ground. A cut in my leg still oozed, and my jaw throbbed from a punch I took. Despina's clicking bones sounded behind me. I scooped a handful of sand from my satchel and tossed it out in front of me. A giant web sprung between two trees, and I leapt through a rectangular gap. I heard the soft thud of her over-sized head hitting the fine strands, but I was already sprinting. It wouldn't hold her long, but I only needed a head start. Once I reached the stairs, I could better deflect her attacks. She wouldn't want to break what was left of the Weaver's home which meant she would pull her punches. At least until I reached the top where she would have me cornered, but by then I should have the thread I needed.

An explosion of terror shot through me. Not mine, but his. The Weaver's fear, close and undiluted. I spun around, grabbing another handful of sand. Despina was still untangling herself, but there wasn't another living nightmare to be seen. My brows lowered, and I scanned the area. *Where are you, Weaver? And what are you afra*—

Sharp, blinding pain lanced my chest. Stinging. Burning. My heart sputtered, and the ground rose up to meet me.

I lay there, in the blood and dirt, gasping for what were surely my last breaths. I rubbed a shaking hand over the fatal wound, but there was no mark. A cloud descended over me, wrapping around my mind. No matter which way I looked, I understood nothing. Nothing but blazing agony. Nothing but a desire for it to end.

I flipped to my back to find Despina hovering over me. Only her hair moved, her empty eye sockets focused on the fortress. *Nora.* A crackling breath broke free from my throat. Something went wrong. The Weaver never came... I forced myself up onto my elbows and scrambled out from under the skeletal nightmare.

Despina didn't so much as glance in my direction, and I willed myself onto unsteady feet.

Ice filled my chest, chasing the magic from my center. Each breath threatened to crumble my lungs, each step, my bones. My jaw trembled. Teeth clacked. I wasn't going to make it. I stumbled over my own feet. The ground warped before me, an upheaval, and I flung my arms out to catch my balance.

A scream blasted across the battlefield, nearly sending me back to my knees. Then another scream. "Sandman!"

"Nora," I tried to call back, but my voice was gone. Lost. I sucked in air. What was he doing to her? What had she done to him? Despina's bones clacked again. Quick. Erratic. I tried to move faster, to run, but my vision blurred. The nightmare zipped past me, the wind she kicked up the only thing to touch me. A blur of ivory bones snaked up the side of the black wall.

The pain gripping my chest faded. This was surely what dying felt like; the bliss before the nothing. But then my vision cleared. The shaking in my legs dulled to a tremor. Heat exploded behind my tattoo, branching out through my arms. The sand at my hip buzzed through the satchel with new vigor. I flexed the numbness from my fingers.

A cry rang down from the distant sky. Something large and angry was coming. I could question everything later, after I found Nora and we were out of danger. My boots pounded across the lawn, the memory of pain slowing my movements, and my ragged breath echoed in my ears.

"Nora?" I propelled myself up the outer stairs. Despina clicked and scraped her way over the domed roof. We reached the door at the same time, and I threw a handful of sand at her. It exploded in a series of tiny white fireworks. She reeled back. I flung myself inside and slammed the door behind me.

"Nora?"

Blood was everywhere. Splattered on the walls. The loom. Pooling beneath the bodies. *Bodies.*

The air left me, wringing my lungs. Suffocating me.

I was wrong. I hadn't been dying before. *This* was dying. This was death.

I slid across the soaked floor on my knees and scooped Nora into my arms. Her skin was like ice, her face white as a sheet. Blood matted her hair and speckled her face like a second layer of freckles. Tears pricked my eyes. "Nora?" I smoothed her hair back, wiped at the blood on her skin. It smeared, the streak reaching all the way down her jaw. "No, no, no. Open your eyes. Please, Nora. Please, wake up."

Another screech joined the first outside. Let them come. Let them see their master dead on the floor. Let them see who did it. Let them rip me apart so that my body matched my heart.

I glared at the knife in Nora's hand with its red, glowing center. Recognition struck, and my stomach churned. I hadn't seen it in a thousand years. The Weaver and I had agreed... My mouth ran dry. It was supposed to be lost. Buried. Burned. At the bottom of an ocean. Destroyed. Somewhere neither the Weaver nor I would ever find it and try to demolish the balance. I hooked my arm under Nora's shoulders and leaned forward, yanking the blade from her grip. No one should have this much power. No one. I leaned away from the Weaver's body, resting on my heels.

"Why?" I choked. "We had a plan."

She answered with a groan.

"Nora!" The knife clattered to the ground, and I lifted her up. "Nora? Can you hear me?"

She winced. "Sandman?"

I crushed her against me. Hot tears spilled down my cheeks. "You're alive."

"Debatable," she mumbled into my chest.

"What happened? You were only supposed to get the thread. Where did you find that knife?" I blurted, the words overlapping.

"I..." She shifted, and I loosened my grip. "Rowan and Kail gave it to me to kill him. I wasn't sure I would be able to do it, but he... I had no choice."

Rowan and Kail. But how did they find it? My fingers dug into Nora's shoulders, and she sat up gingerly. We were supposed to bind the Weaver. That was it. Anything else had the potential to destroy the Night World, and now... My eyes locked onto the Weaver's waxen face, and I stilled. My friend. My enemy. Emotions funneled through me faster than I could register them. My entire life was woven with strands of his existence, and now... Now it felt as if my heart was cleaved in two—his half gone and Nora's hemorrhaging. "You killed him," I rasped.

She nodded, and her hands flew up to press against her temples. Beneath the Weaver's blood, her fingers and hands were black, the mat color reaching up toward her elbow like a glove. Each of her frantic heartbeats sent a visible pulse of gold along the veins beneath. Thread coiled around her wrist like a manacle, the other end still attached to the loom. My blood drained to my feet. *Magic.* The Weaver's magic. The pain I felt outside... That was the Weaver's death, and the release of it was because the balance was restored. My connection to the Weaver wasn't gone—it was transferred.

To her.

My jaw hung open, my voice raw. "No."

"I'm sorry. I know it wasn't the plan, and I should have told you."

I pried her hands away from her head, holding them between us. "Look."

Her eyes flashed. She snatched her arms from my grip and scrubbed frantically at her skin. "What is this?"

Outside, the creatures had arrived, screeching over our heads. Others came too. Bellowing and shouting and roaring. No one had come close to killing one of us before, and with the nightmares, there was no way to know if they were here for revenge or to welcome Nora as their new lord. *Lady*. But whatever their reason, now wasn't the time. We had to get out of here and regroup.

"We have to leave," I said. She didn't move except to continue scratching at her arms. "*Now.*"

I scooped the blade off the floor, tucking it into my belt, and hauled her up by her elbows. A low moan beat against my eardrums. The Blood Army. Rowan and Kail had come to claim their prize—whatever they hoped it would be. I grabbed the thread where it connected to the loom and raked it across a sharp metal edge. It whipped itself free of me and fastened around Nora's arm, melding into the sleeve of her black T-shirt.

"Sandman," she cried.

The terror in her voice cut like glass, gouging my soul. Pain poured from the wound and spread its acidic burn through my body until every beat of my heart made it feel as if I would combust. Nora... My Nora. What had she *done?*

I spared a final glance at the Weaver's corpse and regret pinched my chest. Surely, this wasn't real. He would open his gold eyes and bark out a loud curse any moment now. Much worse had happened to us in the past and he—*we*—survived. Except I'd seen too much death since our creation not to recognize its pallor. My power pulsed at the brutal realization, threatening to knock me off my feet.

The Weaver, my friend, my nemesis… was gone.

But this wasn't the time to mourn. If I should mourn at all. So I steeled myself and gripped Nora's hand. The color on her arms would fade as the magic sunk deeper into her being, but the consequences of her actions—never. "I'm sorry," I whispered and ripped her from the Nightmare Realm.

Her realm.

Chapter Thirty

The pain continued to tremble through my body. A pinch here, a poke there. My muscles cramped, and joints ached, but the worst of it had faded. My vision was clear by the time the Sandman escorted me back to the beach. He released his grip on my elbows, and I fell to my knees into glorious, glorious sand. A sob stuck in my throat.

"No," the Sandman shouted. I snapped my head up to find Baku crouching low, a hungry gleam in his eyes. "No." His voice was softer this time, his hands held out in my defense.

Baku flicked a look between us but didn't straighten from his position.

A cold sweat broke out on my skin. "Sandman?"

"*No.* She's not... She... You can't." His shoulders slumped, and he stepped between us. "Give us a few minutes, Baku."

I didn't see Baku get up or walk away, but I sensed his distance growing on the other side of the Sandman. It was a small weight lifted from inside. A sprinkle of calm amid the chaos. "I'm so sorry," I blurted through building tears. I wanted to reach out to him but found I didn't have the courage to try. "I didn't know. I thought..." *I thought I would fix everything.* I held my arms out in front of me, stained and foreign. They prickled with a power I couldn't explain, the threads holding me in a vice grip. "What's happening to me?"

The Sandman shook his head once. Dirt and debris were caked in his hair. A smudge of something else marked his face. His chest was covered in mud and tacky blood, his legs drenched. The fabric of his pants clung to his thigh where a large gash continued to bleed, but most of it came from somewhere else. I looked past my arms to the blood splattered over my entire body, and my heart shuttered.

My eyes sought his, desperate for answers, but even with all the signs of a vicious fight, they were the worst to look at. Stars danced a duet across the vibrant violet—love and hate, relief and fear.

Despair shook through me like an earthquake. Whatever this was, whatever was happening, it was as bad as it seemed. Worse. "Stop looking at me like that," I said, sounding as broken and desperate as I felt. "Tell me what this is before I find a saw and start—"

"The balance." His eyes fell to my arms, and he reached out to stroke his fingertips over my tense wrists. "I wasn't sure what killing him would do exactly, or I would have warned you." He ran his hands through his hair. "Or, maybe I wouldn't have because I didn't know you were planning this. And the knife?

You had it on you when you came back? No." He winced. "Don't answer that. I know you did."

"It wasn't like that." I inched closer, still not daring to reach out. But it *was* like that. It was a conscious decision to lie and betray. "I wanted the Weaver dead, Sandman. I *needed* him dead and for this to be over. I knew you would've stopped me if I told you. I second guessed myself until the end, but he wasn't going to let me go."

"I know he wasn't," he mumbled, his head hanging. "I know, I know. But, Nora... I told you the universe kept the balance. You could've..."

I stared at him. The words were all over his face, his body, aching to be free yet too afraid to surface. "Just say it."

He shook his head, his eyes pressed shut. "It doesn't matter. It's done."

"But what's happening to me?"

"Apparently to kill the Weaver is to become the Weaver," he said, his voice dead. He met my gaze, his pupils wide. "To become the Weaver is to become a target."

I shook my head. He couldn't mean that. This was a trick, a nightmare. This wasn't the beach, but another mind game the Weaver's world was playing on me. I couldn't be the Weaver. The Weaver was the Weaver, dead or alive.

"What are you saying? That I'm a nightmare now?" I sucked in the lilac-scented air and almost gagged. *Sweet. Too sweet.* "Why would I be a target?"

"You're the Lady of Nightmares. Not quite a nightmare, but not quite human either. Someone has to rule over them, keep them in line, create them."

"No. Rowan said they could—"

"Rowan used you. She was no match for the Weaver, but you? If killing the Weaver makes you the next ruler of the Nightmare Realm, you were never meant to last long."

"No..." But it rang true. Once I killed the Weaver, she planned to kill me. I leapt to my feet, scrubbing at the stain on my arms again. "*No.* There has to be something we can do. Can't I just pass the torch or something? If Rowan wants this, she can have it."

The Sandman shook his head. "If there is a way, I know nothing of it."

The beach spun, and I latched onto his arm. My lungs cried for air but no matter how much I drew, no matter how quickly I drew it, there wasn't enough. My pulse hammered through me. *Weaver.* I blinked through wet eyes. "There has to be *something.*"

Thunder boomed overhead. Lightning followed on its heels, outlining a thousand different shapes, all coming straight toward us. A splash of orange, a towering set of horns, a slithering figure in the sky. The low moan of the Blood Army.

The Sandman reached into the satchel still hanging at his hip. "You have to leave."

"You can't face that many alone," I cried. The volume of their march alone was unlike anything I'd ever heard. The ground trembled with it.

The Sandman scooped up enough sand to make a pair of scissors and snipped the thread from my wrist, then again at the sleeve of my shirt. I felt naked, weak, wrong without it. I wanted to snatch the long tangle from his hands. Protect it. Keep it. But the deep need for it scared me more than the Sandman destroying it did. I curled my hands into fists. "If I really am the new Weaver, I'm going to stay and fight."

"You have no idea how to use the magic coursing through your veins," he said, not unkindly. "Besides, they're coming because I kidnapped their new leader. If you're not here, they'll look for you somewhere else."

The black and gold thread writhed in his arms, reaching for me, but I stepped back. "You didn't kidnap me."

"Technically, I did," he said. "And whatever their feelings are about this power shift, they won't stand for it. What they will do after they have you back… is anyone's guess."

"But…" I blinked at the mass of creatures coming toward the Dream Realm and something swelled in my breast. A sickening hope. A brimming hate. I clamped a hand over my mouth to keep from speaking about things I didn't understand.

"I'm going to put the entire Nightmare Realm on lockdown until you've gained enough strength to face them. The nightmares already can't get out, but I'll make it so that no one can get in. Who knows what they'll do to a Dreamer without someone to enforce the rules, as few as they are. If you're here, you'll be bound too. And…" He slammed his mouth shut and swallowed hard. "And, that means you need to wake up."

I tore my eyes away from the darkening sky. "You can do that? Stop everyone from having a nightmare?"

"It will take everything I have, but without the Weaver fighting me, it's possible." He stepped closer and lifted my chin. His lips pressed against mine, hard and unapologetic. "Everything will be fine, okay? I'll see you later. I promise."

Baku appeared at his side again, shifting between his paws, and the hoard slowed. Slowed but didn't stop. Even if I wasn't here, if they believed he had taken me, they would want their pound of flesh. Both their anger and anticipation tingled along my nerves.

"Distract them," he said to Baku.

Baku snorted his agreement, if only out of excitement for having caged prey, and an irrational spike of anger hit me. I focused on the Sandman's hands, and he called sand up to encase the long, thrashing strand of thread. Invading it. Stealing its allegiance. I balled my hands into fists. The nightmares were close enough to the thinning barrier now that flashes of muted color broke through the darkness. A wicked gleam filled the chimera's eyes.

"Wake up, Nora," the Sandman warned.

I crossed my arms, saw the darkness there, and slipped them behind my back instead. "Baku gets a choice."

"Baku knows what he's doing." The Sandman whipped the coil of thread out and it fell to the ground, limp.

I could help him. I could fight or order the nightmares back to where they belonged. They should have to listen to me now. It was worth a shot anyway. The Dream Realm didn't have to be the only safe place for a Dreamer. Not anymore. Together, the Sandman and I could destroy everything on the other side of the beach's barrier. I saw the walls clearly now—a dome of shimmering magic—and felt the strain of its fading power.

"I love you," he said in a final tone.

"Wait—"

Before I could finish my plea, he shoved me awake.

***

Waking up felt like having my soul ripped away, torn to shreds, and stuffed back into a body that no longer fit. I flew up in bed, crisp white sheets pooling in my lap. A scream lodged in my throat, and I fought to breathe. Monitors beeped furiously all

299

around me. Wires streamed out from the neck of a white and blue hospital gown, and a needle was stuck in my arm, delivering IV fluids. I reached up to tear the wires from my chest and froze. My hands and arms were still as black as night, my veins glowing gold beneath. The place where the thread had circled my wrist was raw and aching.

A nurse in colorful scrubs flew into the room with my mother two steps behind. Katie rushed in beside her dressed in a pair of jeans and a plaid shirt, not the hospital clothes I last saw her in. Her hair was dyed dark brown, her face free of makeup.

My heart dropped. What was I doing here? It couldn't be later than mid-day. The pills I took shouldn't have been enough to warrant a trip to the emergency room. My mother broke down just inside the door, clinging to Katie, whispering *thank you, thank you, thank you.*

"What am I doing here?" I asked in a hoarse voice.

The nurse stuck her head out the door, calling for someone to page the doctor, and rushed over to check the monitors. "How do you feel?"

Like I got hit by a truck. "Someone better tell me what's going on," I said, harsher than intended.

"You've been unconscious for two days." The nurse spoke calmly as she checked the IV bag. "We almost lost you twice."

"Almost lost me?" I looked to my mother with her wrinkled sweats and greasy hair, the old mascara trails running down her cheeks. *When?* My eyes lost focus, my thoughts turning inward. What were the things that almost killed me? Becoming the Weaver, probably, but what else? "I..."

Katie slipped past the nurse and placed her hand in mine. "We thought it might have been a reaction to the pills you took, but they pumped your stomach and everything." Her eyes bored into mine. She knew. "The doctor said your heart gave out a couple times this afternoon but righted itself somehow."

"It's all over now." I squeezed my sister's hand. It was only partially a lie. The Weaver was gone, our torment over, but there was so much more to think about. How long could I stay with my family? The Sandman never lasted long in the Day World, and he was stronger than I was, but I forced a weak smile for their sake. "I'm awake now. Everything can go back to normal."

"Normal?" my mother asked. "We're moving, and you're never leaving the house again. Either of you."

"Mom," Katie groaned.

She glared, her face tight. "You think I'm kidding?"

I blinked, forcing my smile to stay put. Even if it wouldn't be for long, I wanted to stay in our house, surrounded by a lifetime of memories. When I left them for the Nightmare Realm, my mother would be glad for them. I gripped the railing of the bed. Or maybe she was right—maybe moving was better. She deserved a fresh start away from the things that would remind her of her delusional, runaway daughter.

Already I felt the strain of this place. It clawed at me like a drowning man would claw at the surface of a lake. The bright fluorescent lights stung my exposed skin, and my pupils constricted against the faint sunlight filtering through the tinted window.

But no one noticed my arms. They couldn't see the power raging beneath my skin or comprehend my ability to bring a nightmare crashing into their slumber. It was my new secret, the hidden truth that mortals couldn't see, just as no one had noticed the Sandman's tattoos or his starlit eyes. Even then, before I knew the Sandman was real or who Ben really was, I wasn't completely human. I carried a piece of the Sandman inside me.

I still did.

Now I belonged to something darker though. It lurked beneath my skin, grinning as it spread. The idea should have terrified me. By my own hand, I created a different identity for myself. Something new. Something legends never spoke of. A Weaver. *The* Weaver. Ruler of all things that go bump in the night.

Yes, I should have been terrified, and a large part of me was.

But another part of me grinned back, and that terrified me more than anything else.

I flopped back on the flat pillow and slammed my eyes shut, ignoring the sudden rush of medical staff that flooded into the room. While they thought I slept for two days, I was awake.

Running.

Fighting.

Plotting.

Killing.

And I was exhausted.

Please come, I plead silently to the Sandman. *Please help me. I need you.*

Chapter Thirty-One

The Sandman

I ripped myself out of the crazed darkness, back to the Dream Realm. The force of my back hitting the ground knocked my teeth together. The sand reached up to cradle me, a few grains sneaking beneath my clothes. The binding was done. I had no way of knowing how long it would last, but it bought me some time. Enough to recharge and prepare. This wouldn't be like last time. I would check the binding every day and tighten it down.

Baku glared at me, shaking his head. Blood stained the fur around his mouth and paws.

"I know, Baku." I sighed. "I'll train her. She'll learn and take up her rightful place. A year—"

He huffed.

"Six months," I conceded. The nightmares needed someone to lead them before they tore each other apart. "Six months, and she'll be ready."

He gave a laugh-like grumble and walked away, disappearing through the barrier.

Nora wouldn't be ready in six months, nor would she be in a year. Or two, or three. Being trapped would only fuel the nightmares volatile behavior. The mindless ones wouldn't be much of a problem if she proved she wouldn't put up with their behavior, but the others... They would undoubtedly line up for an opportunity to crush her, either for her power or because they were angry she abandoned them. I had the knife now, but they wouldn't need a special weapon to kill the Weaver like everyone else did. They were her and she was them. It would be nothing more than severing a limb to them now that they knew without a doubt what a Weaver's death meant.

I shifted into a sitting position, setting my elbows on my knees, and my chin hit my chest. There was nothing I could do to protect her there. Not anymore. So, I closed my eyes and called on the sand that Nora's presence tainted, working it through my fingers while trying not to crumble.

***

It took nearly four hours to regain enough strength to Day Walk and another to track down Nora's location. Our cord was severed now, dead and dull, but I was connected to her in another way. As my opposite, I could feel her proximity, her feelings. The fear and confusion laced with a near giddiness, which brought on a stronger wave of fear.

I almost didn't recognize Katie staring at the wall in the waiting room of the hospital. Her hair was dark now, and the brightness gone from her expression. She clasped the leather bag I gave Nora in one hand. The other toyed with the strings, the knotted ends fraying under the constant touch. I tucked my hands in my back pockets. Did she believe now? It would be easier for Nora if she had someone on this side to confide in now that I... Now that she couldn't come to the beach without infecting it.

"Where's Nora?" I asked, cringing at the clear misery in my voice.

Katie looked me up and down slowly, recognition filtering in through her pain. "Ben, right?"

I nodded.

"I'll show you." Katie stood, her movements stiff and slow, and motioned me to follow her down the hall. "She's awake now."

I didn't trust myself to speak so I nodded again.

"Fair warning. She's a little off right now," she added. Her fingers curled around the bag, squeezing. "The doctors keep ordering more tests and someone is constantly in and out to poke at her, so I think she's just tired but..." She shrugged.

"Is she alone now?"

"Our mom and Paul are in the cafeteria, and Nora threw the last nurse out before she got halfway to the bed." She stopped outside of an open door. "This is her."

"Thanks." I gave her a wisp of a smile. "I'll take my chances."

"Good luck."

I waited for her to walk back down the hall and turn into the small seating area before slipping inside. A blue curtain was drawn across the room, but I shut the door anyway. I wiped sweaty hands on my pants and stepped around the cloth. Nora stood in front of a monitor with colored lines, pressing button after button with her charcoal fingers. A thin line of blood ran from the crease of her elbow where she must have ripped a needle out.

"What are you doing?" I asked.

She jumped and slammed a hand to her chest. "Sandman." Her shoulders squared. "I thought you were one of them."

"One of who?"

"The hospital staff. Or maybe Detective Bell. I overheard him talking to my mother in the hall about wanting to personally apologize, but I pretended to be asleep." She bit her lip, turning back to the screen. "Help me shut this thing off so I can sneak out of here."

My mouth ran dry. I moved slowly to her side and guided her hand away from the machine. She jerked against the touch, then squeezed my fingers, clinging to me while she trembled. "The Nightmare Realm is bound," I said. "It should last for a few months, at least, but I'll keep reinforcing it to give you more time."

"More time," she echoed and started jabbing the buttons with her other hand.

I watched her, unsure what to say or do. "You should make the most of it with your family. They need you."

"Well, *I* need *you*," she shouted.

My lips pressed into a frown. She was still Nora, my Nora, but for the first time, I was at a loss of how to react. How was I supposed to make this better for her? "You have me," I promised.

"I called for you." Her fingers stilled on the monitor. "You didn't come."

I closed my eyes and twisted my neck so that she couldn't see my face distort. If I heard her, I would have come the second

I was able. But I couldn't. I never could again. "I won't be able to hear you anymore," I said gently.

A small, pained sound escaped her throat. "Now that I'm the Weaver, you mean? Now that we're enemies?" Her voice cracked.

"No." I spun and gripped her face, forcing her to look at me and me at her. My stomach clenched. "I will never be your enemy, Nora. I'll train you so when the time comes you're ready to go back, but you will never be anything but *you*. Forever. You will have me no matter what."

Tears brimmed in her green eyes, and she tugged me closer, burying her face into my shirt. "I'm scared."

My words were trapped beneath a heavy blanket of sorrow. I tried to stomp the feeling down, to move beyond it. There was already enough suffering inside her that she didn't need to confuse mine with her own, but it was a boulder. A mountain. Immovable. She was what everyone feared now—she should fear nothing. She needed to fear nothing if she was going to survive.

"It'll be okay, Nora," I finally managed. My fingers shook, and I ran a hand over her head. "We'll get through this."

Her tears soaked through my shirt, her back shaking with each sob. "I'm going to have to leave everyone, even you, and live in that horrible place for the rest of my miserable life."

I held her so tight she had to feel my heart pounding against her cheek. It was true she would have to leave this world, but she could learn to Day Walk to visit her family. I didn't know what it meant for us yet, but I didn't want to give her up. I wouldn't. No matter what it took, we would find a way for it to work. "You'll never have to leave me. I'm always yours, remember?"

She tilted her head back to study me, her chin trembling. I would have given anything to know what she was thinking in that moment. Disbelief raged across her face, then a softer flash of hope, followed by a tiny crease between her brows. She wanted to believe me, but I understood the hesitation. It seemed impossible to me right now too, but things would settle down. A path might open to us when our minds were clear. It had to. A block of ice formed in my gut, frozen guilt and shame. I drew a shuddering breath.

"And I'm always yours," she finally whispered.

I kissed her, tasting the salt from her tears, and let myself forget everything for that brief moment. Nora would be okay. We would be okay. Eventually. Six months would have to be enough time to become who she needed to be—no longer a mere Dream Keeper but a powerful new entity. A Lady of Nightmares with kindness in her heart and steel in her soul.

Acknowledgements

Now's the part where I say thank you and pray I don't forget anyone!

First, my editor, Kate—you're an absolute gift from the editing gods!

My endlessly supportive critique partners: Lauren, Kalyn, Loretta, and Candace.

As always, my Saltmates!

Lindsay & Judy.

Priscilla, Katie, Elle, Melissa, Stacy.

And, of course, all the thanks to my family! My husband, my boys, Nonny, Kathy, Mom, Dad, Heather, and my Georgia family.

Thank you, thank you, thank you!

Also by Amber R. Duell

Young Adult

The Dark Dreamer Trilogy:
Dream Keeper
Dark Consort
Night Warden

When Stars Are Bright

New Adult
Fragile Chaos
The Prince's Wing

Faeries of Oz series (co-written with Candace Robinson):
Lion (ebook prequel short story)
Tin
Crow
Ozma
Tik-Tok

Vampires in Wonderland (co-written with Candace Robinson):
Rav (ebook prequel short story)
Maddie
Chess
Knave

Once Upon A Wicked Villain (co-written with Candace Robinson):
Spindle of Sin
Tower of Shadows

About the Author

Amber R. Duell was born and raised in a small town in Central New York. She does her best writing in the middle of the night, surviving the daylight hours with massive amounts of caffeine. Her favorite stories are dark with a touch of romance and a villain you either love to hate or hate to love.

When not reading or writing, she enjoys snowboarding, embroidering, snuggling with her cat, and staying up way too late to research genealogy. She loves to travel and has visited more countries than states. Kissing the Blarney Stone and hand-feeding monkeys in the mountains of France will be hard to beat, but that doesn't stop her from trying to find the next real-life adventure.